Her pulse had jumped  the m hand touched his for arm.

Max's entire body had responded—a visceral reaction to her touch. Her kind words. The admiration he saw in her eyes, when he explained the complex security system to protect his son.

He forced himself to step back, allowing Grace to examine the blade. She lived next door and she cared about his son. His son cared about her. There couldn't be some random one-night stand between the two of them. It would be the destruction of one of his son's most important relationships. And that could not happen.

But she just traced the outline of your tattoo with her fingers.

No. That didn't matter. They were cut from very different cloth, and she knew that from the start on moving day. Grace didn't think she was of his caliber, and she was right. There were plenty of reasons to avoid Grace Bennett.

He just had to remember them, which was proving difficult.

Dear Reader,

Life is full of surprises, isn't it? It seems the things we remember most are the times when something didn't go as expected. And not necessarily in a bad way—it might be the weekly game night that ended up making you and your family laugh more than you ever have before because of some silly joke, and you all still laugh about it years later.

It might be that blind date you didn't want to go on thirty years ago, but you went, and you found your soulmate in a townie restaurant that's now a gas station. And life was never the same again.

And yes, sometimes those surprises aren't the happiest. Those events also become waypoints in our lives, where there's a Before and an After. This is a story about two people dealing with life-altering changes. Single dad Max and his uptight neighbor, Grace, don't think they have room in their changed lives for romance.

But the surprises keep coming for Max, Grace and five-year-old Tyler, until a holiday children's pageant, complete with astronauts and dragons, helps them see that happily-ever-afters often come along when least expected.

Books don't happen in a vacuum. I want to offer special thanks to my editor, Gail Chasan; my agent, Jill Marsal; and especially to that guy I met on a blind date thirty years ago and fell in love with—Himself. Because HEAs, in books and in life, really can come out of nowhere!

Jo McNally

A CAPE COD HOLIDAY

JO McNALLY

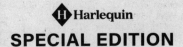

SPECIAL EDITION

Harlequin®
SPECIAL
EDITION™

Recycling programs
for this product may
not exist in your area.

ISBN-13: 978-1-335-40212-7

A Cape Cod Holiday

Copyright © 2024 by Jo McNally

 Harlequin Enterprises ULC
22 Adelaide St. West, 41st Floor
Toronto, Ontario M5H 4E3, Canada
www.Harlequin.com

Printed in Lithuania

MIX
Paper | Supporting
responsible forestry
FSC® C021394

Award-winning romance author **Jo McNally** lives in her beloved Upstate New York with her very own romance-hero husband. When she's not writing or reading romance novels, she loves to travel and explore new places and experiences. She's a big fan of leisurely lunches with her besties. Her favorite room at home is the sunroom, where she enjoys both morning coffee and evening cocktails with her husband while listening to an eclectic (and often Irish) playlist.

Books by Jo McNally

Winsome Cove

A Cape Cod Summer
A Cape Cod Holiday

The Fortunes of Texas: Fortune's Secret Children

Fortune's Secret Marriage

Harlequin Special Edition

Gallant Lake Stories

A Man You Can Trust
It Started at Christmas...
Her Homecoming Wish
Changing His Plans
Her Mountainside Haven
Second-Chance Summer
Expecting His Holiday Surprise

The Fortunes of Texas: The Wedding Gift

A Soldier's Dare

Visit the Author Profile page
at Harlequin.com for more titles.

This book is about the changes and surprises that come along in life—both positive and not. It's dedicated to everyone who has faced unexpected challenges and found their way through them with love. If you're in the middle of something like that right now, then it's especially dedicated to you.

Prologue

Max Bellamy wondered for the hundredth time if he was doing the right thing as he pulled his pickup truck into the parking lot of a hotel outside of Buffalo. He was towing a twenty-foot trailer, so he had to park in the back. He turned off the engine and sat for a moment, staring out the windshield at the commercial office park surrounding the hotel.

"Is this Cape Sod, Max?" his five-year-old son asked. "Is this our new house?"

"It's Cape *Cod*, like the fish," Max answered, still staring straight ahead. "And no, Tyler, this is not a house. It's a hotel." Anticipating the next question that was sure to come—the kid never ran out of them—Max added, "We can't get into our house until Friday, after the closing." He cringed, knowing he'd just opened himself up to more questions. Max was still learning to edit his answers to avoid being stuck answering questions for an hour.

"What's a *closing*? Why do we have to wait for it? What if it's already closed?" Tyler's brown eyes went wide. "Will we have to live in the truck?"

Max gave his son a quick smile, which was, of course, not returned. "Tyler, we won't have to live in the truck.

Your new grandma owns a motel, remember? We'll be there tomorrow night, then I'll go pay for our new house Friday morning. Once that happens, we can move in." Assuming the moving truck arrived on time with the scant amount of furniture he owned, but he knew better than to mention that to Tyler and give him something new to fret about. Luckily, he'd managed to buy some of the existing furniture from the sellers, so it wouldn't be *too* empty.

"I liked my *old* house and my *old* grandma. Will she come to Cape Cod, too?"

Max bit back a very bad word. At the moment, he wouldn't mind if he never saw Tyler's grandparents again. Not after they tried to keep his son from him. First, by supporting—and possibly encouraging—Marie's decision not to tell Max that Tyler even existed while she was alive. Then, after Marie's sudden death, they'd fought the social workers who'd insisted on tracking down Tyler's father—Max—instead of automatically handing *them* permanent custody of the boy. If Marie hadn't put Max's name on the birth certificate, he may have never found out he even had a son.

But Sally and Ed Cosma *were* Tyler's grandparents, and, as angry as Max was, he knew it would be wrong to keep them out of Tyler's life.

"Sure, they might visit. Or maybe we'll visit them."
When hell freezes over...

Tyler perked right up. "When? Tomorrow?"

"Uh, no. First, we need to get settled in our new house, and you need to get registered in your new school. But... someday."

Tyler let out a huff and threw himself back against the seat. Great. The kid was ticked off. Again.

Max opened his door. "Come on, Ty. Let's get some dinner. You can watch a little TV before bed."

Like a yo-yo, Tyler bounced from sulking to excitement. But not happiness. Smiles came very rarely to the dark-haired, dark-eyed boy.

"What are we going to watch, Max? A movie? The new cartoon one?"

"Maybe." He was new at this fatherhood business, but he'd learned the magic of that word—*maybe*. It wasn't a no but wasn't exactly a yes. It seemed to satisfy Tyler, and the boy hopped out of the truck and came to the front, where Max waited. Max held out his hand, but Tyler shook his head sharply. There were no cars around to worry about, so Max let it go and followed his son across the lot.

He couldn't help wishing the boy would call him "Dad," but the social worker told him not to push too hard, since Tyler was dealing with so much grief and upheaval. *Pick your battles*, Sandy said. The problem was he had no idea which battles to pick. He wanted his son to be happy, but right now, that seemed a long way away.

Insta-father or not, whenever he thought of Tyler as his son, it did something funny to his heart. They were virtual strangers. They didn't have the same last name— Tyler's birth certificate gave him his mother's last name, Cosma. But this boy was *his*, and Max would do anything for him, even if it might feel like the wrong thing. Like buying a house in Winsome Cove and settling down like an actual grown-up, instead of traveling from Renaissance fair to Renaissance fair with a portable forge, making knives and swords and the occasional art piece.

Being a nomad was no life for a little boy.

Max's mother and sister both lived in Winsome Cove, and they'd vowed to help him with Tyler. It had been an impulsive move, but things had been moving at light speed for months now. He could have bought a place near the small rural town in southern Ohio where Tyler had lived with his mom. But Marie's family had been so grief-stricken over the car accident that took Marie's life—and so hostile to Max's arrival—that he'd decided to give Tyler and him a fresh start away from them.

Maybe Winsome Cove would work its magic on Tyler, just as it had on Mom and Lexi. His big sister had only gone there temporarily, to help their mom get settled in the old motel she'd inherited a year and a half ago. Then Lexi ended up opening a restaurant and falling in love while in the little seaside town. Those family ties would be good for Tyler, and Lord knew Max needed the help—no matter how much he chafed against the idea of settling down and buying a hundred-and-fifty-year-old house sight unseen in some little New England tourist town. That had never been part of his plan.

Of course, fatherhood hadn't been part of his plan, either.

Chapter One

Grace Bennett was not happy. She was sitting on her front porch, which was one of her favorite places to be. She had her favorite mug in her hand, filled with her favorite Italian roast coffee. She had the day off from work. And it was a glorious September morning, with a brilliant blue sky. A gentle sea breeze brought fresh salt air wafting across the five blocks from the beach to her home on Revere Street.

Her cat, Mozart, was curled up inside his felted wool igloo by her chair. The Siamese was not at all fond of cool weather, but he'd yowled at her when she'd poured her coffee, knowing where she was headed. So she'd snapped the lightweight outdoor leash onto his harness. He'd immediately tunneled under the plush blanket inside the igloo. Outdoors, but not really. He'd managed to get his way, as usual, so he was content and quiet.

Yes, this should have been a perfect Friday morning.

Except for the moving truck sitting next door.

These old lots were narrow, so the neighboring driveway abutted her driveway, which was right next to her porch. There was a large box truck sitting there, blocking her view of the Hendersons' house. She frowned into her coffee. It wasn't the Hendersons' house anymore. Walt Henderson died a year ago, and Lucy Henderson's children had convinced her to sell the large home and move to a senior-living apartment closer to them in Boston. Grace couldn't blame them, since Lucy was eighty-five.

But Grace had purchased her own home from her parents when they'd retired to Florida, meaning the Hendersons had been her neighbors for her entire life. Until now. She glared at the bright yellow moving truck. She'd pressed Devlin Knight, the real estate agent who'd sold the Hendersons' place, for information on the buyer. All he would say was that the buyer was from out of state and had found the property online. That was the worst possible scenario. Someone who didn't even *live* on the Cape would have no appreciation for the historical significance of the homes on Revere Street in Winsome Cove. They'd probably want to put some ugly addition on. Or worse, they might plan to tear down the house completely and build some modern monstrosity. It was happening in small towns up and down Cape Cod.

Her scowl slowly worked into a smug smile. What they *wanted* to do and what they'd be *able* to do were two very different things. As chairperson of the Winsome Cove Historical Society, she knew the Henderson house, along with all the homes on this section of Revere Street, had strict regulations in place that would protect the home's integrity from being harmed, at least externally. But she'd heard horror stories from other towns where out-of-state buyers with deep pockets had found ways around ordinances. In one case two towns over, the buyers demolished a hundred-year-old home in the dark of night. They paid the fines without a care, then built a contemporary home that looked obscene surrounded by graceful vintage houses. She'd have to keep a close eye on these new neighbors of hers.

Grace supposed it was a positive sign that they were actually moving into the house. If someone was living there, they couldn't very well tear it down. She froze, her coffee mug halfway to her lips. What if this was a *renter* moving in? Everyone knew renters didn't always take care of properties. Or worse, what if they were going to try to flip it into a short-term vacation rental? Oh, God, was she going to have groups of college students renting the house next door for wild summer parties? Her chin rose. She'd put an end to *that* in a hurry.

Five hours later, the movers seemed to be finished and were folding up stacks of quilted packing blankets. Grace had been doing her best not to be obvious about watching what was going on. It was tacky to be seen spying on neighbors, new or otherwise. But her kitchen window was far enough back in her house that she'd been able to see some of the activity. Who could blame her for deciding it was time to wash all the crystal in her antique hutch? Coincidentally, that task had her standing at the window quite a bit. And since it was a greenhouse window that extended out from the house, facing the adjoining driveways, she had a pretty good view.

There was a man who appeared to be in charge, directing the moving crew. He was tall and rugged looking, as if he'd lived in the mountains somewhere, maybe as a lumberjack. Or maybe he was in a biker gang, with those tattoos. Grace knew tattoos didn't mean "criminal," but this guy had a *lot* of them on his arms, or as much of his arms as she could see under his rolled-up sleeves. He had longish light brown hair and quite possibly the broadest shoulders she'd ever seen on a man. Maybe he was some macho gym rat, popping steroids and lifting weights all day. He looked to be around her age—midthirties—and there was a dark-haired young boy with him. The boy didn't seem very happy to be there, moping around the porch and backyard.

Where was the mom? Maybe she'd left moving day to her husband, but then…why have the little boy there? The moving truck roared to life, making Grace jump back from the window so no one would spot her. As the truck pulled away, she saw a large black trailer hitched to an equally large gray pickup truck in front of the house. Tattoo Man went out to the truck and, to Grace's horror, backed that ugly, commercial-looking trailer into the driveway and all the way back to the carriage house. Right next to Grace's picket-fenced backyard and garden. Oh, no. That wouldn't do at all. She was out her back door before she even had time to think about what she was doing.

"Yoo-hoo!" She waved to the man as he left his truck. She'd been raised to always be as pleasant as possible when beginning a conversation. "Hello, may I have a word?"

His jaw tightened, but he walked over to the white picket fence dividing their properties. He didn't speak, just stared as if to say *you're the one who wanted to talk, so talk*. Rude. Still, she continued to smile.

"Hi, I'm Grace Bennett, your neighbor. Are you the new owner here?"

At first he just nodded, then he finally spoke. "I am.

Max Bellamy." He looked down and grimaced. "I'd offer to shake your hand, but I'm dirty and sweaty and it looks like you're going out somewhere." He gestured to her pale green linen trousers and lightweight sweater. She'd tied a jaunty navy blue scarf around her neck this morning—it was one of her favorite classic looks. But she didn't consider herself *dressed up.* After all, she'd been washing crystal all day.

"That's fine." She didn't want to touch his dirty hands, anyway. "I just wanted to say welcome to the neighborhood, and also...you can't park that there."

His thick eyebrows rose sharply. "I can't park my own truck in my driveway?"

"Oh, you can park the truck—" though she'd prefer he didn't "—but the trailer needs to go."

His mouth stayed open for a moment as he digested what she'd said.

"Go *where*? It's *my* trailer."

She did her best to hold on to her we're-all-friends-here smile, ignoring the edge in his voice. "I'm afraid we don't allow commercial trailers, campers or that sort of thing to be stored on properties in the historic district. You don't have to move it this instant or anything—I know you're just moving in. But by tomorrow..." He started to object, fire glinting in his eyes, and she talked over him, trying to show she was willing to be reasonable. "Well, it is the weekend, isn't it? Let's say by Monday, then."

He muttered something under his breath about small-town busybodies, and she let go of her phony smile.

"Mr. Bellamy, you need to read your deed and the historical district covenants that I'm sure you received at closing." Devlin Knight was very thorough with documents for his clients.

"That trailer holds my livelihood." He gestured toward it. What kind of man made his living out of a trailer? "Who can I talk to about this supposed rule?"

"There's nothing *supposed* about it. No trailers here, period. And you can talk to the code enforcement department, or to *me*, since I'm the chairperson of the Winsome Cove Historical Society."

"Of course you are," he muttered.

She ignored him. "I'd be happy to help you understand the responsibility you took on when you purchased this beautiful property."

He grumbled again at the little jab she'd just given. He met her gaze, clearly angry now. "Oh, I understand, alright. I understand that I'm lucky enough to be living next door to someone who's going to try to tell me what to do on a property *I'm* paying the mortgage and taxes on."

"Again, Mr. Bellamy, I'm sure it's all spelled out in your property documents." The man looked exhausted—his face was drawn and the lines around his eyes were tight and deep. That wasn't really her problem, but she felt a small pinch of guilt. He'd clearly had a long day, and she'd introduced herself by reciting rules and regulations to him. She took a breath and dialed down her sarcasm. "I don't want us to start off on the wrong foot as new neighbors. I'm just trying to protect you from a visit from the code department."

Before he could respond, the boy called out from the side porch. "Max! I'm hungry. When are we going to eat something?"

Max? So the boy wasn't his son. Perhaps a nephew?

The man's broad shoulders sagged. "I'll order pizza for us, buddy. There should be chips or something in that big box on the counter…" He seemed to reconsider the wisdom of a small child reaching into a packing box on top of a counter. "Never mind. I'll come get it for you." He looked back to Grace. "I don't want to be fighting with my neighbors, either. It's been a long-ass week, and clearly I had no idea the trailer was going to be a problem, but… I'll figure something out. Right now I need to feed my kid."

"Your son calls you by your given name?" That seemed odd.

"Yeah, he does. Is that against the regulations, too?"

"No, I just—" She stopped when Max turned and walked away from her. Grace didn't want to be enemies with her new neighbor, but if today was any indication, they'd never be friends, either.

Max poured a splash of whiskey into his glass, then reconsidered. One splash wasn't going to be enough tonight. He added a few ice cubes and a lot more whiskey. His sister, standing at his side by the vintage bar cart in the dining room, huffed out a short laugh.

"You really *did* have a bad day, huh?" She snagged the bottle from his hand and poured some into a glass for her husband, Sam Knight. Three months pregnant, Lexi was drinking sparkling water. Their mother, Phyllis, was in the kitchen, trying to enlist Tyler's help in getting dessert. Lexi sat next to Sam at the old dining room table, across from Max. "So what's going on? How can we help?"

He took a drink. "You know how they say the devil is in the details? Well, I've learned how true that saying is over the past week. A million decisions to make about where stuff goes in this house and what we still need and how I'm going to pay for it. Getting Tyler registered at school—I had to jump through hoops to get that done." So many questions from the administrator about where Tyler's mother was, why their last names were different, why they'd come to Cape Cod, why Max hadn't been in the boy's life until now. They went over the court papers with a microscope. He understood they wanted to protect Tyler, but the whole process made him feel like they thought he'd kidnapped the kid. He took another sip of whiskey.

"Plus, I've discovered this house is in a historic district, meaning all kinds of rules to follow, and I can't figure out a way around them." Having never owned his own home before, he'd had no idea that people could tell you what you could and couldn't do with your own damn property. He was sure getting an education on it now.

Sam frowned, exchanging glances with Lexi. The two had met just over a year ago and had married in the spring, which was when Max had met his brother-in-law for the first time. Max was hosting this meal, but restaurant chef Lexi had brought dinner, and Mom had made her lazy daisy cake, a favorite of Max's.

"Devlin didn't tell you it was zoned historic?" Sam asked. He and Devlin Knight were cousins, as well as best friends.

"He mentioned something about it, and sent some paperwork, but…" Max shrugged, making his sister laugh.

"But you never read the papers, did you?" she asked.

She turned to Sam. "My brother is allergic to fine print, among other things—like commitment, a steady job, owning a house—"

He felt a rush of annoyance only his big sister could ignite. "Seriously, Lex? You're sitting in the house I just bought, I'm self-employed, and there aren't many *commitments* bigger than being a father."

She started to snap back at him, but Sam rested his hand on her arm. She hesitated, then nodded. Max felt a newfound admiration for the man who could calm his sharp-tongued sister with just a touch. She looked over at Max.

"You're right. I'm sorry."

He snorted. "This place really *has* changed you if you can say those words without looking like you're eating lemons."

Sam chuckled softly, but Lexi just gave a little shrug. "I guess we've all dealt with some changes this year."

Before Max could agree, their mother came back with three dessert plates with cake on them. Instead of frosting, the cake was topped with a layer of toasted coconut and nuts. Tyler was right behind her, carrying the other two plates. Not smiling, but not actively resisting her, either. He'd seemed charmed by Phyllis Bellamy from the moment he'd met her at the Sassy Mermaid Motor Lodge the day they'd arrived.

The first thing he'd said that day, while still in the truck, was, "Why is her hair *pink*?"

That was a really good question, and one Max had no answer for. For the majority of his life, Phyllis Bellamy had been a model mom in suburban Des Moines, Iowa. Always neat as a pin, dressed to the nines, hair perfectly coiffed. She'd hosted the ritziest fundraisers at the country club, standing next to the husband she *knew* was sleeping with anyone who'd take him. When Max's father had the audacity to fall in love with, and leave her for, a woman younger than Max, Phyllis had been stunned. Then angry. And then she'd just…changed.

She'd chopped her brown hair short and dyed it hot pink. She'd traded her age-appropriate mom-wear for skintight tops and miniskirts, along with her beloved leopard print ankle boots. While in the midst of this metamorphosis, she'd learned an uncle she'd barely known had died and left her an old motel on Cape Cod. Instead of selling it immediately as her three children begged her to do, she'd sold their four-bedroom colonial back in Iowa instead, moving here to Winsome Cove to claim the small apartment above the motel office as her new home.

Mom and Tyler sat at the table, and Tyler stared dubiously at the small square of cake in front of him. "Why doesn't it have frosting?" he asked. "Cake should have frosting."

Mom leaned toward him, dropping her voice to a conspiratorial whisper. "It's so yummy that it doesn't *need* frosting."

"I don't think I'll like it." Tyler was gripping his fork, staring at the cake like it might attack him. He'd eaten a pretty good meal, so Max wasn't going to press the issue. His mother met Max's eyes and smiled.

"Well, that's fine, but there's only one way you'll know for sure, and that's to try it. It's your daddy's favorite." That would *not* be a selling point to Tyler. Sure enough, he set his fork down and sat back in his chair.

Mom just shrugged and took a big bite of her cake, moaning loudly in ecstasy, knowing Tyler was watching her every move.

When Max had introduced them, he'd told his mother not to take anything personally. "He's pretty shy," he'd said, "so don't be surprised if he doesn't open right up. And when he *does* start talking, he may ask more questions than you'll be able to handle."

His mother had laughed out loud at that. "More than I can handle, huh? Are you forgetting I raised three children, including a little boy who wanted to know *everything* from the minute he could speak?"

A weird emotion rippled through Max at that. He didn't remember being that inquisitive, but if he was, that meant Tyler got the trait from *him*. Which meant there was some of him in his son after all. The son who wouldn't even call him *Dad*.

Lexi smiled at the boy. "So, Tyler, how do you like Winsome Cove?"

Tyler wrinkled his nose. "It smells funny here."

"It does, doesn't it?" Mom laughed. "This town smells like salt water and fog and seals and sharks…"

"Sharks?" Tyler looked around like he expected to see a great white in the doorway. The kid worried about everything. "There are *sharks* here?"

Sam grinned. He owned a marina and did charter boat trips so people could fish or see whales, seals and— occasionally—sharks. "There are sharks in the ocean, buddy, but you don't have to worry about them on land." Sam's thick New England accent made *sharks* sound like *shahks*. "I can take you out on my boat sometime and show you where they are and where they aren't."

Tyler didn't look thrilled at the idea of a boat ride. He'd grown up surrounded by cornfields. He watched as everyone ate their dessert, and Max smiled to himself when the boy picked up his fork and took a small bite of cake. And then another. Tyler looked up at his grandmother, his voice small as he reluctantly admitted, "It's good, Nana."

Mom had told Tyler he could call her Grandma, but he'd refused, saying he already had a Grandma. So she'd suggested Nana, and he'd agreed. She whispered something in a silly voice to Tyler now, and the boy actually smiled briefly.

When Tyler smiled, Max got that same indefinable emotion he'd felt when Mom suggested Tyler got his curiosity from Max. He and his son were still virtual strangers who looked nothing alike, but there was a connection there. A bond.

"Hey, who's giving you a *hahd* time about the zoning?" Sam asked. "Maybe I can help." Sam was a fifth generation Winsome Cove resident, and he knew just about everyone in town.

"I think my biggest problem is going to be my next-door neighbor, Grace Bennett. She's the president of the historical society or whatever, and she's keeping a very close eye on everything I do."

He'd spotted the icy blonde at her kitchen window more than once, spying on him.

"Oh." Sam's voice was flat. "Grace."

"That doesn't sound good." Max set his fork down.

Sam grimaced. "Well, for one thing, I don't know her well, so I can't help much. I know her brother, Aiden. He's a dentist, and he's friendly enough. But Grace and

I don't exactly move in the same circles. I've seen her at a few business owner meetings in town. She has a reputation for being...um...stubborn. She runs Aiden's dental practice a few blocks from here. I've heard she's a stickler for doing things a certain way."

"Perfect." Max rolled his eyes.

He could hardly wait for Grace Bennett's reaction when he finished setting up the forge in his carriage house. As soon as the electrician finished rewiring the old building and the new propane tank was installed, Max would be getting back to work hammering out metal blades and sculptures. He had online orders stacking up, and he needed to get some money flowing again to pay for this place.

"But," Sam continued, "I *do* know that the restrictions in this neighborhood are mostly external and cosmetic. In other words, you can't alter the exterior of the house if it changes the historical accuracy. The committee needs to approve things like new windows, paint, roofing. There are a few truly historic landmark houses in town that have tighter controls about the interiors, but not here. Revere Street is unique because of the variety of styles and ages of the houses. This house is a late 1800s colonial, but Grace Bennett's bungalow is probably from the 1920s. Joe and Loretta's saltbox house—the brown one a few houses over—could be as old as the 1700s. But I don't think anything here is considered all that precious that anyone other than Grace Bennett would give you a hard time. We New England*ahs* tend to mind our own business."

"Yeah, well... Grace seems to be the exception to that

rule." Max finished his last bite of cake. "She stands at that kitchen window and watches every move I make."

His mother snorted. "That greenhouse window? It's probably over her kitchen sink, and she's just washing dishes. You're sounding a little paranoid, honey."

"Mom, I've *seen* her leaning forward to look around. And you didn't see the way she came trotting out on moving day, all sweet and sugary, to tell me I couldn't park my trailer here. She's a busybody, and I don't like busybodies."

He'd ended up parking the trailer at his mom's motel until he could figure out what to do with it. He'd probably end up selling it, since his traveling days were over for now.

His mother stared at him for a moment, then shook her head. "I know you've never had long-term neighbors— you just hopped in your motor home and drove off if you didn't like someone. But you can't do that anymore. You don't have to be best pals with this Bennett woman, but trust me—you don't want to be outright feuding with a next-door neighbor. Figure out a way to make peace."

"What do you want me to do—bake her a pie or something?"

Lexi came to his defense. "Isn't *she* the one who's supposed to do that, Mom? Welcome him to the neighborhood? Has anyone else welcomed you here?"

He nodded. "The Lanfreys next door—the *other* next door—brought a plate of brownies. Maya and Leon King from across the street brought me—" he glanced at Tyler "—*us* a casserole over the weekend. Baked ziti. It was good, wasn't it, buddy?"

Tyler started to give Max a typical who-cares shrug,

then he looked at his Nana. All she did was arch one eyebrow and the kid cracked. "It was okay."

Max chuckled, winking at his mother. "He polished off two pieces. They have a daughter Tyler's age—she's in his class at school."

Sam nodded. "Chantal, right? Leon works in construction—he did some work at our place this summer. He built that new deck across the back of the house, and he brought Chantal with him a few times. Cute kid."

Lexi stood and started to collect the dessert plates. "She's adorable. And if you need any work done here, Leon's the one to call. I love our new deck." She paused, glancing at their mother. "My point, though, is that Leon and Maya did the right thing by welcoming you to the neighborhood. You shouldn't have to kiss up to a neighbor who *didn't* welcome you."

Their mom's eyes narrowed. "I raised you all better than that. So far, all I've heard is that this woman introduced herself and warned you about something you could get in trouble for, which sounds pretty neighborly to me. Would you have preferred she let you get a zoning violation instead?" Max started to answer, but she talked over him. "And if she was a little abrupt in the two minutes that you spoke to her, there may have been a reason you just don't know about. Maybe she was having a bad day, or had just burned her finger on the stove, or couldn't get her afternoon nap because your movers were working right outside her window. It's not like you to judge someone that quickly, Max." She rolled her eyes toward Tyler. "Think of the example you're setting."

He wanted to argue, but…he couldn't. As usual, his mother was right. He and Grace had been immediately bristly with each other for some reason, but technically she hadn't done anything wrong.

Grace seemed to be the type of person who'd promptly report any violations she might spot, though. He'd seen her watching out of that window, and she acted like someone who'd do that.

The narc next door.

Chapter Two

One of the many things Grace loved about living on Cape Cod was the weather, even beyond summertime. Yes, winters could be frigid, and the occasional hurricane or nor'easter came blowing through, but autumn on the Cape was generally delightful. Like today, with temperatures in the seventies and bright sunshine.

It was a perfect Sunday afternoon for cleaning up her vegetable and flower gardens. Some of her backyard flowers were still going strong, thanks to the moisture-rich ocean air. The petunias from the front porch were getting a little straggly, but they were still blossoming, so she'd moved them to the back patio. She'd replaced them out front with a mix of potted mums and petunias. As long as she was in the backyard, she'd decided to cut back the vegetables in her raised beds. The tomatoes were done for the year, but she had cabbage, brussels sprouts and squash still going strong.

The beds were set into four raised rectangles along the south fence to get the most sun. Each was about two feet high, framed with thick cedar planks and four-by-four corners. Her father had built them thirty years ago for her mom, and then her brother, Aiden, had rebuilt them for Grace a few summers ago. She sat back on her heels and looked around the yard she'd loved her entire life. She knew every inch of it. Every plant. Every stone. It was orderly and productive, yes. But it was also… beautiful. Familiar. Soothing.

"Whatcha' doin'?" The voice, from only a few feet away, startled her so much that she dropped her hand trowel. The little boy, son of Tattoo Man, was standing at the fence, staring at her. His features were darker than Max's. He had wide brown eyes and tousled dark hair. He could barely see over the top of the picket fence. He nodded at the pile of uprooted plants at her feet. "That's not how you pick tomatoes, you know."

She couldn't help giving him a quick laugh. "Yes, I know. I'm not picking them. I'm pulling the plants up for the winter. Have you picked tomatoes before?"

The boy nodded. "My mom and grandma had a garden. They let me help."

"Where was that?"

"Ohio." His voice dropped so that she almost didn't hear him.

"That's a long way from Cape Cod. This was a big move for you, huh?"

He shrugged, then pointed to the plant bed behind her. "What's that?"

"That's acorn squash." She groaned as she stood and stretched, gesturing to the garden beds. "And that's brussels sprouts. They're like baby cabbages."

The boy made a face. "Gross."

"Sounds like someone hasn't had brussels sprouts roasted with bacon and balsamic glaze. It's yummy."

She walked over to the fence. "My name is Grace Bennett. What's yours?"

"Tyler Cosma."

Interesting. Max's last name was Bellamy. She'd done some inquiring after their first meeting. Maya King from across the street told Grace that it was just Max and his son, who was five, just like Maya's daughter, Chantal. No mom in sight. Maya also said Max was the son of Phyllis Bellamy, who'd inherited the old Sassy Mermaid Motor Lodge last year. Which meant he was the brother of Lexi Bellamy Knight, head chef at the newest restaurant in town, 200 Wharf. Lexi had recently married into one of the town's oldest seafaring families.

Phyllis encouraged local residents to use her motel property to access the beaches—a tradition her uncle had started—and Grace had taken advantage of that offer. But she and Phyllis weren't any more than waving acquaintances.

"Nice to meet you, Tyler." She looked around. He was young to be out here alone. "Where's your dad?"

"He's making a sword." He was so matter-of-fact that she laughed again.

"Really? Is he planning on slaying a dragon later?"

Tyler's eyes went wide. "Are there dragons here?"

"No, honey. I was making a joke, like you."

"I wasn't joking."

"Your dad actually makes swords?" Surely that was a joke.

He nodded. "He makes knives and axes and spears, too. In there."

He jerked his head toward the carriage house behind him. The square two-story building sat about twenty feet behind Max's house, not far from Grace's much smaller detached garage. The Hendersons had used the pretty old carriage house as a garage and for storage. It was painted blue and white, just like the house. Walt Henderson had kept his vintage Thunderbird in. Now there was smoke billowing up out of the small chimney.

Oh, great. She lived next to a guy who made actual weapons. Her eyes narrowed… Surely that was against one of the neighborhood covenants?

"What's your cat's name?"

She looked around quickly, thinking Mozart had gotten out somehow, but he was nowhere to be seen. He was probably curled up on the rocking chair on the screen porch. It was one of his favorite spots on a warm, sunny day.

"How do you know I have a cat?"

"I saw it in the window." He pointed at the greenhouse kitchen window. Another favorite sunning spot.

"His name is Mozart. He likes to sun himself in that window."

"Why Mozart? What does 'sun himself' mean?"

This was one curious kid. "Mozart is a music composer I like. Sunning himself means he likes to sleep in the warm sunshine."

"What's a composer?"

"Someone who writes music."

"Do you eat the food from here?"

"What?" He was zigzagging between topics. Where was his father?

"The *garden*," Tyler said, in a tone that said *duh*. "Do you eat the stuff? My grandma canned her garden food, and we ate it all year."

Tyler boldly opened her gate and walked into the yard,

looking around as if inspecting the gardens. Cheeky little kid.

"Well, I don't do any canning, but that was smart of your grandma. I freeze some of it and eat the rest or give it away." Her friends dreaded zucchini season.

Tyler nodded as if in approval of her answer. "What's your favorite?"

She thought about it. There was something about his seriousness that made her want to be honest with him. "I guess it would be green beans. And yellow beans, too."

His nose wrinkled again. "I don't like beans."

Hardly unusual for a five-year-old. "Well, *my* grandma used to make a dinner of yellow beans and potatoes cooked in milk, served over white bread. It was delicious."

That little nose remained wrinkled. "Beans on bread? Yuck."

She looked beyond him toward the carriage house. Where was Max Bellamy? This little boy was way too friendly with strangers to be wandering around by himself.

"Do you think your dad would like some acorn squash?" She'd picked some of the deep green squash and stacked them in the corner of the bed.

"That's not an acorn." There was the scolding tone again. "Acorns grow on trees."

"You're right, acorns do grow on trees. But this is a squash that's named for acorns because it's round like they are. See?" She held one up.

He was unimpressed. "Max doesn't cook as good as my mom. He doesn't do a lot of *veg-tables* like that. He said it's because he's been a one-man show too long." He took the dark, ridged globe from her. It was one of the smaller ones, but he still had to grip it with both hands. "What does it taste like? What do you cook it with?"

"It's delicious. I bake it with maple syrup and brown sugar."

He studied it. "Why is it black? It looks like it's rotten."

"Look closer. It's actually very dark green."

He held it up and studied it in the sunlight. She couldn't help smiling. The boy was smart, and genuinely curious about things.

"Oh, yeah, you're right. It's green."

"Tyler!" Max's voice called out sharp as a whip. He was in the doorway of the carriage house. His sandy brown hair was slicked back in thick waves, as if he'd just pushed it there with his fingers, and his faded T-shirt was sweat-soaked and clinging to him. He stepped out of the shadows and into the sun, looking around.

He was *so* not her type—she preferred a quieter, more studious man—but...*oh, my.* The guy had muscles for days—thick biceps, broad shoulders and six-pack abs that the shirt defined very clearly. Even his *neck* had muscles. He *looked* like a man who spent his days sweating over a hot forge, hammering on steel blades and...

Get it together, Grace!

She blinked and looked away, shocked at her visceral reaction to her new neighbor. Admiring his physique simply wouldn't do. Completely unproductive. He called his son's name again, with a tinge of worry on the edge of his voice. Tyler was silent. This wasn't a game she was going to let him play.

"He's over here!" She waved her hand to get his attention. "We were just talking about vegetable gardens."

Max hurried over to the fence, his expression easing when he spotted Tyler. But he was still frowning.

"I told you to stay in the backyard. You can't just wander off."

The boy looked around and shrugged.

"*This* is a backyard."

Grace bit her lip at his cheekiness, knowing she shouldn't encourage it. Max's eyes narrowed.

"You know damn—" he grimaced and took a breath "—you know I meant *our* backyard. I told you very clearly to stay in *our* yard, Tyler. You disobeyed me by coming over here and bothering Ms. Bennett in *her* yard."

The boy's sass was gone in the face of his father's scolding, and he dropped his head to stare at the ground, mumbling, "I know."

Grace bristled at Max's tone. "Maybe you should have been paying more attention. You can't expect a little boy to just follow orders without being supervised." She may not have children, but she knew that much.

"He's old enough to know what 'stay in the yard' means." Max wasn't backing down. "Look, I'm sorry he bothered you. It won't happen again." He looked down at Tyler. "Will it?"

His only answer was a quick shake of his head. Grace found young children to be chaotic, and she didn't do chaos well. But this intelligent, and somehow terribly sad, little boy tugged at her heart. She put her hand on his shoulder.

"That's my fault," she said. "He came to the fence and asked what I was doing, and I showed him my garden beds." She didn't mention that Tyler had invited himself in. "I was just asking him if he wanted to take home an acorn squash for you to cook."

Tyler held up the squash with a quick grin. "It's *green*!"

Max looked between Tyler and her, as if deciding if he should stay angry or not. "Uh...yes, it is green."

"You know how to cook it, right, Max?" Tyler had just finished telling Grace his dad wasn't much of a cook, so she knew he was setting a little trap to embarrass his father.

"Sure he does," she cut in before Max could answer. "*Everyone* knows how to cook acorn squash."

Max stared hard at her, then gave her a brittle smile. "Sure. Everyone knows that."

"Can you make it tonight?" Tyler asked.

Max hesitated, then nodded. "I guess so."

"Grace said—"

"You don't call adults by their first names without permission, Tyler. It's Ms....." He walked through the gate and looked at Grace. "Mrs.?"

Was he fishing for information, or giving Tyler a manners lesson?

"Tyler, I'm Miss Bennett," she answered. "But I give you permission to call me Grace." She emphasized the *Miss* for Max's benefit.

"You play the piano." Tyler said it as a statement, not a question.

"Um, yes. I do. You've heard me?"

Her father had bought the baby grand piano for her mother and then created a music nook in the corner of the living room, where bookshelves lined the walls. They'd made sure Grace started lessons at an early age.

She'd continued in college, and even thought she might play for a living...until the night that changed the course of her life forever. It took a while, but after the attack, she'd found comfort again in music. There was an order in the clearly defined notes on the lines of her sheet music. Grace liked things to be orderly.

"I hear you a lot!" Tyler said.

His father seemed surprised. "I've heard music, but I thought it was a recording, not you playing."

"I'll take that as a compliment," she said, not at all sure he meant it that way. "I give lessons, too, so sometimes you're hearing my students." She was selective about who she taught, because she took her music so seriously. At the moment, she had three students—two high schoolers and an older woman who'd taken classical piano when she was younger and was trying to refresh her skills.

"My mom played piano."

Grace didn't think much of the four simple words until she saw the effect they had on Max. He stared at Tyler in what seemed to be shock.

"I... I didn't know that."

This was one of those moments when Max wished he could just suspend time and call the social worker back in Ohio and ask her what to do. Tyler didn't speak of his mother often. The social worker, Sandy, told him it would be healthy for the boy to talk through his emotions and grieve his mom properly. The brief, but intense, custody battle had prevented some of that grieving process from happening. Sandy had promised Max that it was going to have to be dealt with sooner or later.

"She was teaching me." Tyler's eyes lit up, and he turned back to Grace. "Can *you* teach me?"

Her face froze briefly, then she shook her head sharply. "Oh…um… I don't teach children your age, honey. But maybe when you're older…"

The joy was gone from his son's face in an instant, and Max felt a pain in his heart as sharp as if someone had stabbed him with the saber he'd just been working on in the forge. He was still getting used to these emotions that came out of nowhere as a parent. Tyler's pain was *his* pain. His joy was Max's joy.

When Max had looked out at his yard a few minutes ago and hadn't seen Tyler there, the panic nearly buckled his knees. Fatherhood felt like the world's best, and scariest, roller coaster.

"Tyler," he started, "do you really want to learn how to play?" There was an old upright piano in the house that the sellers had left, along with some of the furniture he'd agreed to buy. Max figured the piano was something he'd get rid of once he bought more furniture of his own for the place.

He got the shrug from hell in response. Max hated that particular shrug—the one where Tyler paused, but instead of telling Max what was on his mind, he'd just lift both little shoulders and let them fall. It felt like a slap in the face, but Sandy had told Max it would take time for Tyler to trust him with his true feelings. Max took a deep breath, blowing it out slowly and trying not to look or sound as frustrated as he felt. He put his hand on Tyler's shoulder and waited until he looked up.

"If you want piano lessons, we'll find someone to teach you. I'll get that old piano tuned and you can play it, just like your mom did." He glanced at Grace, who looked confused and very curious. "Maybe Miss Bennett can give me some names of other teachers if she can't do it. I play guitar, so you and I could play music together. Would you like that, son?"

Max braced himself for the dreaded shrug, but Tyler gave a slow nod. It was lacking in enthusiasm, but enthusiasm was an emotion Tyler didn't show Max very often. A nod was about as good as it got.

"Okay," he said. "Say thank you to Miss Bennett, and take that squash into the kitchen."

"Thank you, Grace." He glanced at Max. "She said I could call her that." Tyler mumbled the words so quickly they were barely comprehensible, then ran past his father and over to their back door, clutching the small round squash in his hands.

Max watched until Tyler was inside, then turned back to Grace. "I'm sorry if he bothered you—"

After their first run-in, he hadn't pictured her as a woman who'd give her time—and produce—to an impatient child. He'd assumed she was going to be a neighbor like Mrs. Shastin from his childhood. Every neighborhood had one—the grumpy old person who yelled at the kids for being too loud and refused to return any balls that landed in their yard.

"He wasn't a bother," she answered. "Although I was surprised to see him outside by himself."

"I *told* him to stay in our yard." He couldn't help being defensive, but the woman was right. It *had* taken too long for him to realize Tyler had disobeyed his instructions. He didn't think he'd ever get used to people judging his parenting skills, though. It reminded him too much of Tyler's grandparents arguing that Max didn't know how to be a father. He was doing the best he could.

He gave her a pointed look. "Maybe you shouldn't have been hiding him over here. You could have sent him back to his own home, where he belonged."

She went ramrod straight. "I wasn't trying to hide him." She paused, brushing a loose strand of hair from her face. "But you're right. I should have told him to get your permission. I'm sorry."

Had his nosy, critical neighbor just *apologized*? Max gave her a nod of acknowledgment. His mother told him he didn't want to make enemies of neighbors, even if they were busybodies. And Grace *had* been kind to Tyler. Tyler didn't warm to strangers easily, but he'd walked right over to Grace's yard and spoken to her.

She didn't look as prim and proper today as their first encounter. Her thick honey-blond hair was pulled back into a low ponytail, and she was wearing ankle-length trousers and tennis shoes, with a dark gold sweater that almost matched her eyes. She was attractive, with her high cheekbones and wide smile. Not that she'd smiled at Max much since they'd met, but she had with Tyler, and it was a showstopper of a smile.

She had a smudge of dirt on her cheek, and he was suddenly tempted to reach out and brush it away. Max rubbed the back of his neck instead and realized exactly how sweaty he was. Ugh. His shirt was stuck to him. He picked at it, then made a face.

"I need to apologize, too," he said. "Once again I'm not looking or smelling my best. I was working in the forge and—"

"Tyler said you made swords, but I thought he was exaggerating."

"No exaggeration. I make blades of all kinds."

"As a hobby, right?" One eyebrow rose, as if she was hoping he'd say yes.

"Uh, no. It's how I make my living." At least, he hoped it would continue to be his livelihood. Without traveling to fairs, he was going to have to rely heavily on word of mouth and his website. And maybe pick up a part-time job. Cape Cod was expensive.

She hesitated. "You make *weapons* for a living. In a residential neighborhood."

Here we go.

"Are you going to report me to the town about *that*, too?" His irritation rose. He'd been right about her after all. "Because that's something I *did* check on when I bought the house. In fact, this town is so old that there are specific ordinances spelling out where blacksmiths can operate. They have to be in freestanding buildings—" he started counting off on his fingers "—the forge must be vented to the outside, and there needs to be at least two points of egress from the building."

She didn't look convinced. "Isn't there a lot of noise and hammering with blacksmithing?"

"Not the kind of noise that would be against the law, at least not before ten at night. And I'm insulating the power hammer as much as possible." He'd created a booth for the pneumatic hammer, but the foam insulating tiles hadn't arrived yet. Despite what Grace Bennett thought, he intended to be a considerate neighbor. He folded his arms on his chest. "Any more questions before you call the town offices to verify what I've said?"

"I didn't say I was going to report you." She tugged at the hem of her sweater, her voice softer. "I wasn't aware the town had blacksmith laws in place, but it makes sense, since Winsome Cove is over three hundred years old. I'm glad you did your homework on that, but it's still a business operating in a residential neighborhood. And I'm not happy that you're making *weapons*."

He scrubbed his hands down his face, not sure if he should laugh or scream. "I am not a freakin' serial killer, Grace. Most of my blades are ornamental—they hang on people's walls. I make a few functional axes and kitchen knives, but those are for domestic use, not as tools of war. Besides, how is what I'm doing any more commercial than getting paid for piano lessons?"

"That's different…"

"How is it different?"

"Well…" She started to sputter. "The lessons are private. And I have three students total, not a parade of customers coming to buy something from me."

"Have you seen a parade of people at my place?"

"Not yet, but—"

Oh, man. She really was a Mrs. Shastin after all.

"I sell my blades online," he explained, trying to keep his voice level. "Very rarely will any customer live close enough to come to the forge. I won't be opening a showroom here, so relax. If that's something you know how to do."

That last bit was unnecessary, and he regretted it as soon as the words left his lips. He didn't know this woman well enough to make a jab like that. Seeing her puff up in indignation told him she felt the same way.

"I beg your pardon? Just because I believe in following the rules doesn't mean I'm not capable of relaxing. In fact, I'm the *most* relaxed when rules are followed. Laws and regulations are there for a reason. They're a way of maintaining order." Her cheeks were turning pink. Max had clearly touched a nerve, and he had a feeling this wasn't the first time she'd given this little speech.

"Okay, okay. I get it." He held up his hands. "Rules make you happy. Fine. I just think it sounds boring to go through life worrying about every little rule that might exist. Breaking the rules once in a while can be fun."

She looked down, her eyes clouded with some emotion he couldn't identify. She was holding her gardening gloves in one hand, and her fingers were so tight around them that her knuckles were turning white.

"It's *not* fun."

He barely heard her words, spoken so softly. But as soon as they sank in, he knew something had happened to her or someone she knew. It must have happened because someone broke the rules. Max had enough problems dealing with his *own* life right now to ask about her issues, but it would be cruel to push her any further.

"I'm not sure how we ended up debating life philosophies here, but... I didn't mean to upset you. There's nothing wrong with following rules. That's exactly what I'm doing with my forge." He tipped his head to the side and smiled at her, trying to break the tension.

There was a long pause before her face softened and she returned from whatever dark place her thoughts had taken her. Okay, he was officially curious, even if he shouldn't be. Grace was more interesting than he'd assumed at their first meeting. He liked interesting women. But...nope. He'd sworn off women for the time being.

Tyler needed all of his attention. The kid did *not* need any more strangers coming into his life.

"Do you know how to cook that squash I gave Tyler?" There was just the slightest hint of knowing in her voice, and his face heated. Had Tyler said something about Max's cooking skills? Sure, his specialty was single-guy food, but he did well enough to keep them alive, and he was watching a ton of online cooking videos to up his game. He was also grateful for his talented mom and sister, who both dropped off meals regularly. One of them could tell him what to do with that squash.

"I'll manage," he answered. She didn't look convinced, but she didn't press him.

"I cook mine with butter and maple syrup, if you have any." She looked across the two driveways to his house. "I'll bet Tyler will love it."

"He wouldn't tell me so, even if he did." He was whining about his own son. Not a good look. "I didn't mean that. Sorry. Thanks for the squash. I should, uh, go make sure he hasn't started playing soccer with it."

Chapter Three

"I just can't figure Max Bellamy out." Grace scowled into her coffee cup. She was in the break room at her brother's dental practice. Aiden was at the counter pouring coffee for himself. He glanced over his shoulder at her.

"Do you need to?"

"What do you mean?"

"He's just a neighbor. As long as he minds his own business, do you need to know what makes him tick? It's not like you have to be friends." Aiden paused, then turned dramatically, pretending to be some valley girl teenager, with a scandalized look on his face. "Oh. My. God. Do you *like* him? Is he hot?" Aiden breathlessly took a seat at the table, resting his chin in his hand. "Tell me *everything*."

"Don't be an ass." Grace stuck her tongue out at her big brother. "I don't like *or* dislike the man. He's just hard to read. He was rude the first time we met, but then on Sunday he was…different. Mad about losing track of his little boy, then he chatted nicely, then he got prickly when I asked a few questions about him operating an actual forge in the carriage house, and then he turned nice again."

Aiden had gone still when she mentioned the forge. "Define asking a *few questions*."

"They were legitimate questions, Aiden. Excuse me if I'm not thrilled that my new neighbor is manufacturing actual *swords* next door. What kind of guy does that in this day and age? Is he obsessed with weapons?"

"Sis, there's a hit cable show where bladesmiths compete against each other for money, so it's not *that* uncommon. Just think how popular Dungeons & Dragons is, or *Game of Thrones*, not to mention all the Tolkien books and movies. The Renaissance fairs draw big crowds. It might be a niche thing, but it's a pretty big niche." He gave her a shoulder nudge. "I don't think people use them for actual sword fights. They're probably made to hang on a wall. Relax."

Relax. That was the same thing Max had lectured her about.

"I'm perfectly relaxed, Aiden. I'm just…curious."

"Right." He stood with a sigh. "Mrs. Niven is coming in for a root canal, so I'd better make sure we're ready for her. She can be a handful. You said this Max guy has a kid, right?"

"A little boy, Tyler. He's cute. Very inquisitive. But there's a weight on him. More weight than a five-year-old should carry. I don't know their family situation, so I'm not sure where the mom is. Maybe Ohio?"

Aiden patted her shoulder. "I'm sure you'll find a way to get their story."

"You make me sound like some sitcom busybody neighbor. I'm genuinely concerned, Aiden."

Her brother had started to turn away, but he stopped. "I know that, Grace. But sometimes you come across so serious that *other* people don't know that. You've built some mighty high walls around you."

"With good reason," she pointed out. She absently rubbed her fingers on the front of her shoulder, feeling the scar from a bullet wound beneath her blouse.

"Again, *I* know that. But I worry about you protecting yourself so much that—"

The break room door opened behind him, and Allison Davis poked her head around it. "Sorry to interrupt, but Mrs. Niven is here, and Therese says she's already starting to hyperventilate out in the waiting room."

Grace stood. "I should get back to the front desk so Therese can have lunch."

Aiden put his hand on her arm to stop her, then gave Allison a smile. "Bring Mrs. Niven in and set her up in exam room three. I'll be right there." He waited until his dental assistant left, then turned back to Grace. "This conversation isn't over. I worry about you shutting everyone out...being alone..."

"Shutting one new neighbor out is not exactly a crisis." And she did *not* want to talk about what happened twelve years ago. She'd moved on and had no interest in going back. "I'm fine."

But apparently she hadn't even managed to shut the new neighbor out, because Max Bellamy was sitting on her front porch steps when she got home that evening. Her car's headlights caught him there, and he stood as she pulled into the driveway. She had motion lights facing the driveway, and they lit up the whole side of her house as she parked. Max waited for her at the front corner of her house. She took a deep breath and opened the door. Tyler wasn't with him.

"Is everything okay?" she asked. Had Tyler wandered off?

"Yes," he spread his hands wide and didn't move any closer. "Sorry to be lurking here, but I was hoping to catch you before I headed over to bring Tyler home from my mom's place. I need a favor."

"O-kay…" Grace grabbed her bag and locked the car. It was silly to be so hesitant. Max wasn't doing anything wrong. Her neighbor might be rough around the edges, but he'd never once felt threatening. Not even now, waiting for her in the near dark. She gave him a polite smile as she walked toward him. "How can I help?"

"Do you remember the other day, when Tyler talked about playing the piano, and how his mom played?"

"That's right—you wanted me to get some recommendations for a teacher, didn't you?"

"Well…no." He rubbed the back of his neck and stared at the ground for a moment before looking up at her. "I want you to teach him."

"Oh, no. Sorry." She shook her head sharply. "I honestly don't teach beginners. My youngest student right now is sixteen—"

"Tyler insists he won't go to anyone but you."

"What? Why? We only talked for a few minutes…"

Max shook his head with a heavy sigh. "Do not ask me to explain the workings of a five-year-old mind, Grace. I'm new at this, and I honestly have no clue."

He was *new* at this? How could the father of a five-year-old consider himself *new*? Maybe he meant new at being a single father. There must have been a divorce.

Maybe that was the weight she'd sensed on Tyler. And the way he lit up when he talked about his mom playing piano. He must miss her. But that wasn't Grace's concern. Not that she didn't care about the boy, but she didn't want to be involved in whatever was going on. It sounded messy, and she didn't do messy.

"I'm sorry, but I wouldn't even know where to begin. I'll check around and see if—"

"The kid has made up his mind, and it has to be you. There are very few things he cares strongly about, and he is adamant that you need to teach him. He does know some basics, so maybe not exactly a beginner...?"

"He's *five*." She shifted her bag on her shoulder. They were still standing outside at the base of the side steps to her kitchen door. There was a fine mist in the air— an ocean fog was rolling in. "Come inside."

She should have thought the invitation through before offering. Once she'd unlocked the door and Max followed her into her cheery orange and white kitchen, she realized how imposing he was. Again, not threatening, but the man filled a doorway. Hell, he filled the whole room. His faded jeans and well-worn leather jacket were starkly casual in her bright, organized space.

The stubble on his chin. The faint line of dirt beneath his nails. His calloused hands. The thick, messy waves of brown hair. The faint smell of smoke and sweat as she'd opened the door for him. The base energy that radiated from him. He was unlike anyone who'd stood in here before. All of her senses felt heightened. It was as if his energy was amping hers up just by sheer proximity. She cleared her throat and tried to corral her emotions.

"No offense, but every parent considers their child

to be exceptional. I highly doubt a boy Tyler's age is at an intermediate level—"

"Maybe not what *you* consider intermediate, but he can read music, he knows the scale and he seems to have a good grasp of music in general. He gets how it works and knows when it doesn't. That kind of musical sense can't really be taught." Max was still at the door, as if aware of how out of place he was in her house. "He sat at the old piano in our front room, and I was genuinely surprised. And he *wants* this so bad—more than I've seen him want anything. He said his mom was teaching him…"

Grace knew she'd sound condescending if she told Max that children don't always get what they want. There was more to it than that. She could tell by how almost *desperate* Max seemed. But for her to take on a young child as a student… She had nothing against kids in general, but they were so unpredictable.

"Why can't his mother teach him?" She was running out of reasons to say no.

Max blinked a few times, then sighed, staring at the floor.

"His mother is dead."

There were only so many ways to share that fact, and Max believed in being direct. But Grace's sharp gasp told him that maybe he should have softened the news a bit. Her left hand went out to the counter to steady herself. Yeah, he could have been smoother. But how else do you say it? Marie *was* dead. Still, he felt obliged to apologize.

"Sorry to just blurt that out, but that's the situation. That's why she can't teach him."

"I'm *so* sorry, Max. How awful for you and Tyler. She must have been very young."

Marie *had* been young. That was one of the reasons he'd had no interest in pursuing anything long-term with her. He was pretty sure the age gap was also one of the reasons her parents had been so hostile. It wasn't like she'd been a child, though. She'd been out of college and living on her own when they met.

"She was twenty-eight. It was a car accident."

A heavy silence filled the aggressively cheerful kitchen. It was bright—oranges and yellows, with white cupboards and stone counters. The corner where a small breakfast table sat was wallpapered in big, bright daisies. It was a sharp contrast to his own kitchen, with the dated golden oak cupboards. It was dark outside, but this space felt fun and inviting. It showed a side of Grace he hadn't imagined. Miss Prim and Proper liked things modern and playful in her house. Who'd have thought?

There were two small dishes on a place mat on the floor in the corner, one with kibble and one with water. Tyler had mentioned that she had a cat. Somehow, Grace being a cat lady made perfect sense.

"Do you have time for a cup of coffee?" she asked, snapping his attention back to her. She'd set her bag on a chair and was shedding her hooded raincoat. Sam said she managed her brother's small town dental office, but she looked like she could walk into any corporate boardroom up in Boston. Her burgundy wool trousers picked up the dark red in her hip-length plaid blazer. Beneath the jacket, she wore a silky beige top with a softly draped neckline. Gold jewelry completed the look—every last detail carefully selected. The look suited her, but was way too buttoned-up for his taste. His *usual* taste, anyway.

Max glanced at his watch. Mom wasn't expecting him for another hour, and the Sassy Mermaid Motor Lodge was five minutes away. Tyler was beginning to bond with Phyllis Bellamy, and he liked hanging out at the old motel with her. Maybe more than he liked being with Max. Which brought him back to why he was standing in Grace's kitchen. If he could convince her to give Tyler lessons, maybe the boy would realize how much his father cared about making him happy.

"Max? Coffee? It's a Keurig, so I can make whatever you want—regular, flavored, decaf?" Grace had an orange polka-dot mug in her hand, waiting for his answer with one eyebrow raised.

"Um…yeah. Sure. Regular. Black."

She nodded toward the table. "It's okay to come inside. Have a seat."

She made his coffee, then a mug of decaf for herself, before joining him at the table. Her eyes, soft and golden brown, were still filled with sorrow and concern.

"Tell me about her."

"Who? Oh… Tyler's mom? I can't tell you much, really. I didn't know her that well, or for very long."

Grace sat back, fully focused on him now. "You weren't together when she passed?"

"We were never together at all."

He started to give her the abridged version of the story, but found himself sharing more than he intended. How he and Marie had met at a Renaissance fair outside Cincinnati that ran for four weekends in September. She was part of the entertainment, dancing around in a corset and flowing skirt slit to her thigh while she played the tambourine and sang. Her family was Romanian, and she had long black curly hair and big dark eyes, like Tyler. Max had rented a vendor's booth and was selling decorative swords and axes, as well as kitchen knives and some garden sculptures—stylized dragons and castles. When he did fairs like that, he always set up a portable forge and worked the steel right there for people to watch.

Marie made a point to keep dancing by his booth, singing and laughing. They'd flirted playfully at first. By the third weekend, they shared a few glasses of mead, and she'd followed him to his motor home for a night of lovemaking. They'd used protection. They'd made their intentions very clear—it was a temporary fling. Nothing more. He'd had another fair waiting in Alabama, so they'd said their goodbyes and that was that. Until six months ago, when social services tracked him down with the news that he was a father.

Grace was hanging on every word at this point. "You didn't know she'd had Tyler?"

"Not a clue. But she put my name on his birth certificate, thank God. Otherwise, her parents would have ended up with custody, and I never would have known." He quickly hit the highlights—or *low*lights—of the custody fight and the bad blood between Marie's parents and him. Including that they'd made him take a paternity test in the hopes that he *wasn't* the father. Which didn't say much for their trust of Marie. "And that's one of the reasons I ended up here," he said, taking one last sip of his coffee. "The move was hard on Tyler, but I thought he needed a complete change, away from the drama. Away from people poisoning him against me." He frowned down into the empty mug. "It's hard enough learning to be a dad out of the blue. I didn't need people telling Tyler or me how lousy I was at it."

"I don't think you're lousy at it." Grace's voice had a different tone, one he couldn't quite identify. It wasn't pity or sadness. It wasn't fake positivity. It was...kindness. The realization did something odd inside his chest. His pulse jumped and skipped, then settled into a strong, steady rhythm, as if finally finding safety and truth and...

What the hell?

He sat up abruptly. He hadn't had anything to drink, but he was clearly under the influence of something. The influence of Grace? Or just the unfamiliar feeling of support from someone who wasn't an immediate relative? He told himself it had to be the latter. But his heart never changed its beat, whispering to him that it was the woman making him feel this way.

Her shoulders straightened. "I'll give Tyler piano lessons."

Before Max could do something stupid like cartwheel across the kitchen, she held up her hand in caution. "I'm not committing to anything long-term, but I can assess his skill level and knock the rust off his fingers—I'm sure it's been a while since he's played. Then we'll discuss what's next. If I decide to introduce him to another instructor, I'm sure he'll be okay with it."

Max had his doubts. Tyler was a very determined little boy. He either didn't care at all, or he cared one whole hell of a lot. And once he'd learned Grace gave lessons, it was all he'd talked about. But this was a start, and Max was grateful for it.

"I really appreciate this, Grace. It's the first thing I've seen him get excited about, so I want to show him I've noticed and did something about it." She didn't look enthusiastic, and his smile faded. "Why so hesitant? Do you really not like teaching young kids?"

She gave a quick, embarrassed smile. "I don't dislike children, if that's what you're thinking. I just…" She shrugged. "Young children can be chaos monsters, and I'm not a fan of chaos. They're so…unpredictable. I understand that they're just being normal kids, and pushing boundaries is how they learn and all that, but—"

"But you like it when rules are followed and people behave themselves," he finished the thought for her. And she didn't bother disagreeing. This much he knew about her, if not much else. "You're not wrong about the chaos. The lack of adult logic has been one of my biggest learning curves with Tyler. My work in the forge can be dangerous, and I believe in safety first. But just telling him 'that's dangerous' doesn't seem to get through. I have to lay out exactly what *could* happen, without being graphic, and then answer his fifty questions about what I've just explained." Had he just given her a reason to change her mind? He leaned forward. "But Tyler's mature for his age in a lot of ways, and he loves music. I had no idea until I saw him talking to you in the backyard."

It wasn't for lack of trying. Max had asked all kinds of questions about what Tyler liked and didn't like. And Tyler had seen Max's guitars and heard the blues music Max liked. But he'd never said a word, not even when he saw the upright piano the Hendersons had left in the house. It was like Tyler refused to give any ground at all to Max, even if he was spiting himself in the process. *Chaos monster.*

"I hope I can live up to his expectations," Grace said, suddenly looking concerned.

"I have no doubt that you will. And really, anything you do will be a step forward, and that's all I can ask." He glanced at his watch and stood. "I'd better go get him from Mom's. Tomorrow's a school day. What time is good for a lesson? Oh, wait, you work… Maybe before dinner one night a week?" He felt like he was babbling all of a sudden, desperate for her to commit to lessons before she changed her mind.

"I have Friday afternoons off. I could probably fit Tyler in at four o'clock, if that would work. His lessons would only be about thirty minutes to start."

Grace's New England accent was much softer than Sam's or other locals Max had spoken to. There was a refinement to Grace's voice, as if she worked at controlling her pronunciation. *Typical.* But she still softened her Rs enough that *start* sounded more like *staht*. He liked it.

"Fridays are perfect. I really appreciate this."

She nodded, jotting something in a planner sitting near her place at the table. "I'll order a book for him to use, and you'll need to make sure your piano is properly tuned." She pulled a business card from the back of the planner. "I use Jeff, and I think Lucy Henderson did, too. He's from Falmouth, and his prices are reasonable." Her expression had changed from concern and sympathy to all business. This was the Grace he was more familiar with. In control. She stood to face him. "You're the one who will have to make sure he practices. He can't just come to lessons and then blow it off until the next lesson. And if he decides he's not that interested, we'll bring it to a close. I'm not going to nag a five-year-old."

"One skill I've managed to perfect this year is nagging a five-year-old, so I'll handle that part. But he seems genuinely enthusiastic about this."

"They're all enthusiastic to *play*," Grace answered. "But *learning* to play isn't quite as much fun as they think it will be."

Yes, she was back to prim and organized. Grace-in-Control. But there was something softer about her eyes. Pity for him? For Tyler? Or genuine caring—he wasn't sure. Whatever it was, it made the woman even more appealing. And distracting. He didn't need distractions right now.

"Makes sense." He turned for the door. "I'll do my best to keep focused around you… I mean, keep Tyler focused on your lessons."

Smooth move, Bellamy.

She just nodded. He left before he could make himself look any sillier. She locked the door behind him—two locks?—and it took all his willpower not to look back to see if she was watching through the window. Whatever hold that woman had on him, he was going to have to resist it. For one thing, she didn't seem at all interested. And for another, his son needed Max's complete focus right now. He was off the dating market. He was a big boy, and perfectly capable of, and experienced at, being unattached. Even if he had been free, prim Miss Grace Bennett was not his type.

He opened the door to his truck. Then again, maybe it was time for his type to change.

Nah. He was doing just fine.

Chapter Four

All parents thought their children were prodigies. Or at the very least, exceptional. It was another reason Grace avoided teaching piano to children—the parents. They hovered, they pushed, they expressed their disappointment over any perceived lack of progress. They wanted their child to be ready to compete on *America's Got Talent* after six months of beginner lessons. It was frustrating having to break the sad news to them that little Johnny or Nancy would *never* be in a music competition. *Ever.* No matter how much they practiced.

But now, as she stood watching Tyler playing a relatively advanced melody from his lesson book, she couldn't help thinking of the way she'd mentally rolled her eyes at Max nearly a month ago, when he'd suggested Tyler might be at the intermediate level. Was he a prodigy? No. He wouldn't be playing in concert halls any time soon, if ever. But Tyler's mother had taught him well, and Max had been right about the boy having an intuitive understanding of rhythm and timing. He knew what quarter notes and half notes and whole notes were. He even understood what the basic rest symbols meant. She'd bought a popular children's lesson book for him with a zebra on the cover and was happy to learn his mom had started him on the same book. But he was almost finished with it, so she was going to have to find something more challenging for him.

"That was a boring song, Grace." Tyler's shoulders slumped when he hit the last note. "I liked last week's song better."

Grace smiled down at him. "This song was closer to a nocturne—" on a child's level, of course "—which means it's a song inspired by nighttime, when things are soft and quiet. There are some very pretty nocturnes, though."

"Do you know any?" Tyler liked to watch Grace play the piano. She wasn't sure if it was a stalling tactic, or if it reminded him of his mother. Maybe a bit of both.

"Sure I do. One of my favorite Chopin pieces is a nocturne. It reminds me of a warm summer night. Do you want to hear it?" He nodded, scooting over on the bench so she could join him. "I don't expect you to be able to play this one yet, Tyler, but there are some shorter passages I could teach you. So listen, but also watch my fingers."

She began to play, and the hypnotic rhythm of the music filled the room. Tyler was watching her closely, and his face lit up when she hit the measure with the distinctive quick trill of notes. He didn't say anything for a moment after she finished, then he breathed a soft "Wow."

Grace chuckled. "See? Nocturnes can be fun, but they're not for everyone. Would you rather play something more lively and modern? Is there a type of music you like?" His answer would help her decide which lesson book to order for him.

He stared at the keyboard, then glanced up at her

through his long, dark eyelashes. It was as if he was embarrassed to tell her.

"Blues?" he finally said quietly.

Her heart jumped a little at the single word. She'd been hearing Max's speakers playing at night when he was in the carriage house. It was very definitely blues music, but more guitar than keyboard. Some songs were slow and sultry, and some were closer to classic rock, with long guitar riffs. Max had told her how fragile his new relationship with his son was. How unimpressed Tyler seemed to be with him. And yet...his son wanted to play the music Max loved. She gave Tyler a quick hug. She didn't want to make a fuss and risk making him recant. There was only one problem... Were there lesson books at his age level with blues music? Blues was usually four-four time, but with a unique syncopation and often with flattened chords. That would be a challenge for a five-year-old. As it was, his hands were too small to play most regular chords.

"In other words," she started, "you aren't crazy about my beloved classical music?" His nose wrinkled, making her laugh. "I can definitely move you to more contemporary stuff—maybe some Disney tunes?" He nodded. "And I'll look for some beginner blues, too, but I'm not sure what's available. If you really want to step up, it may take more lesson time." A full hour lesson would be too much for someone so young. "Maybe two half-hour lessons and lots of practice time at home?"

His head bobbed up and down. "I can do that!"

In a matter of a few weeks, this shy little boy had started to blossom. Tyler was still calling his father by his first name, but he'd just asked to learn the same music that Max enjoyed. That couldn't be a coincidence. It's not that Grace was crediting the piano lessons as the answer. Tyler had mentioned having a new friend, Isaac, at school, and liking his teacher, Miss Kelleher. Grace wasn't surprised at that—she knew Mary Kelleher from the community chorus. Grace played accompaniment and Mary was a first soprano.

And she'd seen Tyler playing with young Chantal from across the street the other day. Chantal's mother—and one of Grace's best friends—Maya King had watched Tyler a few times for Max when he needed to go somewhere. It looked as if this fresh start Max wanted to give Tyler was beginning to take hold.

"So can I come back tomorrow for another class?"

Tyler's question brought her back to the present. As usual, whenever her thoughts wandered to Max Bellamy, they tended to linger there, and she'd almost forgotten about the child at her side.

"Not tomorrow, Max—I mean, *Tyler*. First I have to talk to your dad and make sure it's okay. Remember, he's paying for these lessons. Because he loves you." It was a heavy-handed oversell, but she couldn't resist. Tyler's nose wrinkled again.

"Can I pet Mozart now?"

The boy was fascinated with the aloof Siamese cat. Mozart was *not* fascinated by the boy, and usually bolted when Tyler came thumping into the house.

"I think Mozart is sleeping upstairs." She'd meant that as a way of saying Mozart wasn't available. Tyler took it as an invitation.

"I'll find him!" He ran up the staircase before she could react.

"No! Tyler, don't disturb…"

She was talking to an empty room. She reminded herself for the hundredth time that this was why she didn't teach young children. They were inherently out of control. She followed him upstairs to make sure child and cat were safe.

She found them in her bedroom at the back of the house. Mozart was standing on the pillows on the bed, glaring at Tyler. His back was arched, but not much. This was his *how dare you?* pose, not his *I will cut you!* pose. Tyler was lying on his stomach on the bed, talking quietly to the cat.

"It's okay, Mozart. I won't pick you up. My grandma and grandpa have a cat named Fluffy, and he doesn't like to be carried, either. He scratched my arm once, and it bled. My mom got mad but Grandma said Fluffy was just being a cat and I was just being a boy and that he and I would figure it out." He belly-crawled closer to a wary Mozart. "I just want to be your friend. I miss Fluffy." His voice dropped. "I miss everyone."

Grace swallowed the emotions rising in her throat. Tyler reached out one hand, and Mozart sniffed at it before dropping his head to rub against Tyler's fingers. The boy giggled. She coughed lightly and stepped into the room.

"Looks like you two are becoming friends." Mozart let out a drawling meow and jumped off the bed to come rub her ankles until she picked him up.

"I think he likes me!" Tyler slid off the bed and hurried toward her. The quick movement made Mozart go very still in her arms, but he allowed Tyler to stroke his fur a few times before jumping to the floor. Tyler started to follow, and the cat bolted. Grace caught Tyler's arm.

"I think he likes you, too, but Mozart needs some quiet time, honey. Why don't we go back downstairs?"

"Why?" His favorite word.

"Because your lesson is over and I need to eat my dinner, and you need to go home and eat *your* dinner."

"Did you make something for us to eat?"

She couldn't help laughing. "Just because I sent one dish of chicken marsala home with you two weeks ago doesn't mean—"

"But *did* you make something?"

Tyler had mentioned more than once that Max wasn't the world's greatest cook. And she always had leftovers. She'd sent a plate of chicken home with him one time. Max had texted to thank her, although he made it clear that it wasn't *necessary*. She didn't want to offend him with any more pity meals, but she'd discovered neither man nor boy refused desserts.

"Do you like chocolate chip cookies?"

Tyler nodded enthusiastically.

"Well, I have some in the kitchen. Let's go."

"Explain to me exactly what I'm looking at here." Max gestured toward his mother, who was behind the bar at the Salty Knight, arguing loudly with the owner, Fred Knight.

His sister started to laugh. "Oh, that? That's our mother and her arch-nemesis-slash-future-boyfriend, Fred. They've been doing this for over a year now. Devlin, Sam and I can't decide if they're going to kill each other or fall into bed together."

Max and Lexi were seated at a corner table in the townie bar, near the window overlooking Wharf Street. He'd learned the short waterfront street used to be the main drag in Winsome Cove decades ago, until the current Main Street was developed up above it. That's where the tourist shops and boutiques were, along with a few chain restaurants and stores closer to the edge of town. Wharf Street had become a dead-end street, with one side a parking lot for the tourist section, and a line of older buildings on the water side.

But Lexi and her pals were determined to bring Wharf Street back to some kind of glory. Her successful restaurant, 200 Wharf, was connected to the bar. It had helped make the street a destination, but there were still empty storefronts between it and the seafood market near the top of the hill.

Max set his beer down and grimaced at his sister. "Fall into bed? That's our *mom*, Lexi."

"Yeah, well—this is Mom 2.0. You know how much she's changed since the divorce." Lexi sipped her sparkling water and gestured toward the bar. "Look at her, for heaven's sake!"

She was right, of course. The sweet, conservative mom of his youth had been replaced with this vibrant, sassy, confident woman who had apparently won over the entire town of Winsome Cove. Everywhere he went, as soon as people found out Phyllis was his mother, they went on and on about how much they loved her. She'd saved the Sassy Mermaid Motor Lodge, she volunteered on just about every committee there was on Cape Cod, she was the new president of the business owner's group here in town…

"Frederick Knight, I can out-mix you right now on any cocktail you care to mention!" His mother slapped her hand on the bar. Her pink hair was spiky on top, as if she'd overdone the gel that morning. She was in a skintight blue and red top and black jeans tucked into high black boots. Not the mom of his childhood, but he couldn't look away. And apparently neither could her nemesis.

"Damn you, woman!" The older man, built like a stout fireplug, slapped *his* hand on the bar, too. "I've told you a hundred times I don't care about them fancy drinks the damn tourists want! *My* friends drink beer, and you can't pour a good pint to save your ass. So there!"

Fred was a fourth-generation native of Winsome Cove, so his accent was thick. It came out more like *yah cahn't po-ah a good glahss of be-yah t'save your ahss! So they-ah!*

Mom tugged her apron off and threw it on the bar. "Fine! I came in here to help, but I quit!"

"You can't quit—you're *fired*!"

She waggled her index finger right under her boss's nose. "You be careful, old man. I'll leave you working on your own this Friday night."

"Don't threaten *me* with a good time, you overgrown hippie! Don't you have beds to make or something?"

Max straightened in his seat, but his sister shook her head at him. "This is just how they communicate, Max. None of us can figure out their code, but trust me—she hasn't really quit and he isn't really going to fire her."

Their mother worked Friday and Saturday nights, running back and forth from the restaurant to the bar with diners' drink orders. The two businesses shared a hallway and restrooms. Fred's late wife had apparently run the restaurant as a more casual family spot years ago. He'd tried to keep it going after her death, but the restaurant side had been empty for a couple years when Lexi took it over and took it upscale.

Mom didn't need to work as a cocktail waitress. The old motel she'd inherited and fixed up had started turning a decent profit over the past year. But she insisted she enjoyed the work, despite the heated arguments that seemed to be standard operating procedure with the bar owner. She marched over and threw herself into a chair at the table he and Lexi were at and flashed them both a bright smile.

"So how are my two favorite Winsome Cove residents today?"

"Mom," Max started, "are you okay?"

She looked incredulous. "Why? Oh, *that*?" She gestured toward the bar. "Phhfft! The old goat doesn't have a clue. How's my sweet Tyler doing?"

Lexi gave him a pointed *told you so* look from across the table, and he shrugged. "Tyler's good, Mom. He's still pretty quiet, but he likes his teacher, and she says he's doing well in class. He's made a couple of friends. He's taking piano lessons next door."

"With the woman you called a busybody?" Mom asked.

"You can be a busybody and still teach piano," he pointed out. "She's okay, and Tyler likes her. I had to beg her to do it, though."

"I would have liked seeing you beg. How did you win her over?" Lexi sipped her water and checked her watch. Her kitchen staff handled lunch without her, but she'd have to head over to the restaurant before long to get ready for dinner hour. "And why didn't she want to do it to start with?"

"I had to tell her Tyler's story and get her feeling sorry for him. Or for me. I may have laid it on too heavy, because she's been sending food home with Tyler, as if she's afraid we're starving." He was making light of it, but he couldn't shake the memory of her telling him he was a good dad. She was virtually a stranger, but those words meant something to him. "She says she likes kids, but she doesn't like teaching them. She called them chaos monsters."

His mother let out a loud, sharp laugh. "She's not wrong there! You know, I didn't connect the name with the face when you first mentioned her, but she's one of the regular walkers at the beach. They use the motel access on Tuesday and Friday mornings. There's five or six of them."

Their great-uncle, who Max and Lexi never met, had owned the Sassy Mermaid for decades. Despite having no contact with his family in Iowa, he'd left the 1940s motel to Phyllis in his will. He'd been a bit of a town hero for making sure the locals had access to the beach the motel overlooked. He even used to host cookouts there, and Mom was continuing both traditions.

"She's a blonde, right? About Lexi's height?" His mother continued after he nodded. "She always waves toward the office when she walks by. Like a little thank-you. She doesn't seem like a busybody at all." She leaned forward, lowering her voice. "I asked around, and I learned that house was her parents' place. She bought it from them. Caroline Curey at the gift shop—she's a student up at Berklee—heard that Grace wanted to be some sort of concert pianist, but she came home after college and went to work for her brother instead. Caroline didn't know why, but she would have been just a kid then."

Max shook his head. "A perfectionist like Grace probably couldn't hack it. She's too uptight." He looked up to find his mother and sister staring at him. "What?"

Lexi held up one hand and ticked topics off on her fingers. "You say *she's* a busybody, but *you* spilled your whole life story to her. And I heard you're accepting *cooked meals* from her. You think you know her well enough to offer an opinion on why she's made her life choices—even if that opinion wasn't very generous." Her hand dropped to the table. "If you ask me, you seem pretty invested in this neighbor of yours."

Sure, Grace was interesting. But he didn't need interesting women in his life right now. Nothing against the fairer sex, but his life had to be centered around his son.

"I wouldn't even be talking to the woman if Tyler hadn't formed some sort of bond with her. I have no idea why. She gave him a squash and suddenly they're besties." He sighed heavily, and his mother placed her hand over his on the table as he continued. "You've both seen it—he opens up more to women than men. Or at least to *this* man." He put his other hand on his chest.

"He'll come around, honey." His mother patted his hand. "And if Tyler likes your neighbor, that's okay. Just…be careful. You're dealing with a lot, and she's a lovely woman, but getting involved with a next-door neighbor could end up being worse than being enemies with one."

"Mom, trust me—there's no way anything's gonna happen between me and Grace Bennett."

Chapter Five

Grace wasn't sure what to expect when she opened the door to the old carriage house at nine o'clock in the evening, but she was unprepared for the sight of Max Bellamy sweating in front of a blazing red furnace. The sleeves of his dark flannel shirt were rolled up, exposing a tattooed forearm with taut veins creating a raised roadmap under his skin. He was wearing a thick leather apron, and he pulled a long piece of glowing metal from the gas-powered furnace with a pair of tongs and slapped it onto an anvil before grabbing a large hammer and striking it. Sparks flew, and she didn't know if her face was heating up from the temperature or if it was Max—hot, sweaty, muscular Max—making her flush.

He glanced her way, and his thick eyebrows rose in surprise.

"Close the door!" he barked. "The cold air will cool this too fast, and I'll have to start…" He scowled down at the metal. "Aw, hell. Too late." He slid the metal back into the furnace, glowing bright orange with heat.

Grace felt some kinship with that furnace right now. She quickly closed the door behind her, muttering an apology. Max couldn't hear her, of course. Between the

the furnace and the guitar riff blasting over the—she quickly counted—*four* speakers mounted in here, it was no wonder he hadn't responded when she'd knocked on the door to the carriage house.

He was busy trying to fix whatever disaster she'd created with the open door, so she took a moment to look around. The open beams of the old structure were visible in the shadows above them and were a contrast to the modern equipment and bright lights of Max's forge area below. Everything was organized, which appealed to Grace, even if she had no idea what these tools did. She knew what an anvil was, though, and it was mounted on a massive square butcher block. A strip of leather wound around the wood, nailed down to create loops where tools hung. Tongs of all sizes, along with an assortment of hammers and rasps. More tools hung on the wall behind him. The furnace—was that what he called the forge?—was a modern-looking contraption wrapped in black powdered steel. Ceramic bricks lined the inside to hold and direct the intense heat. There was a smaller anvil in the corner, and a heavy workbench stretched across the back wall. Attached to it was a series of vertical tubes of PVC and metal in various lengths, from one foot to more than four feet high. There was a small walled-in enclosure in the far corner.

Max yanked the length of steel from the forge and began to hammer it. She could see the near-molten metal grow thinner and longer with each powerful strike. He didn't bother looking up when he spoke next.

"Give me a minute." It sounded more like an order than a request. "I need to get at least another inch on this." He hammered a few more times, then held the blade against a metal yardstick attached to the anvil base. Satisfied, he dunked it into one of the long tubes of PVC pipe, and smoke rolled up as water or some other liquid boiled around the hot steel. He set the now darkened blade on the anvil and finally looked at Grace.

"Sorry," he said gruffly. "I was right in the middle of something." It was an apology that sounded more like an accusation.

"I didn't realize you'd be doing all this stuff in the evenings, too." Prudish? Maybe. But she didn't like the way the sight of him hammering away on red-hot steel made her feel. She pulled her shoulders back. *Focus.* Before she could continue, he held up his hand, slid off the heavy leather gloves, then grabbed a remote and turned down the loud music.

"This *stuff* is how I make my living, and I need every order to afford living here. Did you come out here to complain about something?" Now that he wasn't doing hot stuff like hammering molten metal, Grace could see that there were deep lines around Max's eyes, as if he hadn't been sleeping well. Or was stressed—perhaps about money? The Cape *was* an expensive place to live.

"No, that's not why I'm here. To be honest, with my windows closed I could barely hear you. But now that I'm here, I do have one concern…"

"Which is?"

"Is Tyler staying at his grandmother's, or…? I mean, you didn't hear me knocking, and you didn't know that I'd come inside. So if he's home…"

He put his hand on his hip and scowled, but the frown faded quickly and his hand dropped to his side, as if he'd swallowed an angry response. He gestured toward a flat screen she hadn't noticed, suspended on the wall over the workbench, where he could see it easily. On the screen, she could see a night vision capture of a bedroom, with a twin bed and what appeared to be a sleeping child.

"It's a fair question," Max admitted. "I wait until I know he's asleep before I come out here in the evenings. I'm only twenty feet from the house, and I've installed a security system that alerts me if his bedroom door opens. I have a few other cameras and motion sensors around the house, inside and out—it's nanny cams taken to the next level. If he gets up, I'll know it. If anyone goes near the outside of the house, I'll know it." He gave her a quick half smile. "I guess I need to add monitors to the forge, too. I never heard you knocking. What's up?"

"I wanted to see if it would be possible for Tyler to take two lessons per week. He's actually quite good. He's not crazy about classical music, though, so we compromised on moving to a book of Disney music for his age level. He wanted me to teach him the blues, but…"

Max's eyebrows rose, and his smile deepened until she could see it sparkling in his gray-blue eyes. The man didn't show it often, but he had a stellar smile. "He *asked* to learn the blues?" He paused. "Maybe he's paying attention more than I realized, not that he'd ever admit it. But the chords and the syncopation…"

"I know. He's not ready to go too far with it, but there *are* some very basic books out there for beginners, and we might try one of those, just as a change of pace. I don't want to push his lesson to an hour, because it feels like too much for a young child. But I was wondering if we could add another half-hour class, maybe one evening a week before dinner?"

"Sure. He's been happier since he's started playing. Less anxious."

"I'm glad. He told me he has made some friends at school, too. He's settling in here?"

Max nodded absently, putting some of his tools away. "I think going to a small elementary school like the one in Winsome Cove has been good for him. He's a smart kid. And kindergarten was a good age to make the move. He didn't have a huge circle of friends back in Ohio to miss." He glanced up at the monitor, where they could see Tyler sleeping. Max's expression was so rich with emotion that Grace's breath caught. She found herself moving closer to the anvil. To him.

"Tyler's doing well, Max, considering all he's been through this year. You're a good dad." She put her hand on his arm, and they both froze.

Grace tried to remind herself that this man had disrupted her quiet neighborhood with his swords and his hammering and his music and...and...his mere *existence*. Her subconscious argued back that she was simply being a compassionate person expressing concern for another human being. Even if no other human sent this zap of energy through her at the simple touch of her fingers on his skin. Max's eyes darkened, as if he'd felt the same chemistry.

His skin was warm from working near the forge, and she could feel a sheen of sweat on the surface. There was a sharply intricate Celtic band tattooed around his forearm, and she stared at it, figuring it was safer than looking into those eyes any longer than necessary. An ornate dagger was on the inside of his arm, with the tip ending at his wrist. Her finger started to trace the outline, and Max inhaled a sharp breath. Grace snapped out of her stupor and yanked her hand away from him.

"S-sorry," she mumbled, with no idea what she was apologizing for.

There was an awkward beat of silence between them before Max cleared his throat.

"Uh…yeah. So…what day is good for Tyler's second lesson?"

She was so grateful for the quick change of subject that she almost laughed in giddy relief. Whatever that weird moment was when she'd touched him, it was over.

"Oh, my schedule's pretty flexible. The office is open late on Thursdays, but other than that, whatever day works for you. Is five o'clock Tuesday okay? Too late? Too early? I can move it—" Oh, God, she was babbling.

"Tuesday at five is fine," Max cut her off, as if to stop the list of options she was reciting.

"And…he'll need to practice, of course. But it seems like he has been doing well with practicing so far."

"I still need to get that old piano tuned, but he's on that thing every chance he gets." A pause. "So we're set for Tuesdays and Fridays, then?"

"Yes, definitely." He was telling her it was time to go. She needed to turn on her heel and walk out the door. Their business was done. They'd survived that odd little moment with their dignity intact. She should go home. Right now.

But the forge was still blazing, and the blade he'd been working on was cooling on the anvil, its color now a dull, dark gray. It was long, maybe a couple of feet, and narrow, with a slight curve.

The conversation was over. *Time to go, Grace…*

She reached for the blade instead. What was this thing he was creating from solid steel with fire and a hammer?

Max reached out to lightly take Grace's wrist before her fingers touched the blade. Just because it wasn't glowing red, that didn't mean it wasn't still hot. And there it was again. That ridiculous surge of…something…through his veins the moment he touched her. He bit back a curse, then put his free hand on the blade. It was warm, but safe enough to touch. He released Grace like she was burning his skin.

"I wasn't sure it had cooled enough," he explained. "It's warm, but you can touch it."

Why did those normal words sound suddenly suggestive?

Grace put her hand on the blade, and God help him, he felt his body reacting to the woman touching his artwork.

"It's not sharp," Grace said.

"The grinder will put the cutting edge on it. I can make it sharp as a razor." He realized he was boasting and dialed it back a bit. "Well, not like a razor. This one is supposed to be more decorative than functional. Most of my blades are, other than the smaller knives."

His clients usually hung his work on their walls as art. It wasn't good business to sell customers an ornamental sword that could slice a tomato without causing a dimple in it. Those people had children and grandchildren who could injure themselves just touching the shiny blade on the wall. He was capable of making those razor edges— he'd won competitions with his blades—but that didn't mean everything he'd made was razor-sharp.

Through the years, he'd shown his work to hundreds of potential customers. But watching Grace Bennett run her fingers along the length of the blade was intoxicating in a way he'd never experienced before. She wasn't some sword groupie at a Ren fair. She was his neighbor in small-town Cape Cod. She taught his son. He could *not* screw this up by listening to the voice in his head screaming *KISS HER!* in bold letters. Such a bad idea. The *worst*. So messy. So unnecessary.

Then she ran her fingers down the length of the future saber again, and he groaned out loud. Was she doing it on purpose? Was the uptight, follow-the-rules piano teacher *flirting* with him? Or was it all a coincidence, blown out of proportion by his admittedly horny brain? He didn't want a woman in his life. But damn, he missed a woman's touch. More than he'd realized, considering the strong reaction he had to Grace's touch, and her kind words earlier.

His pulse had jumped the moment her fingers brushed his forearm. His entire body had responded. A visceral reaction to her touch. Her kind words. The admiration he saw in her eyes when he explained his complex security system to protect Tyler.

He forced himself to step back, allowing her to examine the blade. She lived next door, and she cared about his son. His son cared about her. There could not be some random one-night stand between the two of them. It would be the destruction of one of his son's most important relationships.

He reminded himself of their first conversation— how she'd recited the rules he had to follow in order to live in his own damn house. Her immediate disdain for him, just by looking at him.

But she just traced the outline of your tattoo with her fingers.

No. That didn't matter. They were cut from very different cloth, and she'd judged him right from the start on moving day. And the afternoon when Tyler went into her garden. She obviously didn't think he was of her caliber, and she was right. There were plenty of reasons to avoid Grace Bennett. He just had to remember them, which was proving difficult.

She said you were a good dad.

She'd also questioned him tonight about how he could be out here without Tyler, as if she thought he'd neglect his son. She'd done that the afternoon in the garden, too. Scolded him for not knowing where Tyler was for five whole minutes.

As a blacksmith, he had a good understanding of science—how metal bonded right down to the molecular level if treated properly. But this attraction he was feeling toward Grace? Well, *that* chemistry was lying. It had to be.

"Look," he started. "I really need to grind this blade tonight. So if we're all set with Tyler's schedule…"

She got the message, stepping away from the anvil with a quick nod. "Of course. Sorry for holding you up. I'll…um…order those music books and…um…get back to it."

He had no idea what "it" was, but she was leaving, so he didn't question it.

"Right. Thanks."

After she left, the old carriage house felt colder, even though the forge was still blazing hot enough to melt steel.

Chapter Six

Grace pulled her scarf tighter and tugged the hood of her jacket up over her head. She loved walking the beach with her friends, but in October the ocean breezes could be downright frigid. Today was one of those days.

Maya King laughed next to her. "You were the smart one, Grace, wearing something with a hood. This wind is *brutal.*"

Maya and her husband, Leon, had lived across the street from Grace for ten years now. They had two children. Chantal was five, and baby Zander was six months old. Maya and Grace had been friends in high school and had both played in the school orchestra—Maya on flute and Grace on piano. It had felt like a band camp reunion when the Kings moved into her neighborhood, and their old friendship had quickly reblossomed.

Genevieve Curey was on Grace's other side, and she huddled in close so Grace could be her windbreak. She and her wife, Amy, had moved to Winsome Cove from Jamaica and now owned a souvenir and T-shirt shop on Main Street. Genevieve's daughter, Caroline, was studying music at Berklee in Boston. Grace had given her piano lessons back when she was in high school.

"Whose idea was this, anyway?" Genevieve shouted over the wind, her clipped island accent sharp. "I'm from the tropics, damn it. This cannot be good for me!"

They all laughed. There were two other walkers in the group today—Marnie Glenn, who worked at the post office, and... Phyllis Bellamy.

Max's mother had surprised them that morning when she trotted out from the motel office in a puffy white jacket and tall, laced hiking boots. Her pink hair was covered with a pink knit hat. "Hey, ladies! Mind if I join in? I could use the exercise."

Of course they'd all welcomed her, since she allowed them to use the wooden stairs from the motel's observation deck down to the beach. It was the most direct way to get to the sand for anyone within walking distance. Waterfront homes had tied up access in other areas, so the only other option was driving to a public access spot outside the town. Grace wondered about Phyllis's reason for joining, though. The woman, in her early-to-mid sixties, was constantly on the move, between working at the Sassy Mermaid and being a cocktail waitress at 200 Wharf.

Grace had spoken to Phyllis and Lexi a few times in passing, at the town's Old Harbour Days festival and at the few business owner's meetings Grace attended in Aiden's place. Phyllis was a fascinating woman. Everyone Grace knew loved her, with her edgy, youthful style and energetic approach to life. She'd embraced Winsome Cove with open arms, and Winsome Cove had clearly embraced her right back. But never once had she offered to join the walking group until today.

Phyllis was striding ahead of them now, laughing

over her shoulder as if she could defy the sharp wind. "Genevieve, you moved to Cape Cod *years* ago, so quit yer bitchin', woman. Besides..." She turned, walking backward and spreading her arms wide in the wind. "This is nothing! You should try walking from your car to the grocery store in Iowa in January with a negative twenty windchill. Makes this feel like a May breeze—" Just as she said *breeze*, her knit cap flew off. She let out a curse and chased after it, looking more like a little girl than a senior citizen.

"Phyllis, you make us all feel *old*!" Maya laughed. "But I'm glad you joined us today."

Phyllis scooped her pink hat up from the sand, gave it a shake, then put it back over her matching hair. "Me, too! So what do you gals talk about when you're not being jealous of me?"

"Sometimes we hardly talk at all," Marnie answered. "And sometimes it's nonstop. Sometimes it's all of us at once, and sometimes one of us really needs to vent." She stretched the sleeves of her Irish sweater down and pulled her hands up inside to keep them warm. "Didn't your son just move to town? How's that going?"

"Oh, Max is such a nice guy," Maya gushed. "And he has a son Chantal's age—Tyler. Your grandson is a little sweetheart, Phyllis."

"Yes, he is. He was a surprise, that one, but he's our pride and joy."

"How was he a surprise?" Marnie asked.

For some reason impossible to identify, Grace heard *herself* answering the question. "The mother didn't know she was pregnant until after Max left town, and never attempted to tell him, but she *did* put his name on Tyler's birth certificate. Max didn't know he had a son until after she died—"

Sympathetic *oh nos* floated on the wind from her friends. Except for Phyllis. She was standing still, giving Grace a look she couldn't read. Not surprised exactly. Not upset. Just...curious. *Very* curious.

"Oh, that's right," Marnie said. "He lives right next door to you! So he didn't know...?"

"Uh, no. But..." She glanced at Phyllis, suddenly aware that she may have shared too much. "Well...of course he has custody of Tyler now, and he's stepped up as a dad."

"Yes, he has," Phyllis said, still staring at Grace. The sun slid out from behind a cloud but didn't do much to warm the wind. If anything, the cold felt sharper against the backdrop of an increasingly blue sky. "You're his piano teacher, right?"

"Shut the front door!" Marnie smacked Grace on the arm. "You didn't mention that! I thought you didn't teach little kids?"

"She made a special exception for Tyler." Phyllis started walking again, and they followed her. "And I heard she sends meals over to the house, too."

Maya gave Grace a long, sideways look, then cleared her throat and looked back to Phyllis. "Oh, the whole neighborhood is doing that. I sent baked ziti over a couple weeks ago myself."

"Oh, that's nice." Phyllis didn't look like she quite bought it, but she was gracious. "Thank you all for taking care of my boys."

"And speaking of boys," Genevieve started. "What have *you* been up to, Miss Phyllis? I saw you laughing it up with Fred Knight a couple weeks ago at the bar, and then Amy said you and Fred came close to throwing beer bottles at each other this week. Is there something going on with you two we should know about?"

Phyllis, normally so brassy and bold, did something unusual. She *blushed.* And quite a bit, considering Grace could see it beneath the rosy cheeks they all had from the wind. She hesitated before answering, and Marnie took pity on her.

"Oh, never mind that. We all know how cranky Fred can be—he'd drive anyone to throwing something at him if you gave him enough time."

They were almost back to the wooden stairs leading up the small cliff to the Sassy Mermaid. There were a few seals sunning themselves on the rocks fifty feet away, ignoring the five women who huddled against the cliff to avoid the wind. Phyllis was suddenly serious.

"This gal's group has a cone of silence over it, right? What's said here stays here?" The other women leaned in, nodding enthusiastically. "Fine. I'll be honest—I have no flipping clue what's going on with Fred and me. We've been bickering since the day we met, but it's usually in fun. I think. At least... *I'm* having fun. But how am I supposed to know what *he's* thinking?"

"What do you *want* him to be thinking?" Genevieve asked, then realization dawned. "Amy was right—you *like* that old crab, don't you?"

"I like him, but I don't know if I *like* like him, you know? All we have in common is arguing about cocktails. But... I look forward to those arguments. I look forward to Friday and Saturday nights, and I think it has a lot to do with him." She stuffed her hands in her pockets. "But maybe it's just that our debates are stimulating. I love running the motel, but my conversations with people there have to be polite, at least on my part, whether it's an employee or a guest. I don't get to use my brain the way I do at the bar with Fred." She paused, then gave an exaggerated shrug and laughed. "That's one of the reasons I wanted to join you ladies today—to have a grown-up conversation with someone other than coworkers and family."

They started up the stairs, offering advice that ranged from telling Fred how she felt about him to finding some other outlet to stimulate her mind. Grace stayed silent, partly because she didn't have a lot of relationship advice to offer, and partly because she suspected the *other* reason Phyllis had joined their walk was to learn more about Grace. Maybe she just wanted to get to know her grandson's piano teacher.

She hoped Max's mom wasn't thinking she and Max were *involved* or anything silly like that.

"Your sister's worried about you, and I'm the one hearing about it." Sam Knight shook his finger at Max on the sidewalk. "You've been here for over a month and you don't even know where the best coffee shop is. Or the hardware store. Or where to go for a drink. Too much work and no play makes Max a dull and lonely boy."

Max had texted his brother-in-law an hour earlier for the location of a good hardware store. Instead of simply getting an address in response, he ended up standing here on Main Street in Winsome Cove, getting a lecture. He should have just taken his chances with an internet search, but he figured Sam could steer him to the best local store for custom ordering tools and supplies. In-stead, Sam said they should meet at Jerry's Java House.

At least it was a nice day, with puffy white clouds dotting the sky. He looked up and blinked into the sun. Sam and Lexi had a point. Max hadn't gotten out much, but he'd been busy.

"What I *need* to do is work as much as possible so I can make a living here." His previous home had been an older forty-foot motor home when he was on the road, and a studio apartment in Des Moines when he wasn't. Selling the motor home had given him the down payment on the house, but the mortgage was still steep. The custody battle back in Ohio took a chunk of his savings, too.

"What you *need* to do—" Sam opened the door to the coffee shop "—is make connections locally. Friends. Hobbies. *Fun.* Lexi and your mom have decided you've been a hermit long enough, and you know that means they're about to make you their project."

He could feel a vein pulsing behind his right eye. His feisty sister had turned into Sweet Suzie Sunshine since she'd married Sam Knight, especially since becoming pregnant. Max was glad she was happy. She'd had a tough few years before coming to Cape Cod, but now she ran a successful restaurant, she and her friends were busy rejuvenating Wharf Street in town and she'd just been elected secretary of the Winsome Cove Business Association, which their mother ran. Sam waved at the man behind the pastry counter, and followed his gesture toward a café table near the window.

"I overheard them saying they're going to get you out of that old house more, even if they have to drag you out," Sam said. "According to your sister, all you do is go back and forth from the house to the carriage house and back again."

"The carriage house is where my *job* is. And the house, which needs work, is where I'm raising my *son*. That's two more full-time jobs."

He looked out at the quiet Main Street. It was a weekday and the so-called *season* on Cape Cod was winding down. Lexi had explained that some tourist business would linger through the holidays, but it was nothing like what the summer months had been. The population of Winsome Cove more than doubled in the summer, between second-home owners and visitors. On his way here, though, he'd seen two or three businesses on Main Street with Closed for the Season signs in the windows.

Max pushed his hair off his face, making a mental note to ask Sam for the name of a good barber while they were here. "I know my way around town—the grocery store is that way, the school is that way, the Sassy Mermaid Motor Lodge is up there, and down that little dead-end street is a halfway decent bar and restaurant." He was pointing over toward Wharf Street, where Lexi's restaurant, 200 Wharf, was a popular destination. Not just for locals, but for diners from Boston who'd drive out to enjoy her locally-sourced cuisine. Sam, his cousin Devlin and his uncle Fred were all part owners of the place, as well as a few other buildings on Wharf Street.

The man from behind the counter was at their table now, looking at Max in disbelief. "So you know where four businesses are, and two of them are owned by your family members. Is that what I'm hearing?"

Max stuttered, and Sam started laughing. "Jerry, be nice. Max, this is Jerry, who owns this place with his much more well-mannered husband, Cliff. Jerry, this is my brother-in-law, Max Bellamy. But you knew that already."

"I know when sexy, tattooed blacksmiths come to town. I'm married, not dead." Hand on his hip, Jerry's gaze swept Max from head to toe. "Even if they *aren't* customers of mine."

Max had no idea how to respond to that, and Sam stepped in again. "The man is a single father who's trying to get settled into his house. Don't hate him for taking a few weeks to find the coffee shop. He's here now, right?"

Jerry, short and wiry with chemically-enhanced orange-red hair, pretended to debate Sam's comment, then he nodded firmly. "Fair enough. Welcome to Winsome Cove. What can I get you gents today?" He winked at Max. "Other than a local map."

They placed their orders for coffee and Danish pastries, then Sam settled back into advice mode. "There's a business owner's group in town that you should join. Devlin and I are in it, and your mom is the new chairperson. Lexi is on the board, too. You've met Shelly Berinson, right? At the design shop?"

Max nodded. "SeaShelly's Designs? Yeah, Mom dragged me there to buy throw pillows and a couple of lamps. And Lexi introduced me to Carm and her parents, who run the seafood market. I've met Tyler's teacher, Mary Kelleher. And I even know some of my neighbors." His voice softened. "I appreciate everyone's concern, but I'm doing okay. And as far as which bars to hit, I'm assuming *your* family's bar is at the top of the list, and I've been there. More than once. You're welcome."

"Don't tell my dad I said this, but the Salty Knight isn't exactly the best bar to meet people, unless you're interested in meeting Uncle Fred's card-playing pals, like John and Steve. Some of the tourists are starting to wander down there for the so-called 'authentic local flavor,' but it's hardly a nightclub atmosphere."

"Yeah, well, hanging out in nightclubs is a little tough with a five-year-old. I'm not interested in hitting bars to meet women, anyway. Those days are over."

Sam studied him for a moment, as if weighing his answer. Then he shook his head with a sad smile. "You don't have to be celibate just because you have a child. Lexi says hitting the bars used to be one of your favorite things to do. I'm not suggesting you should go on a drunken pub crawl every weekend, but…"

"But what?"

Sam grimaced, rubbing his neck, then looking up to the ceiling with a groan. "Remember that I got roped into this conversation by my wife and mother-in-law, okay? From what Lexi said, your life has been spent in a different town every few weeks, and a different girl more often than that."

Max set his coffee mug down. "My big sister exaggerated just a bit. Covering all those miles isn't easy when you're driving a bus-sized motorhome and towing a trailer. Plus I worked my ass off hammering steel during the day at the fairs and festivals, so at night all I wanted to do was shower and crawl into bed. *Usually* alone."

"So I can report back that you're doing okay so far? The move? The house? Small-town life and PTO meetings?" Sam grinned as he popped the last bite of his cherry Danish into his mouth.

Max had told Lexi about the parent-teacher group meeting he'd attended last week. He was determined to be a hands-on father. There'd only been two other dads at the meeting, and they were married to each other. As the new single dad in town, he'd felt like a slab of meat thrown to a hungry mob. The moms were almost falling over each other to get to "know" Max. If he wanted an active dating life, all he had to do was skim through the three or four phone numbers that had been pressed into his hand on scraps of paper. But that wasn't what he wanted, or needed, right now.

"Tyler's had enough to deal with without me running a parade of women in and out the door. He needs to know that he comes first for me." He leaned forward. "You just wait until your kid gets here, man. The minute I saw Tyler and knew he was mine, that was it for my so-called old life. I did all of this—the move, the house, small-town life—for *him*. He may not see that now, but eventually…"

Sam agreed and stopped grilling Max. The conversation shifted to Lexi's pregnancy and the plans they were making. Lexi didn't want to know if it was a boy or girl, although Sam thought it would make planning easier if they knew. They were converting his boyhood room into the nursery but were arguing over what color to paint it. Max told him how he'd let Tyler pick the color for his bedroom. He was still trying to get used to the neon green the boy selected. At least he'd managed to win a compromise on the bold color, painting only two walls green, and the other two a soft gray to tame it a little.

He and Sam finished their coffees and walked back down to Wharf Street, where Max had parked. They went past a few freshly-painted, but empty, storefronts. Sam explained that he and Devlin were working on getting commercial tenants into the Knight family buildings. They had a guy interested in one space for a used bookstore.

Max listened, but only partially. He was thinking about what they'd discussed earlier. He *had* been missing grown-up conversation. He was either alone in the forge or alone with Tyler. Maybe that's why he couldn't stop thinking of the effect Grace Bennett had on him whenever she came into his space.

She'd stopped by the forge a couple of evenings since that first night when she'd touched his arm. She'd give him a quick update on Tyler's progress, perhaps mention some zoning covenant Max or someone else in the neighborhood might be breaking, and she'd drop off a plate of baked goods. They'd both been careful not to get too close to each other—she stayed firmly on the opposite side of the anvil while he was working. She didn't even hand him the desserts directly. She'd set the plate on the workbench. No more fingers moving across his tattoos.

Even so, he always had a harder time falling asleep after those visits and found himself looking forward to the next one. Maybe it wasn't Grace herself he looked forward to, but having an adult to talk to.

He and Sam stopped in front of his sister's restaurant, and Max extended his hand. "Thanks, Sam. I admit my life is lacking adult companionship, and I'm not talking about one-night stands." They shook hands. "You can report back to the ladies that there's no need to worry about me, though. I'll do better at being a model citizen of Winsome Cove, if they'll cut me some slack for needing to work long hours. I'm not out traveling and working in front of my customers anymore and relying on online sales is tougher than I anticipated. Pretty soon I'll be asking if anyone needs help on their lobster boats."

Sam snapped his fingers. "Oh, that reminds me— Shelly Berinson wants to talk to you about some interior design project she's working on. She and Devlin had dinner here the other night, and she told me she has a client who wants a custom iron railing on their staircase. She asked if I thought you could create some artsy panels for it. This is a client with very deep pockets, so if you can do it, it might help with your finances." He grinned and slapped Max's shoulder. "Trust me, you don't want to work on a lobster boat."

Max had never attempted anything like a wrought iron bannister, but that didn't mean he couldn't do it. He'd done some custom iron sculpture work for gardens, and people seemed happy with it. He had all the welding supplies he needed. Maybe he could put his metalworking skills to use in a new way and ease his cash flow concerns.

Chapter Seven

Grace had just sat down and opened her book when she heard the banging sound. At first, she assumed it was a car driving by with the bass blasting on their radio. In the summer, those cars made her windows rattle, but this was more muffled. After ten minutes, she set down the book and went to the front door. Was someone parked out front? She didn't see any cars. She didn't hear any music. But she could hear the pounding sound. It was coming from behind the house—maybe the next street over? She went to the edge of the porch. No. It was coming from the carriage house next door. Max.

She checked her watch before going inside to grab her jacket. It was eight o'clock at night, and that was just too much noise. Certainly enough that she needed to go speak with him. Even if it wasn't one of Tyler's lesson days.

She'd visited Max out there a few times now, usually to update him on Tyler's progress. She could have texted. She could wait until the following day. But then she would miss seeing him in full swordsmith mode. She'd stopped fighting the truth—she enjoyed watching Max work at the anvil, forcing steel to obey his will.

It didn't mean anything other than that she was a

woman who appreciated handsome men doing…powerful things. Making tools with his hands. She'd never been one to thirst after "bad boys" like bikers and other tough guys. She preferred her romance novels to have small-town heroes, not mobsters. But that didn't mean she couldn't admire someone who was out of her normal realm of attraction.

She knocked briefly on the door to the carriage house, then pushed the door open, closing it quickly behind her. She'd learned her lesson after that first night when he'd scolded her for letting the cold air in.

"Hi, Grace!" She was surprised to see Tyler sitting on a wooden stool near the back of the shop, at the far end of the workbench. He had some sort of horseshoe contraption he was studying. It had a piece of wood, a short chain and some iron rings, like a puzzle.

"Hi, Tyler," she answered, looking around for Max. "I don't usually see you out here, especially on a school night. Where's—"

She stopped when Max stepped out of the odd wooden booth in the corner. He was frowning at the gray, twisted length of steel in his hand, and his eyes briefly glanced toward Grace, then back down again. "Hey, Grace. Do you need something?"

He didn't stop for an answer, walking to the workbench and laying the twisted piece against the yardstick fastened to the bench. He nodded in satisfaction, then used the tongs to slide the metal back into the forge. He brushed his hands on his leather apron and finally looked at her in earnest.

"Grace?"

Something sultry was playing over the speakers, with

a low, rhythmic beat and a soft guitar playing. A raspy voice singing about flood waters. But it didn't have any of the pounding bass she'd heard earlier.

"I...uh, wondered what was going on out here. It sounded like blaring rock music, or drums, but..." She looked around.

"Ah," he nodded. "That was the power hammer." He jerked his thumb toward the corner structure he'd walked out of. "I finally got it set up last week. I insulated the booth, but that thing is pounding with about 120 psi— that's pounds per square inch—so it's got some juice." He paused. "Was it bothering you? I tested it, and it was within the decibel limits."

"Max let *me* start it," Tyler said with a proud grin. "It has a foot pedal that you can just step on, and I got to step on it."

Max smiled warmly. "That's right, buddy. You did a good job, too."

"Isn't that dangerous?" The boy was *five*. She looked at her watch. "And isn't this a school night?"

The joy vanished from Max's face immediately, and his shoulders tensed. She'd spoiled a warm moment. Maya had told her more than once that she could sound prissy, and she knew she'd done it again.

"You just can't help yourself, can you?" Max asked. She felt his scorn as much as heard it. But it seemed to go over Tyler's head.

"It *is* dangerous!" Tyler beamed at the wonderful news. "Max says everything in here can be dangerous. That's why I have to sit here while he's working. He said that anvil over there is just my size, and someday he'll teach me how to make knives on it!"

He was pointing to an anvil much smaller than the one Max was using. None of that information made Grace feel any better. In fact, she felt fully justified now in asking in the first place. Hand on her hip, she turned back to Max.

"Knives? Seriously?"

He had the good grace to look chagrined. "I said *someday*. I did not substantiate a definition of that particular timeline with any specifics."

It took her a moment to realize he was using big words to avoid Tyler understanding that he meant it would be years before *someday* arrived.

"Huh?" Tyler asked. "But...someday, right?"

"That's right, son. Someday." He gave Grace a quick, pointed look. "As long as Miss Grace doesn't report me to the authorities."

She rolled her eyes. "Just because I told you I'm chairperson of the Historical Society, that doesn't mean I'm going to tattle on you for everything. In fact, I haven't reported you to *anyone* for *anything*."

"Yet."

A light of laughter was in his eyes. Was he...was he *teasing* with her? That was new. Even newer? She was fighting a smile in response.

"Grace," Tyler piped up. "Did you come over because of the hammering? Did we wake you up? Are you mad? Did you bring cookies? Do *you* know how to make knives? Max could teach you! You give me lessons, and he could give *you* lessons."

She was relieved at the distraction. She'd learned that Tyler expected direct answers to his questions, even when they came in a flood like this.

"I *did* come over because of the hammering. You didn't wake me up, but you did interrupt my reading. I'm not mad, I'm…concerned. I didn't plan on coming over, so no, I didn't bring cookies. And no, I haven't ever made a knife, and I don't intend to."

"Why not?" He hopped off the small stool and hurried to her side. His dark hair was getting long, and his curls were bouncing. She reached out and ran her fingers through them with affection.

"Because I prefer to buy my knives already made. Isn't it past the time for you to go to bed? It's a school night."

"Nuh-uh!" Tyler folded his arms proudly. "That's why Max said I could come watch him hammering."

"Before you call the truant officer," Max said, "he's right. It's a teacher conference day tomorrow."

Grace threw her hands up. "I wasn't going to call the school!"

Sly. That was what his smile was. Sly. Amused. Teasing. If she didn't know better, she'd think it was even flirtatious. It was *very* attractive on him.

Tyler looked to Max. "Is it hot enough yet?"

Max turned to the hearth and picked up the tongs again. "Thanks for reminding me, pal. And where do you have to be before I can do any work?"

"Sorry, Max!" Tyler scampered back to his perch near the bench.

Max pulled out the bar of dimly glowing steel. He looked at Grace and set the piece on his anvil, then turned off the hearth. "You know what? I'm going to wait until morning to finish working on this one. The power hammer might be a little loud to use at night. If it bothered Miss Grace, it's probably bothering other neighbors. Even if she is a little more sensitive than most."

There was that grin again. He was in a strange mood tonight. Less serious. Lighter. He turned his smile toward his son, and she realized that was it. Tyler was with him and seemed genuinely happy to be there. Max was making headway with his son, and it was bringing a sense of joy to him that showed.

It was a good night. Max hadn't seen that light in Tyler's eyes very often, if *ever*, around him. He was excited, interested in what was happening. Interested, for maybe the first time, in what *Max* was doing. No shrugging. No mumbling. No avoiding eye contact. The kid was laughing with Grace right now as he showed her the horseshoe puzzle Max had made him. When he'd presented it a week ago, Tyler had just stared at it before setting it down with a mumbled thanks. But Max had caught him a few times since then, working on how to move the rings from the horseshoe down the chain to the wooden dowel. And tonight he'd *asked* to come out to the shop to watch. It was progress. Maybe not a huge win, but it made Max feel like he'd just won a very special prize—the admiration of his son.

"Your dad made that himself?" Grace was asking Tyler.

"He made all of it," Tyler answered. "Even the horseshoe! It's a game—I have to get the rings off the horseshoe and onto the wooden stick. He said I can take it to show-and-tell at school." He gave her a big grin. "As long as I don't conk anyone in the head with it."

A new wave of emotion washed over Max. Some invisible corner had been turned with Tyler. It didn't mean they wouldn't have setbacks, but the boy was dropping his guard around Max. He was less secretive about his feelings. Less likely to shrug Max off. More likely to smile, like he was now.

Grace was laughing as she studied the puzzle. "That sounds like a reasonable condition." She glanced over to Max, and it felt like the icing on the cake. Not only was Tyler smiling, but so was Grace.

She was in trim corduroys and a sweater, with a light, open jacket. Casual, but composed. Her signature look. He'd rolled his eyes at her neat and tidy fashion choices at first, but the look worked for her. It was soft. Practical. Attractive. A lot like her. He blinked. *No, no, no.* How could he even think that when he'd just had this break-through with Tyler? *No distractions.* And yet, when she'd run her fingers through his son's hair with that warm expression, it had made something inside of him down-right flutter.

"I'm gonna be a dragon for Halloween!" Tyler told her. "Nana is helping with my costume, and Max is going to be a knight with a sword and everything. Are you giving out candy? What kind?"

Grace laughed at the new flood of questions. "I can't wait to see you on Halloween night. What kind of candy are you hoping for?"

"I like peanut butter cups!"

"What a coincidence—that's exactly what I'll be handing out to trick-or-treaters." She winked at Max over Tyler's head. His son was settling into life here in Winsome Cove. Which meant he had a decision—and a phone call—to make later.

* * *

"Oh, Max…are you serious? You're not playing with us, are you?"

He took a slow breath, thankful he hadn't made this a video call. It was hard enough extending the invitation to Max's grandparents. At least he didn't have to worry about what his face was doing. But this wasn't about him. It was about Tyler.

"No tricks, Sally. I'm inviting you and Ed to Cape Cod for Thanksgiving. My mom will reserve an ocean-front room at her motel." He wasn't ready to have them stay in his house. "It's only a few minutes away. Tyler wants to see you, and I want…" What Max really wanted wasn't important. This wasn't about him. "I want Tyler to be happy. He needs to stay connected with his mother's family. With you and Ed. So… Thanksgiving?"

"Yes!" Sally Cosma shouted the reply so loudly that Max held the phone away from his ear.

It was late, and he was sitting in the living room, with only one lamp on. Seeing Tyler so happy in the forge earlier made him realize just how precious that happiness was. And Tyler missed his Cosma family, despite Max's reservations.

"I just want to be clear," he started. "I don't want to bring any more agitation into Tyler's life. No arguments. No insults. No drama. Can you and Ed agree to that?"

"Of course." Sally's voice was lower now. Calmer. "We can do that. Max…we've had time to consider everything that happened. Ed and I have been speaking with our priest, and he's helped us gain some perspective." She paused. "We only ever wanted what was best for our only grandchild."

"And you didn't think that was me." He couldn't get past the insults they'd hurled at him. Yes, much of it came from grief and shock, but that didn't make the words hurt less. There was silence on the line, then a ragged sigh.

"We didn't *know* you. We'd just lost Marie. The thought of losing Tyler, too…" Her voice faded, and so did some of his anger. If someone showed up at the house right now and tried taking Tyler from him, he'd fight them with everything he had.

"Max? Are you there?"

"I'm here, Sally. I'm glad we agree on no drama. You can spend as much time with Tyler as you want."

"Oh, we miss him so much. I appreciate the video calls, but to hold him again… I can't thank you enough." Those weekly video calls had been tough on Max, but he was glad his mother had encouraged them. They'd helped Tyler feel less disconnected from the life he'd known before.

"Okay, then." He cleared his throat, anxious to get this over with. "I guess I'll see you in a few weeks." Time to prepare himself and Tyler. "Let me know the dates you'll be here, and I'll have Mom reserve the room for you."

Sally was crying again by the time they said goodbye. Max poured himself a stiff drink. He was doing this for Tyler. He could get through anything for his son's happiness.

Chapter Eight

Grace set her coffee cup down on the table at Jerry's Java House with a heavy sigh. Heavier than she'd intended, because her best friend started to laugh.

"Girl, you look like you have the weight of the world on your shoulders! What's going on?" Maya arched one of her brows at Grace, then leaned forward. "Is it something at work? What's got you so all up in your head?"

"Oh…nothing, really. Or a lot of little things that don't amount to anything. Sorry." Grace gave her friend a reassuring smile. "I told you about the new receptionist at the dental office. Therese has some challenging ideas. So many opinions and suggestions, but some of her ideas might actually be worth exploring."

"And that annoys the hell out of you, doesn't it?"

Grace laughed. "You know me too well!"

"Rules are there for a reason." Maya held her hand up, straightening in her chair as if she was giving a speech, emphasizing with one hand. "Putting procedures in writing makes them easy for all to follow and helps avoid confusion. An organized office is a more efficient one…"

"I do not sound that uptight." Grace paused. "Do I?"

Now it was Maya's turn to laugh. "Well, you *would*

if you strung all those platitudes together like I just did, but no. You don't usually sound that prissy."

"Which means I *sometimes* do." It was no secret, and Maya had mentioned it before. Maya knew why, too. Breaking the rules had nearly killed Grace twelve years ago. "I know the staff rolls their eyes at me. I think my brother does, too. In one breath, Aiden tells me he likes that he doesn't have to worry about the business end of things so he can focus on patients, but then he turns around yesterday and tells me to try being more open-minded. I think he has a crush on the new girl."

"Or...and just hear me out here... Aiden wants you to try to be more open-minded. What has this new girl suggested that's so awful?"

"Nothing is *awful*. It's just...she worked for a much larger, multi-office practice in Boston, and some of those procedures won't transfer to our little office."

"But some of them could?"

Grace finally conceded. "Some of them could, yes. I suppose if we tackled the ideas one at a time..."

"And maybe not think of it as *tackling* but as giving them a chance?" Maya prodded.

"Yes. Fine. I'll work on my open-mindedness. In my defense, I *am* looking into a scheduling tool Therese suggested. It will let Aiden and the hygienists schedule appointments themselves, right from the exam rooms."

"Good girl. I was worried it might be your new neighbor keeping you up at night." Maya sipped her coffee, watching Grace over the rim of the mug. "I had to run out to the car for something after dinner last night, and I could hear the pounding coming from his carriage house. It sounded like a pile driver."

Max Bellamy was keeping her up at night, but not because of noise from the forge. He kept wandering into her dreams, rough and smelling of heated steel. Veins popping on his biceps as he swung a hammer and barked orders at her about keeping the door closed and taking her dress off and… Well, that's usually when she woke up in a sweat, wondering what was broken in her brain to be going there.

"That's his power hammer," Grace explained. "He said he's going to try not to use it in the evenings."

"Did he now?" Maya stared. "I assume you've already checked the covenants for that?"

Grace's face heated. Did everyone—even her best friend—think of her as some sort of tattletale? But the truth was…

"Yes, I checked. As long as he follows the noise ordinances, it's legal. And he does follow them—he keeps that power hammer in a soundproofed corner. He's not out there after ten o'clock, when the town's sound ordinances take effect."

Maya studied her face intently. "I thought you hated this guy? But now you're defending him?"

"I don't *hate* anyone. I miss the Hendersons, and it's… different…having Max and Tyler living there, but I can't change that. I'm trying to be…"

"Open-minded?" Her friend laughed softly. "I'm glad to hear that. I talked to Max the other day when Tyler and Chantal were playing outside together. He seems like a good guy. Overwhelmed, maybe, but he's devoted to Tyler. And he mentioned you're giving Tyler piano lessons. I knew that already, but… I thought you didn't teach kids because they were so unfocused?"

"I tried to turn him down, but Tyler likes me for some reason and he insisted, so Max insisted, and I agreed to give it a shot. I didn't think it would last this long, but the kid's actually pretty good. His mom taught him how to read music and play a little."

"His mom's dead, right? So sad." Maya sipped her coffee. "Max is kinda hot, don't you think?"

The question left Grace sputtering.

"What? I never… Why would I…? I mean…" She tried to regroup. "I've never thought about it."

A huge smile spread on Maya's face. "Oh, my God, you're lying to me right now."

"I am not!" She totally was, but she wasn't going to admit it to anyone, even her best friend.

"You *are*! You always do that little nose thing—barely a wrinkle, more like a tiny twitch—when you're embarrassed and when you're lying." Maya laughed so loudly that other customers glanced their way and smiled, even though they weren't in on the joke.

"Stop it! That's not true, and I'm not lying."

"Ha! You just did it again!" Maya looked around and mouthed *sorry* to the people in the café, then lowered her voice. "And what's up with his mother saying you're cooking meals for him? Are you just admiring this big ol' hottie from afar, or have you two been doing something about it?"

"There is no *us two*, Maya. We had a run-in the first day we met, and now he thinks I'm some obnoxious snob out to get him in trouble all the time." He kept her at arm's length, sending her home whenever things got too close. Which was totally fine. It also stung for some reason. She frowned. "The food is usually just cookies or cupcakes, because Tyler says Max can't cook. I feel sorry for the boy. The only thing we have in common is caring about Tyler. He's a smart little kid, and you're right—Max is a devoted father." She thought of the high-tech security system he had protecting the house. And the way he'd humbled himself, despite their disagreements, to plead with her to give Tyler piano lessons. She also thought about Max leaning over the anvil, swinging a hammer with sweat glistening on his tattooed forearms...

"Oh, wow," Maya breathed. "You're actually blushing right now. For what it's worth, I don't think it would hurt you to be open-minded about the hot single dad next door."

That hot single dad next door was definitely *on* her mind. But that was as far as it would go.

"How many boxes do you have in here, Mom?"

Max was helping his mother pull all the holiday decorations from storage at the Sassy Mermaid.

"A lot," she answered with a laugh. "I put a little something in each guest room, and last year I went all out on decorating the office. Plus your sister is storing a few boxes of holiday stuff here for the restaurant."

"Isn't it a little early? Halloween was just two days ago."

That had been an experience for Max. He was used to grown-ups playing dress-up at fairs, but the kids raised it to a whole new level. They were all so excited. Or amped up on sugar. Or both.

Tyler's dragon costume, thanks to Mom, had been a standout. Everyone loved the shiny green fabric and the sparkly blue wings. The "flames" were made of red and yellow chiffon glued to a hand fan. When Tyler flipped the switch and held it near his face, it looked like glowing dragon flames. Sam had worn all black, with tall leather boots and a wide brimmed black hat. He had a large claymore strapped to his side, but the edges and tip were round and not sharp at all. It was the children's scissors version of a sword. Every few houses, he'd pull out the sword in the middle of the street and roar like a true knight of old, chasing dragons. The kids, and parents, seemed to love it.

Grace had given Tyler enough peanut butter cups to last a month, but her eyes never left Max. She'd insisted that he pull out the sword while on her front porch, and then clapped when he did it. She seemed enthralled with the costumes. And with Max. He was sure he'd seen a spark in her eyes.

He set another box behind the reception desk. When he looked up, he almost didn't believe what he was seeing. He'd just been thinking about her, and there she was—Grace—walking across the lawn of the motel, heading toward the beach. She was almost unrecognizable, bundled in a puffy jacket with a bright blue scarf wound around her neck up to her ears. He watched, then stretched his back.

"Hey, Mom, do you mind if I break away for a few minutes? I want to talk to Grace about Tyler's practice at home last night. He let me play guitar with him, and it was…" He shrugged, not knowing how to put his feelings into words. "It was special, and I want to let her know…"

His mother looked from his face out to where Grace

was walking. "Are you sure you just want to talk with her?" Her smile was playfully suggestive. "She's a lovely woman."

"Stop it." His voice was sharp, so he tried to cover it with a quick, fake laugh. "This is strictly a parent and teacher relationship."

"Really?" Mom asked. "Because your sister tells me she stopped by the other night and Grace was out in the carriage house with you."

Yeah, that had been awkward. He should have known Lexi would go running to tell their mother about it. He'd been showing Grace the process of making a Damascus-patterned blade. Specifically, he'd been demonstrating the twisting and layering of the steel to create detailed swirling patterns in the sword once it was forged. Grace had been standing on the opposite side of the large anvil, as usual. They'd both been careful to keep their distance since that first night, when she touched him and set his skin on fire.

Lexi had waltzed through the door just as he and Grace had each leaned over the blade. So close that he could smell Grace's light floral perfume. It wasn't anything more than an accident of location. They'd ended up with their faces close, like two magnets pulled together. Grace had jumped back so quickly at Lexi's arrival that she'd nearly knocked a tall PVC tube of oil over.

"Mom, Grace just stops once in a while—" two or three times a week "—to update me on Tyler's progress."

"Lexi told me Grace brought you a whole apple pie."

"She brought *Tyler* a pie. He has her convinced I only cook him gruel every day, so she does some pity baking. Please don't make a big deal out of it."

Mom stared at him just a beat longer, then nodded her head toward the door. "Go. She's almost to the stairs. But take your jacket—the wind is sharp today."

"Yes, mother." He grabbed the coat from the office chair. "I'll be right back."

"Don't hurry on my account." She turned away and opened the first box. "Looks like Grace is the only one brave enough to walk in this cold, so she'll probably appreciate your company."

She was out of sight when he got outside, but he knew where she was headed. He jogged toward the wooden steps that led from the motel property down to the beach. There was an observation deck there, next to the long staircase to ocean level. Directly below the deck was a tangle of large rocks, usually covered with seals if it was a sunny day. Today, there were only a few napping there.

Grace had told him one evening how the returning seal population boom had drawn great white sharks back to the Cape, looking for easy meals. During the summer, volunteers often sat on the deck with binoculars, watching for sharks if anyone was swimming. A gust of wind slapped him in the face, and he quickly zipped his jacket. No humans would be in that water today.

He looked down the beach and spotted Grace, leaning into the wind as she walked. He quickly ran down the stairs and hurried to catch up with her, calling her name once he hit the hard-packed sand. She turned in surprise, clutching her scarf tightly over her ears and around her neck.

"Max? What are you doing here? Is Tyler okay?"

"He's fine. I was helping Mom get ready for the next

holiday. She had me pull out about a hundred boxes of stuff, so she can take her time putting it up. At least, that's what she said, but she'll probably have it done by the weekend."

"O-kay. But what are you doing—" she gestured at the ocean waves crashing on the sand "—*here*? Looking for a walk, or...?"

"Um...yeah. A walk would be great." They headed down the beach, into the wind. After a few steps, he remembered what he wanted to tell her. "I wanted to tell you what happened last night while Tyler was practicing. He let me play guitar with him."

"Playing the scales?"

"God, no." Max laughed. "If I heard him play another series of scales in every key, I think I would have lost my mind."

Grace's head was down against the wind, but he caught her smile. "Playing scales is how he learns, Dad."

"If it was as simple as that, he'd be the best piano player in the world, because he definitely has those scales down."

As they walked, he told Grace how he'd asked his son if they could play a song together. Tyler had looked up in surprise. "I'm practicing scales."

"I know," Max assured him. "And it sounds...great. I think you've really nailed them."

Hopefully nailed them into a coffin and nailed the coffin closed. If he heard those do-re-mi notes one more time... Then he noticed the fleeting half smile that went across Tyler's face. The boy straightened a bit with pride. These piano lessons had brought his son more confidence and happiness than Max would have imagined.

Tyler had been confused by Max's offer, and asked him how a piano and guitar could be played together.

"They are both musical instruments," Max told him. "Guitar players read the same sheet music piano players do." Not exactly, but close enough. "We play the same chords. The same notes. It sounds a little different, but music is music." Tyler hadn't looked convinced, but there was a spark of interest in his eyes, so Max sat on the edge of the piano bench with him. "Why don't you pick out a song from your books, and I'll play it with you."

Tyler had hesitated, with that expression Max had come to know so well. The one that showed the walls coming up, refusing to let Max in. His eyes became guarded, and a small wrinkle made the center of his forehead pucker. But then...he'd *nodded*. Max had managed to hold in his sigh of relief, not wanting to overreact and ruin the moment. But his heart skipped a beat at the thought of his son agreeing to play a song together. It was a big moment.

"I agree," Grace said. "For Tyler to want to tackle something like that, with you, means he's confident in his skills. What did you play?"

"He picked 'Bye Bye Blackbird.'"

"Really?" Grace's stride slowed. A flock of seagulls was dancing in the wind out over the water. "We've barely practiced that one."

"Yeah, I could tell that once we started. And it's more jazz than blues, but I knew I could do the harmony. By the way, he doesn't know what that is."

Grace looked over at him. "And you think that's on me? He's only seven weeks into beginner lessons, Max."

"Fair enough. I handled it." He was proud of the moment, and it probably showed. "I told him that harmony is when two musicians don't always play, or sing, the same notes, but the notes they do play complement each other. It's the same song, but with more depth. Two people make one song better." He zipped his jacket a little higher. "I could see I was losing him, so I finally told him it just means if I played a different note than him, it was okay."

Tyler had started to play, and Max had played the guitar softly, adding some freestyle harmony. Tyler hesitated at first, but then he'd continued, bobbing his head. Max added a blues-style slide to the last note. Tyler had looked up at Max with a surprised smile—a *full* smile this time.

"It sounds like the music you listen to!" he'd said.

"Oh, Max, that's great." Grace stopped, turning her back to the growing sea winds. She started back toward the motel. "You must have been thrilled."

"I was, and I have you to thank for it."

"I'm not doing anything that any other piano teacher wouldn't do. I'd like to hear that guitar sometime."

"Maybe I'll bring it over and join one of your classes." He liked the thought of that—the three of them making music together. Max realized he was...*happy*. Not the quick kind of happiness that flitted by when he and Tyler had a good day. This was a richer happiness. Things were getting better with his son on a deeper level, and it made everything else feel lighter and more hopeful. "I meant what I said, Grace. I have you to thank for a lot of things with Tyler, and not just music. You're an important piece of his life, and I think you've helped him accept this move."

Her cheeks turned a deeper shade of pink as she walked. "I'm just the piano teacher, Max."

"You're more than that." To Tyler *and* to him, but he wasn't sure he wanted to go there. He needed to understand his feelings better. "Tyler had no interest in trying to please *me* after I uprooted him. But he wants to please *you*."

She nodded, snuggling deeper into the long wool scarf. "I've noticed that. I don't want to sound weird or presumptuous, but I might remind him of his mom a little? She played the piano, too, and he likes to watch me play." She thought for a moment. "Is that healthy or... not? I don't want to be some sort of surrogate that goofs up the progress he needs to make."

Max was silent. They were almost to the bottom of the stairs up to the motel. Tyler did seem very eager to please the women in his life. Grace. His teacher, Miss Kelleher. Max's mother and sister. Maya King across the street. It made sense, he supposed. The boy had lost his mother, who'd been the only parent he'd known. They'd clearly been very close to each other. Tyler had never *had* a dad in his life, so he either didn't see a reason to impress Max, or was too intimidated.

It was tough for Max to think about, because he hadn't *chosen* to be absent from his son's life. That decision had been made for him. And the person who'd made it would never be able to explain her reasons. Tyler had his grandfather, Ed Cosma, but Ed was a quiet, unassuming guy who followed his wife's lead. Now the kid didn't know how to react to adult men, and it was going to take time—even *more* time—to help him learn.

The social worker had insisted that it needed to happen organically. That he shouldn't expect Tyler to just *know* how to hang out with the guys. That loud men, even if just clowning around, might scare him. Max had learned that lesson early on. He'd taken Tyler to a Renaissance fair a few hours from Cincinnati, to introduce him to Max's world. But Tyler had wanted nothing to do with the loud, hectic fair and the performers dashing up to him and challenging him to sword fights. It was all in fun, and these people were Max's friends, excited to meet his new son. But the afternoon had ended on a sour note, with Tyler in tears, begging to go home.

"I don't think it's harming Tyler at all, Grace." They stopped by the stairs. The wind was partially blocked by the cliffside, and they automatically huddled closer against it. He explained his theory about Tyler not knowing how to relate to men. How he naturally bonded more comfortably with the women in his life.

"That makes sense." She looked out at the gray sea. "But I'm still just his piano teacher."

"I don't know why you keep saying that. You're more than that to him. And to me. You're our neighbor, and you try to keep us on the straight and narrow." She smiled at that. "And you bake really yummy cookies."

She laughed this time, looking up at him through long blond eyelashes. Her skin was wind-kissed, and her hair was sweeping across her face. He brushed it back so he could see those golden brown eyes more clearly. His hand stayed there on the side of her face. Her lips parted, and the air around them suddenly felt still and warm, like they were inside a bubble together. Her hand rested on his forearm.

"Max…" He felt her say his name more than heard it.

He wanted to kiss her. It wasn't the first time the thought had crossed his mind. He'd always talked himself out of it, but maybe he should stop listening to his own voice of reason. Maybe he should just kiss Grace Bennett at last. He moved closer. Their lips had barely brushed together when there was a sudden din of barking.

A bunch of seals had come out of the water and onto the rocks just a few yards away, and the small group of seals already on the rocks were not happy about it. There was nothing sweet or romantic about a dozen seals barking at each other angrily. The moment had officially been broken.

He stepped back, shaking his head. "Saved by the seals."

She smiled nervously, but there was a shadow in her eyes. Was it disappointment he saw? "I need to get going," she said. "Um…thanks for telling me about Tyler. I'm glad he's liking the piano."

Before he could stop her, she turned and jogged up the stairs, leaving him standing alone on the sand with an audience of highly unhelpful seals.

Chapter Nine

Grace had just tugged her sweater off, getting ready for bed, when she heard Max hammering. It wasn't loud enough to be the power hammer, so it had to be just him at the anvil. She hadn't even heard it until she turned off the music she'd been listening to—the Broadway soundtrack from *Wicked*. She checked her watch. It was eleven o'clock. She'd never heard him working out there so late. Had he left Tyler alone in the house all this time? Cameras or not, he told her he always checked on him in person every hour, and he never stayed in the forge past nine or nine thirty.

The hammering stopped, then started again. She did her best to dismiss the enticing image of Max sweating over a length of red-hot steel as he raised and lowered the hammer. Her hand rested on her chest, and she could feel her heart pounding under her fingertips. She was imagining *his* hands touching her. Remembering the thrill pulsing through her veins when his lips had come so close to hers on the beach yesterday. Remembering how much she'd wanted him to kiss her. She licked her lips, then bit the lower one. Well, this wouldn't do at all.

She couldn't lose sleep over a man who so clearly

wanted nothing to do with her. Well, his *body* wanted something, just like hers did. That much was obvious. But his brain refused to go there. Whenever they came close to a personal conversation or even a little flirtation, he shut it down. Did he find her that boring? Was he just a general commitment-phobe? It was obvious they didn't have enough in common to build anything long-term, but it wouldn't kill the man to at least *kiss* her.

They'd come so close on the beach. Then he'd said those words. "*Saved* by the seals." She'd been ready to throw a shoe at the animals for ruining things, but Max felt *saved*.

Her hand slid from her heart to cover her breast, and rested there, her fingertips brushing the lace on her bra. It had been a few years since she'd dated any man, even semiseriously. It took a lot of emotional effort for her to let a man that close. To explain the scars dotting her torso.

That she was feeling this level of desire for a man like Max Bellamy—a tattooed guy with a vulnerable young child and a sword factory behind his house— well, it made no sense. Even though he'd told her some of his own story, she hadn't shared hers. And *her* story tended to change everything in a relationship. But the smoldering desire was there nonetheless.

The hammering started again. What was he doing out there this late? Why was he forcing her to think about him? Suddenly annoyed, she tugged her sweater back over her head. She slipped into her flats and grabbed a jacket from the coat hook near the door, heading out into the cold rain. *Ugh!* She didn't know it had started raining. She hurried across the driveway and barely knocked on the door before stepping inside, brushing her wet hair off her face.

He looked up in surprise when she stepped into the carriage house, then grimaced. "Let me guess. I'm making too much noise."

He was standing at the anvil, a hammer in his hand. Just the way she'd imagined. His face was red from the heat, and he looked distracted. Tired. Frustrated. His flannel shirt was tossed onto the workbench behind him, and he was wearing a sweat-soaked dark blue T-shirt with a Salty Knight logo on it. The blade on the anvil was cooling to a dark copper color as the burning red slowly faded.

"Did you know it's eleven o'clock?"

Oh, God, she really *did* sound prissy, didn't she?

Max grabbed a red handkerchief from his back pocket and wiped his brow with it. "I'm not using the power hammer, and there's no way this is anywhere near breaking the decibel level."

"Is Tyler in the house?"

He set the hammer down and turned to face her. "Yeah, I told him it's going to be a late night, so he called a few of his buddies over and they're playing poker inside."

There was that edge in his tone that made her bristle, or…something. She hadn't come here to argue, so she had no idea why the air in the forge practically shimmered with tension.

She wasn't sure why she'd come here. But the disdain in his voice stung—as if she'd asked something stupid. "It was a valid question, Max. You're working much later than usual."

There she was, sounding prissy again. His face reddened, but then he sighed and rolled his head back and to the side, stretching, before he met her eyes.

"I know, sorry. I've got a hard deadline with this order. The guy needs this custom orc Uruk-hai sword before a comicon this weekend. It has to be Damascus steel." She remembered that was steel made from multiple layers that formed a pattern. "I was polishing the first blade yesterday when I found a crack running down the spine. I had to start all over again from scratch. If I don't get this blade shaped tonight I'll never get it assembled with a handle for him before the weekend." He held up the cooling blade. It was an odd shape—long, thick and straight, with a narrow horizontal spike at the end.

"I'm sorry, did you just say this was an *orc* blade? Like... *Lord of the Rings* orcs? Fictional monsters?"

Max grunted. "Monsters may be a little harsh. They were soldiers of the enemy."

"Yeah—the enemy that happened to be the monstrous all-powerful evil eye of Sauron."

"Not all-powerful. He was defeated in the end."

"Only because a brave little hobbit destroyed the ring."

They stared at each other for a moment, both stunned at the realization that they'd read the same books. A slow smile spread on Max's face.

"Tyler's with my mom at the Sassy Mermaid, by the way. He likes staying there, and I knew I'd be up late working on this thing." He raised the blade, shaped but not polished yet. "The fighting blade of the Uruk-hai."

She returned the smile. There was something sweet and boyish in his expression when he talked about the Tolkien books. She'd loved them, too, as a teen. She'd been alone a lot back then, with Aiden off to college and her parents nearing retirement age. The fantasy world of Middle Earth had been her escape.

Max slid the blade back into the forge. "I just need to quench it one last time to harden it, and then I'll grind the edges tomorrow and reassemble the handle onto it." He paused. "I'm sorry about the noise. Did I wake you up?"

Her anger had evaporated. "I was getting ready for bed when I heard you out here." *And I touched myself.* She felt her cheeks heat up. "It surprised me." *Yes it did.* "I mean, the noise surprised me, but it...wasn't really that loud."

His gaze swept over her body, warming her as it passed. "It's raining out?" She nodded. "Come closer to the forge and warm up."

She was beginning to feel plenty warm, but she did as he asked. She could see the wide container of oil next to the anvil, and stepped to the opposite side, knowing he'd be quenching the unusual blade in that. That was exactly what happened—he pulled out the glowing red blade and thrust it into the oil, causing it to sizzle, boil and smoke.

The steam rose up around Max, and the scene seemed out of some ancient painting, with a hardworking blacksmith toiling over his work. This scene had been unfolding for millennia—man against iron. It was primal. This was the moment when some buxom village wench would stride into the forge and into the smithy's bold embrace. *Not* the local piano teacher. But she couldn't look away. When Max pulled the blade out of the heat, he ran a rasp along its edges and nodded in satisfaction.

"Is it hard?" she asked, before blushing from head to

toe. Had that sounded suggestive? He coughed, trying to hold back laughter. Apparently it *had* sounded suggestive. His steely gaze caught hers, and her lungs froze.

"It's hard enough."

Max knew this was a dangerous game they were playing. Grace's lips parted, and she ran the tip of her tongue along the lower one. Oh, yeah, he was hard enough. More than, actually. But what the hell was she playing at?

She'd busted through the door like she was ready to rip him a new one. But there'd been something in the darkness of her eyes and the high color in her cheeks, despite the cold rain outdoors. Her hair was wet, and surprisingly, curls were forming around her flushed face, softening it even more.

He hit the switch on the forge to shut it down. He set the orc sword down and tugged off his leather apron. She was watching his every move in silence. Of all the people to be fans of Tolkien's books, he'd never have guessed Grace would be one. Another little string connecting them, despite all their differences.

"Why are you here, Grace?" He stepped around the anvil. "If the hammering wasn't that loud, then why did you come running over here in the rain? Is there something you want?"

Her foot shifted, as if she wanted to back away, but she changed her mind. She planted both feet firmly and lifted her chin.

"It was…unusual. You're out of your routine, and I wanted to…to know why, I guess."

He was sweaty and dirty and probably smelly, too. She was in trim wool slacks and a soft sweater. He should step away. But he remembered how soft her trembling lips had been when he'd trespassed there yesterday. And there was a heat in her eyes saying she remembered, too. In fact, she was staring straight at his mouth. Maybe this was her idea of an adventure. Kissing the bad boy next door. Maybe she just wanted to see what it was like to take a walk on the wild side.

Maybe he should give her what she wanted.

"I think you were curious about more than the noise, Grace." He moved closer, just shy of touching his sweaty shirt against her sweater. He lifted his hand but didn't touch her face. Instead, he ran his fingertips through her hair. "I like the curls."

Her nose wrinkled. "They refuse to be tamed. They appear any time my hair gets wet."

"I *like* them," he repeated. Her face was so close. Her nostrils flared as she took a few shallow breaths. She put her hand on his bicep. Was she holding him back or pulling him in? "I'm filthy dirty right now—"

Her lips on his swallowed whatever he was going to say next. Her arms wound around his neck, and her body pressed against his. *Yes, please.* Dirt and sweat be damned. He'd warned her, and if she didn't care, neither did he. Not when she was kissing him like this. Like she couldn't help herself. Like she'd been dying to kiss him.

Max slid his arms around her, one hand on her lower back and the other winding through her damp hair, holding her mouth against his. She may have started this, but he was damn well going to finish it. His lips moved against hers until hers parted, letting him in with a moan that came from deep in her chest. She lifted one leg and curled it around his thigh, and he pressed her back against the anvil with a growl. His hips ground against hers. He was ruining her neatly-pressed trousers, and he didn't care. Not one bit.

They barely broke for air before coming back together, their heads turning for better access. He lifted her body until she could feel his hardness rubbing against her. Her fingers dug through his hair and held on. She was frantic to have more of him. He had more to give, but reality was knocking on the back of his mind.

This was the yes or no moment. Go or stop. They were in the carriage house late on a cold, rainy Saturday night. He could taste wine on her breath. And Max really was a filthy mess. Grace deserved more than a sweaty grope in a barn. His fingers tightened on her buttock. But the groping was pretty damn nice. He lowered her until she was on her feet, his lips refusing to give up on the fun until he forced himself to raise his head.

"No..." Grace murmured, and the plea was almost enough to undo him. But cooler heads had to prevail here. Just because she'd gotten tipsy tonight and decided on this little adventure with a bad boy didn't mean she wouldn't regret it in the morning.

He'd had his share of "blacksmith groupies" over the years. Women who got all hot and bothered when they saw him shaping steel into swords. Women who'd hang around his booth at the fairs and leave their numbers for him to call. Messages left on his phone, with a soft voice leaving a name and address. One even whispered on the phone to "wear that leather apron." And sure, he'd called his share of the numbers. The road was a lonely place. But he knew what they wanted—the swordsman.

Did he think Grace was one of those women? No, he

couldn't imagine her *ever* dropping her phone number off to some random guy. But every time she came out to the carriage house and watched him work, he could feel her eyes on him in a way that didn't happen when they discussed his son in the daylight. He didn't want to be some fantasy for her. It wouldn't feel right for either of them.

"Grace." His hands cupped her face, and he waited until her eyes opened and focused. "We need to stop this. You need to go. You and I might seem fun right now, but we are a very bad idea, and you're going to realize that in the morning."

"You want me to go?"

Her voice was tight with need and hurt. Of course he didn't *want* her to go, but there was no future he could imagine where the two of them were together, and having some one-night stand would cause all kinds of complications he didn't need.

"I do." He lied to her. "Go home. Get some sleep."

She pulled away, and he could tell she was embarrassed. Her cheeks were pink, and she wouldn't meet his eyes. "I'm not a child."

"No, you are an intelligent, grown woman," he replied. "A beautiful woman." She looked up at him. "A *tempting* woman. But this—whatever it is between us—I don't think it's real. And I definitely don't think it's wise." He reached out to touch her cheek, but she pulled away. It was just as well. Touching her again might destroy his resolve.

"Right," she said briskly. "Sorry. I'll go."

She sounded not only embarrassed, but hurt.

"I didn't mean—"

"I know what you meant," she snapped. "You said you

want me to go. So I'm going. You said it was a mistake, and I agree. Let's just…forget this happened."

He couldn't help chuckling at that. "I don't think *that* will happen anytime soon." He meant it as a compliment—it had been one hell of a kiss. But her face flamed red before she turned away and started for the door. "Wait… Grace…"

She was into the rain and gone.

He'd done the right thing. He was sure of it. And yet, he had the feeling he'd hurt her somehow. It didn't make sense, since she was such a stickler for rules and practicality. He started cleaning up the shop to go inside. She'd see the logic once she had a good night's sleep. She'd thank him. And if she didn't—if she stayed mad—it would stop the evening visits to the carriage house. Stop the temptation.

But Max couldn't help wondering if *he'd* ever get a good night's sleep again. He had a feeling he'd be reliving that kiss for a very long time.

"What is eating at you this week, sis?" Aiden stood in the doorway of Grace's small office, arms folded across his chest.

"I have no idea what you're talking about." She moved some folders on her desk. Okay, she *slammed* some folders down on her desk. She looked at her big brother and winced. "Sorry. I'm in a mood."

"I'd say so." Aiden stepped in and closed the office door. She knew she was in for a lecture when he did that. "You read Therese the riot act for trying something new with the records wall, and I heard you agree to let her try it last week, so—"

"I said we'd *try* it. I never actually told her she could go ahead and start moving patient files around without my approval."

"I'm sorry, Grace, but that's BS. Telling her you were willing to try it sure sounded like permission to me. And she only did one row of files, as an experiment." He sat in one of the chairs across from her and leaned back precariously, knowing full well she didn't like it when he did that. She also didn't like when he gave her the paternal stare she was getting at the moment. "Therese hasn't undone your entire beloved system behind your back, but you acted like she did. And that's not like you."

Her jaw worked back and forth as she struggled to come up with an argument in her defense. But Aiden was right. Therese had only reorganized the newest patient files, which were the easiest to manage because they were lighter in volume. And Grace *had* reacted badly, scolding her in front of other staff and even a few patients in the waiting room. She closed her eyes in shame.

"You're right. I owe everyone an apology, especially Therese. I'll go right now and—"

"Hang on." Aiden raised his hand to stop her. "An apology would be nice, but I'm more concerned about what's causing all this."

She loved her brother, but there was no way she was going to tell him about the humiliation she'd experienced on Saturday night. Her whole body tensed just thinking about it. She'd basically thrown herself at Max, and he had kissed her back like she'd never been kissed before. Her blood felt like it was boiling as hot as the quenching oil Max used for his blades. Their mouths, their bodies…it was all so perfect. At least it had been for her.

But not for Max. He'd simply set her aside and told her to leave, making her feel like some overeager teenager.

"Grace?" Aiden brought her back to the present.

"I'm sorry, Aiden. I…uh… I haven't been sleeping well. It's making me cranky."

"Okay. Why aren't you sleeping well? What's on your mind? Are you feeling alright?"

"Oh, it's nothing. Change of seasons." Just the reality of being undesirable. No matter what Max said after he told her to go, that truth had been clear. *You're beautiful.* Yeah, right. Just not *his* type of beautiful. *You're tempting.* But not to him. "I promise I'll apologize to everyone and do better."

"I don't want to leave if you're not feeling well." Aiden was going to a dental conference in Chicago for three days. The office would still be open for dental hygienist work like cleanings and checkups, with Grace in charge.

"I promise I'm fine." And she would be. She needed to shake off her hurt feelings and move on. Who cared what Max Bellamy thought, anyway? "I'll take something tonight to help me sleep and I'll be good tomorrow. Do you need me to take you to the airport in the morning?"

"No, no. Karl's going to drop me off." Karl Whitmore had been Aiden's best friend since grade school. Karl and Grace had dated briefly in high school, but he'd found someone else more interesting and moved on. It was literally the story of her life.

"Grace, why can't I play the song on page ten?"

"Because we work through the book in order, Tyler.

You know that." Grace flipped to the second song in the book. "The books are set up so each song adds to your skills. Why do you want to jump to page ten?"

Tyler shrugged. "It's the song Max played with me."

"Oh, I heard about that. Did you have fun?"

"He played *harr-ny*. On his guitar."

It took a moment before she figured out what he was saying. "Your dad played *harmony* with you? While you played the piano?"

The image made her go soft inside all over again. Max was trying so hard to be a good dad.

"And you played the song on page ten because…?"

"Max said he knew it." Tyler looked up, so serious and sincere. "I thought it might be easier for him. But I couldn't go very fast."

She blinked a few times and looked away. Tyler was still a ways from admitting it, but he felt something for the father who'd suddenly appeared in his life.

"That was very kind of you, Tyler." She smiled brightly. "Maybe we *should* practice that one today, so you can be even better at it the next time Max joins you."

She helped Tyler with the timing. It was a challenge for him, but he gave it his all, finally able to pick up his speed and play more smoothly. It would be a nice surprise for Max.

Grace was doing her best to think of Max as only a neighbor and parent of a student. It was clear he wanted nothing more from her than that. And despite his laughter when she'd suggested they forget that she'd ever kissed him on Saturday night, that was exactly what she intended to do. Forget it. Keep things platonic and civil. They didn't even need to be friends. No more walks on the beach or chats in the forge. He was the parent of a student. That's all Max was to her.

She'd apologized to everyone at the office, but she knew she had more bridge-building to do with Therese. Much to Grace's chagrin, everyone in the office loved the new filing system, just as they'd liked the appointment software Therese had recommended. It gave the techs more autonomy and freed up time for the receptionist to handle phone calls and process payments from patients. Which meant her brother had been right. She'd been resisting it for no good reason other than her dislike of change and fear of chaos. The changes had been positive, and there had been no chaos at all.

"Miss Grace, where's Mozart?" Tyler stopped playing and was looking around the room.

"I think he's upstairs. He likes things nice and quiet, so don't go looking for him, okay?"

"Why does he like quiet?"

"Well, I guess it's what he's used to. It's usually just him and me in the house."

"Why?"

Because your father doesn't like my kisses.

"Mozart and I just like things to be peaceful."

"Why?"

"We just do!" she finally said, with an exasperated laugh. "Are you trying to tell me you're done playing piano today, and it's time for *me* to play?"

His shy grin was all the answer she needed. It had become their tradition—Tyler played for his thirty-minute lesson, then Grace played a piece of music for him while he watched. He seemed to enjoy watching her fingers go across the keys and would watch in rapt attention.

He was probably thinking of his mother, which made the moments bittersweet for her.

"Pick the sheet music, and I'll play it." She nodded at a stack of music off to the side. He couldn't read the titles very well, but he liked making the choice from looking at the sheets. She'd noticed he usually selected something with a lot of musical notes on it, probably thinking he'd be able to stump her. That was unlikely after her years of playing, but she also made sure the choices were songs she knew. This week she'd set out a selection of Broadway tunes.

He handed her a song from *Les Misérables*, his face lighting up when he saw the cover page with the signature young girl with the wide eyes.

"*Les Miz?* Are you sure?"

Tyler nodded and slid closer to her as she began "On My Own." The song was poignant—sad and hopeful all at once. She was almost finished when she glanced at Tyler. He was watching her fingers, as usual. But huge tears were rolling down his face. She barely hesitated on the keys, then decided to play through the ending before putting her arm around his shoulders.

"Did you mom play this one, Tyler?" Grace asked softly. The boy nodded silently. His cheeks were still wet with tears, but he wasn't sobbing. Just leaking sadness on his face. "I'll bet she played it even better than me." He nodded again, and she smiled. She'd never expect to outplay his mother in his eyes. "Do you want me to play it again?" Another nod.

By the time she'd played it the third time, Grace was crying, too.

Chapter Ten

"So Marie played Broadway tunes?" Max's mother was sitting at his kitchen table, sipping a cup of coffee. She'd brought over some prepared dinners for him and Tyler.

"According to Grace, yes. He sure hasn't heard that music with me."

She'd caught Max in the driveway that morning and quickly filled him in on Tyler's lesson before dashing to her car. He had the feeling she didn't want to be anywhere near him, meaning his fears about that kiss had come true. It had spoiled something between them.

"Well, now that you know," Mom said, "you can start playing it more often for him. They say things like sounds and scents are more powerful for memories than words are. It might help him connect to those memories and maybe talk about it with you or his school counselor."

"It's not like I want to erase his mother from his life," he said, staring out the window over the kitchen sink. It faced Grace's house. He'd said something wrong, but he wasn't sure what.

"He's doing better, but Tyler must be missing his momma something awful. Has he opened up at all about her?"

"No." Max joined his mother at the table. "I barely knew her, and Tyler won't tell me anything."

"What about her family? Won't they help?"

Max barked out a sharp, humorous laugh. "*Help?* They tried to keep him from me, Mom. I'm sure they did their best to convince Tyler I'm some evil interloper in his life."

Phyllis Bellamy stared hard at him, long enough to make him squirm.

"What?"

She put her hand over his on the table. "They'll be here in two weeks, honey. They love Tyler, just like you do. Sit down with them and listen to their stories about Marie. They should be a part of Tyler's life."

He looked at their hands together. He was thirty-five, and still comforted by his mother's touch. Tyler would never have that, and it made Max so damn sad.

"They *are* part of his life, Mom. They FaceTime with Tyler at least once a week. And I invited them to spend Thanksgiving here. I'm dreading it, but I did it."

"And I'm proud of you for that. Maybe you'll all get a chance to start healing." She patted his hand, then straightened in her chair. She checked the time. "Oh, I've got to run. I told Fred I'd go to the restaurant supply place in Plymouth and get more napkins for the bar."

"What is going on with you two, Mom?"

His mother blushed, which was something he hadn't seen very often.

"Nothing's going on." She looked away, her lips tight. "He owns the bar. Your sister runs the restaurant. I bounce back and forth between the two and try to keep the peace."

"Keep the peace?" Max laughed. "Half the time, it

seems like you two are the ones who can't have a peaceful conversation."

"Nonsense. We're a little…competitive…but it's never that bad."

"You were yelling at each other last week, Mom. Like, *really* yelling. Something about him not having your Manhattan ready?"

Her face was flame red now, and she stood so quickly that the chair skidded on his floor. He stood, too, marveling at how tense she was at the mention of Fred Knight's name. Was Lexi right about there being some sort of sexual tension between the two? He shuddered. He really didn't want to know.

She took a deep breath, blowing it out slowly with her eyes closed.

"I like fighting with Fred," she admitted. "We're like steel and flint, making sparks off each other. It's fun." She smiled softly at him. "It's different than my former relationship." She was talking about Dad. "Your father and I rarely cared enough about anything to fight over it, especially in those last years we were together. It was all about keeping up appearances and pretending to be a happy couple." Her right shoulder rose and fell quickly. "There's no pretending with Fred. Everything's right out there in the open. And I like that. Honesty is important in a relationship, honey. Even when that honesty might sting a bit. It's better than pretending." She grabbed her jacket and kissed him on the cheek. "Did you hear there's a nor'easter on the way? Your first Cape storm. Give Tyler my love. And say hi to Grace, too."

He didn't say anything about things being off with

Grace this week. Maybe it was time for them to be honest with each other. Or maybe they just needed to kiss some more.

Grace was doing her best not to panic, but if the office lights flickered one more time… Of course, they *did* flicker, and she jumped up from her chair and started pacing.

She shouldn't have stayed at the office so long. She knew that now. Therese had told her that. Aiden had texted her that from Chicago. But there were no appointments after one o'clock on Fridays, so it was the perfect time for her to review the quarterly tax documents in peace and quiet. It wasn't like she had any reason to hurry home—she'd canceled her student lessons because of the storm coming in. She'd decided to balance the checking accounts against receipts and invoices. She'd found a discrepancy of fifty dollars that kept her there longer than she'd planned. It hadn't been all that windy outside during the afternoon, and she thought the hype over the big storm may have been a bust.

But when the nor'easter arrived in earnest, with the high winds whistling loudly around the corner of the office building, she'd looked up from her desk in surprise. She'd just wanted to finish adding the numbers before closing up shop. Now it was dark outside, the lights were flickering and she *couldn't* leave. Not until she knew the power was going to stay on. Every time it flickered off and on, the alarm system beeped and reset. But what if it didn't reset? The building would be open to the thieves who had already hit two other dental offices in eastern Massachusetts recently, looking for drugs.

Not only that, but now that it was dark outside, she didn't feel safe going to her car. What if the lot went dark? How would she know if she was alone or being watched? What if the thieves arrived just as she tried to leave?

Deep, controlled breaths.

Grace was spiraling into a panic attack, and she hadn't had one of those in two or three years. She tried to remember what her therapist had taught her. She took a few breaths—in for four, out for four, repeat.

Deal with facts, not fears.

The alarm system had a battery backup, in addition to the generator backup the entire building had. The dental office thefts had both been off-Cape, so not *that* close. The nearest had been up in Plymouth.

The lights went off for a few very long seconds, then came back on again. The alarm system beeped when it went off, and then when the power came back. The shrill sound set her right back on edge. She did *not* want to suffer a panic attack. She could stop this.

Think of something positive. A happy place.

Oddly enough, Max Bellamy sprang to mind. Which was dumb. That man was *not* her happy place. Her lustful, horny place? Maybe. But certainly not comforting or relaxing when she was facing a panic attack. He was probably the reason her nerves were so on edge in the first place.

She'd felt off balance ever since their kiss last Saturday, and then his rejection of her. A gust of wind hit the side of the office with a whoosh and made the windows rattle. She should leave. She was going to leave. Deep breath. Stick to the facts—home was only two miles away. Everything would be fine. Her home was her happy place, *not* her neighbor's forge. She grabbed her coat and headed for the back door. The office went completely dark. And stayed that way this time.

The security alarm was beeping. The fire alarms were beeping. She held her breath, waiting for the generator to come on. But it didn't. She stood there longer than she should have, but she didn't know what to do. Run? Hunker down? Call for help?

Her phone rang, and she almost screamed. It was the equivalent of someone tapping her on the shoulder in the darkness. She pulled the phone from her bag. It was Max. Had she summoned up the annoying man with her thoughts? And yet, she felt comforted seeing his name on the screen. As if she wasn't alone.

Her voice cracked when she answered. "Hello?"

"Hey, it's Max. Just checking to see if you're okay."

How could he possibly know her situation?

"What? Why?"

He huffed a soft laugh, and her spine reacted with a blast of warmth from top to bottom. *Traitorous spine!*

"Look, I know you're an independent woman and probably have a flashlight in every room, but I wanted to make sure. They're saying the power could be off for a while. If you need anything over there, let me know."

She almost replied that she could really use a sword-bearing hero right now, but she bit that back and swallowed the thought.

"The power's off there?" she asked.

"You're not home?"

"No, I'm at the office." Things kept beeping, begging for electricity and getting on Grace's last nerve. This wasn't supposed to happen. They had a generator. The alarms had a backup. There was a system in place, because she'd made sure Aiden *put* the system in place. Another gust rattled the windows, and she must have made a sound, because Max's tone changed in an instant.

"What's wrong? Is the power off there, too?"

"Yes. We have a generator, but it's not coming on."

"Is anyone there with you?" When she didn't answer, he asked again. "Are you alone?" It sounded like he was outdoors now. Wind whistled on the line. "I'm on my way."

It was ridiculous. She didn't need him to come speeding to the office.

But she very much wanted him to.

It only took a few minutes for Max to get to the dental office. He drove as fast as he could, swerving to avoid the limbs and branches scattered across the road. The office was just as dark as the surrounding neighborhood was, but Grace's car was parked in back.

Of all the emotions he thought Grace might possess, terror wasn't one of them. She was opinionated, sharp, a little fierce at times, fussy, kind with Tyler, critical with Max. But never once had he seen anything that resembled fear in her. When her voice cracked on the phone, he hadn't just heard it—he'd *felt* it. She was scared.

He didn't hesitate to react, hurrying to help her. First, because he wasn't a jerk, and any man should respond the way he was. But more urgently, this was *Grace*. The woman who'd lit him up on Saturday night with a kiss that had wiped all other kisses from his memory. He'd have fought his way out of a lion's den to get to her. He started to get out of his car, then realized that pounding on the office door, or worse, bursting into the dark building, would probably send Grace right over the edge. He grabbed a flashlight from the truck's console while he dialed her number.

She answered, her words clipped and breathless. "You don't need to come. I'm fine."

"I'm already outside and heading for the back door. Is it unlocked?"

"Oh, uh…it's locked. Or it should be. I don't know. I'll…uh…meet you there."

"Stay on the phone until the door's open…"

It opened as he was talking. A small LED lantern dangled from two fingers on one hand, and her phone was in the other. Even in the awful, swinging light, he could see how pale she was. Her soft lips were grayish white. Her eyes were wide and unfocused, her gaze darting at the windstorm behind him. He stepped inside.

"Everything's okay. I'm here. You're safe." She clung to him, but didn't make a sound. No sobbing, no words. His younger sister, Jenny, was terrified of storms, so he figured that's what this was about. "Hey, I didn't know you were afraid of storms. I didn't think you were afraid of anything."

There was a moment of silence, and he didn't push it. He just held her against him and waited for her to find her equilibrium. Grace took a deep, shuddering breath, then stepped back.

"I'm not afraid of the storm. I just…let myself get panicked."

It was an odd choice of words, and he didn't like it. "You don't decide to panic or not. It just…happens. It's okay to be afraid, you know."

Her eyes finally opened, meeting his gaze with a flash of anger. Good. He was glad to see she was aware enough to get mad.

"I'm *not* afraid. It's just…" She rolled her eyes in annoyance. "The generator should have come on. The battery backup is supposed to work. The system didn't—"

"That doesn't matter, Grace. You're safe, and so is your brother's office."

She swallowed hard, biting her lip. "It *does* matter, because I can't leave until the security system is working. There have been robberies at dental offices lately, and I'm responsible until Aiden gets back."

He nodded. "I'm going to take care of it." He turned, checking his phone. He'd called his brother-in-law on his way to the office and asked him to reach out to Aiden Bennett for any advice on the generator. He knew Aiden and Sam were friends. There was an answering text waiting for him.

Aiden says there's a breaker that sometimes pops off when the generator starts. It's the top one in the basement electrical box. He's been meaning to have it checked. Everything okay?

Max made his way down to the basement and found the breaker box. As soon as he flipped the breaker, he heard the large generator firing up outside. Lights came on in the stairway behind him. He answered Sam.

That fixed it. We'll lock up here, and I'll make sure Grace gets home safely.

When he reached the top of the stairs, Grace was tapping on her own phone. She glanced up at him in annoyance. "You called my brother on me?"

"No." He held his hands up. "I called a friend, and *he* called your brother for the information I needed to fix the power situation." He gestured up at the lights that were on. "Now you can go home and not worry. You're welcome. Let's lock up and get out of here while the roads are still passable."

She nodded, then looked around. "Where's Tyler?"

"He's staying with my sister and Sam at the marina with my mom. Tyler was fretting about his Nana being at the hotel during the storm, so Sam and Lexi convinced Mom to come stay with them. And in Tyler's logic, that meant the marina was safer than *my* house, so he insisted *he* had to go there, too. They're having a nor'easter party."

Grace checked the locks on the front door, nodded as if satisfied, then turned to face him. "Oh, no—did I pull you away from the party?"

"No. I figured Tyler would have more fun over there without me, so I stayed home to get some work done. Do you want me to give you a lift?" She declined, saying she'd follow him.

The entire neighborhood was still dark when they drove down Revere Street. The wind howled through the trees, but the rain was letting up a bit. He checked the time when he pulled in. It wasn't even eight o'clock yet. He called out to Grace as she got out of her car.

"Have you eaten?"

She looked over in surprise, shielding her face from the weather so he couldn't see her expression. "Why?"

He shrugged in the rain. "No sense both of us trying to cobble a dinner together without power by ourselves, right?"

He wanted to know where her terror had come from, and he didn't want her to be alone until he knew she felt safe.

She didn't move at first, then her hand dropped and she nodded. "Let me feed Mozart and grab a tray of cookies I baked yesterday."

He thought she was afraid of the dark. "Do you need me to come in with you?"

"I know my way around my own house. I'll be over in a few minutes."

He watched her go in the side door, then saw the beam of a flashlight moving around inside the window. So she wasn't afraid of storms. And she wasn't afraid of the dark.

What had frightened her so badly at the office?

Chapter Eleven

The power came back on just a few minutes after Grace stepped inside Max's kitchen. The wind was still howling, but having light and heat made everything feel better. She looked around in surprise, not realizing Max had repainted the Hendersons' kitchen. Of course it was *his* kitchen now, and the sage green paint made the room feel fresher. More masculine—or at least less feminine. Lucy Henderson's pink and yellow teacup-patterned wallpaper was long gone.

Max's invitation had caught her off guard, but his logic had been sound. Why should both of them be alone in the dark? But being *together* in the dark didn't seem like a great idea, either. She was doubly glad the power had come back on. Now there wouldn't be any awkwardness. Just two neighbors sharing a meal. In a brightly lit room.

His phone pinged with a message, and he chuckled as he read it. "It's from my sister," he explained. "Lexi said Tyler didn't like it when the power went off, but my mother started showing him her famous flashlight finger shadows on the wall—birds and dogs and galloping horses—and he forgot all about the storm." He set the phone down and turned to the stove. "Their lights are back on, too."

"He gets along well with your family, then?"

"Better with them than with me sometimes," Max said matter-of-factly. He looked over his shoulder. "I don't mean to always sound so self-pitying. Things are getting better between us." He lifted the lid on a skillet, filling the kitchen with a delicious aroma. "I hope you don't mind a thrown together skillet dish. I call it goulash, but Lexi tells me it's called American chop suey in Massachusetts. Which makes no sense at all."

Grace began to relax a little more. Surprisingly, it didn't feel strange to be here with Max, chatting about food while he cooked. His favorite music, blues guitar, was playing softly in the background. He nodded toward the kitchen table as he drained some pasta over the sink, and she took a seat there.

"Ground beef, sauce and macaroni? Your sister's right, but don't ask me why. That's just what some people call it here."

He drained the oil from the pan and added the tomato sauce and cooked elbow macaroni, stirring it together. When he brought their plates to the table, she could see that he'd added mushrooms and chopped onions to the meat mixture. Tyler kept saying Max couldn't cook, but he seemed to be doing just fine tonight.

"Beer or wine?" He stood at the fridge. He wouldn't be pulling a nice cabernet out of there, so she opted for beer. His eyebrows rose in surprise. "I didn't picture you as a beer drinker. It doesn't go with the whole classical piano thing."

She took the glass of light beer and shrugged. "I'm an enigma."

His expression was serious when he sat. "Yes, you are."

Those three words felt loaded. As if he'd been thinking about her and her enigma-ness for a while. They began to eat in silence, but after a few bites he set his fork down and looked at her.

"What were you afraid of tonight at the office?"

Oh, she did *not* want to go there. "I wasn't afraid. I just didn't want to leave the office if the alarm system wasn't working, and I didn't know what was happening with the generator. It was…concern, not fear."

"That's bull."

"I beg your pardon?"

"That's bull, and you know it. I heard your voice, Grace, and it wasn't just mild concern. You were practically hyperventilating. But you say it wasn't the storm that scared you—"

She scoffed. "I've lived on the Cape all my life. This storm was nothing."

"And you say you're not afraid of the dark."

She knew where this was going, but she had to cling to some dignity. "I'm a grown woman. It's not like I believe in ghosts or anything like that."

"Then what scared you so bad earlier? Was there someone at the office who frightened you?"

She set her fork down so hard it clanged against her dish. "I told you, I wasn't frightened. I was more… angry." Saying it out loud made her realize how true it was, and her words came out with more force. "I was really, *really* angry that the system wasn't working the way it should have. Systems are in place for a reason."

He studied her face, and when his gaze met hers, it felt like he was looking right into her soul. This wasn't the Max she was used to. This wasn't the hard, sweaty giant hammering on molten steel. This Max had tenderness in his eyes, and warmth, not sparks, where his fingers now rested on her forearm.

"Okay." His voice was soft now, and she felt that familiar flutter in her chest. He was accepting her answer without pushing her, and she was grateful. He looked where his hand was brushing her skin and pulled back. It was a good and logical thing to do. It was also infuriating—did he want to touch her or not?

They went back to eating their meal, and he carefully moved the conversation to the weather, the Cape, the local shops. She recommended a few restaurants, forgetting about his sister's well-known place. He teased her about that, and things got easier between them. They were back to a simple meal between neighbors.

He cleared the table and loaded the dishwasher while she scrubbed the pan and utensils in the sink. Her guard was down.

"So it was the rules being broken that freaked you out so much," he said out of the blue. "You don't just *like* it when rules are followed. You *need* it to happen that way." She turned to silence him, but his eyes were so tender and understanding that something shifted inside of her. She blinked rapidly and looked away, staring out the window at the rainy darkness outside. He moved closer. "What happened, Grace? What made you this way?"

Her skin was alternating from hot to cold. Why did he seem to care so much? How did he know that there had been a *something* that changed her? She blew out a long breath, closing her eyes and struggling with what to do. Storm off to the safety of her own house? She turned away again, silently scrubbing the last pan in the sink, hoping he'd take the hint. She was not about to tell her story to—

"I was shot twice, and it never should have happened." The words spilled out before she could stop them.

She felt him go very still behind her, but he didn't speak. He was waiting for her. And she truly didn't want to talk about—

"There was a mass shooting at my college." She was moving the sponge in quick circles. "A shooter was looking for his ex. He shot five of us randomly before he found her and killed her and himself. Two of the five died. I was one of the lucky ones."

The words sounded robotic in her own ears, like an AI recitation of the story. Max's hand covered hers, and she dropped the sponge to clutch his fingers. His grip made it easier to keep going.

"He never should have been there," she continued. "He'd been arrested that same day for assaulting her, but there was some screwup at the police station. His paperwork got mixed up with someone else, and he ended up being given a desk ticket and was released within hours. When they realized the mistake, they put out a warrant, but it never occurred to anyone to warn his ex. Or the college. It was all so...casual."

"Procedures weren't followed," Max said softly. He was putting the pieces together. He was so close behind her that she could feel the heat of his body on her back.

"It wasn't just the police. The dorms were supposed to be locked at night—you needed a key card to get in after ten o'clock. But some students would prop the back door open with a brick so they could go out and smoke and get back in easily. We'd had meetings about it, and they'd been told it was a security risk, but—"

"That's how he got into the building," Max said softly "Because people broke the rules."

"Yes. Don't get me started on how he was able to buy a handgun so fast."

Max leaned closer, sliding his free arm around her waist and brushing his nose against the back of her neck. "It was chaos," he murmured. "You told me once that you don't like chaos."

She chewed her lower lip before tearing her eyes away from the window and looking over her shoulder at him. His face was so close to hers.

"It took years of counseling to get me to this point. I'm *not* a control freak," she said firmly. "But I want things done the right way. I know that sounds like the same thing, but it's not. It's about doing what's right, not controlling things. It makes me a very good accountant and manager."

It did not make her a great piano accompanist. To do that, you had to be ready to adjust on the fly when things happened, and she couldn't do that. If a soloist stumbled, so did she. It also didn't make her great girlfriend material. Spontaneity was not her thing, and all it took was one *Surprise!* and she was done. And it definitely meant she wouldn't make a great parent. She loved children, but they were so unpredictable that she was always on edge around them. But boy, could she manage. She liked setting and enforcing the rules. She frowned. Maybe that made her a control freak after all.

"And teacher." Max rested his head against hers. What was happening? "It makes you a good teacher."

She'd rarely discussed the shooting with anyone, even her closest family and friends. When she did, people tended to try to convince her to get past it somehow. They meant well. They didn't want her to panic or withdraw. They wanted her to be stronger than she was. They wanted her to be *their* version of normal. But... she wasn't. She was exactly this person in this slightly scarred body with a different view of the world because of one night out of her entire life. Max Bellamy got that somehow. He saw her strength, not her weakness.

"And a good teacher," she agreed. "As long as my students listen to me."

His voice was steady. "Even if they don't, then you just stop being their teacher. There's nothing wrong with setting your own limits, Grace."

Other than her therapist, no one had ever said that to her before. She pulled in a ragged breath, leaning back against him as she straightened.

"I know that. But you'd be surprised by the number of people who find something wrong with it. It tends to make me wary."

He huffed a soft laugh against her skin. All she had to do was turn in his arms and kiss him. But she'd done that once—an uncharacteristic act of spontaneity. And it had ended with Max sending her home. Her cheeks warmed at the memory.

"You weren't wary in the forge the other night." Was that his lips she felt on the skin behind her ear? She willed her knees to stay locked in place.

No swooning, Grace.

"It was a silly thing to do, and I'm sorry. You were right to send me packing."

He went very still again. His hands gripped her hips, and he gently turned her until she was backed up against the sink. His fingers tucked under her chin, lifting it until she was looking right at him.

"Did you think I didn't *like* that you kissed me?"

"Well…you told me to leave." His eyes were dark with some emotion, but she couldn't read it. If he wasn't angry about the kiss, or embarrassed by it, then…what?

"Grace, that kiss ruined all other kisses for me. It was *that* good. I never wanted it to stop." His fingers lightly stroked her cheek. "That kiss made me want us to get naked together."

Something flipped and blossomed inside of her.

"You said it was a mistake."

His mouth twisted in chagrin. "I should have said the *timing* was a mistake. I was a stressed-out sweaty mess, and as much as I wanted you, the circumstances didn't feel right. I don't want to make love to you in the forge. Well, I *do*, but not the first time. The first time, I want to make love to you in a big, soft bed, with plenty of time for us to do it right."

Grace's entire body responded to his words. Her breasts went hard, while her lower belly went soft and warm. His grip on her hip tightened. His eyebrows lowered, narrowing his eyes, but not shielding the desire burning there.

"This could still be a huge mistake. You and I—"

"Have nothing in common," she finished. "Except for this crazy thing between our bodies."

"And a love of Tolkien," he reminded her with a smile. But he quickly grew serious. "Grace, I've done my share of one-night stands and quick flings that lasted as long as a Ren fair did." He cupped her cheek in his hand. "But you don't strike me as a one-night stand woman."

It was true. Despite all her quirks that tended to chase men away, she wanted a relationship that had depth to it. A connection with staying power. This wasn't that. But if they both acknowledged it going in, then it might be okay. Max spoke again before she could say that.

"And I have Tyler now. He's my priority. After I had to fight so hard for permission to raise my own son, there's no way I'll upend his life again, or take any attention away from him, by getting involved with *any* woman. So if we do this, it's—"

"I get it, Max. I'm not going to harass you into a relationship just because we spend a night together. We'll set the ground rules, and that's it. One time. No repeats. No relationship. No regrets. And no one ever knows— especially Tyler."

"And you're okay with that?"

Her head tipped back, and she groaned in frustration. "I told you—I'm not a control freak. I just feel more comfortable when there are parameters and clear expectations. We've done that. We're in agreement. So—"

His lips on hers ended the conversation. His arm slid around her back and pulled her in tight, and it was all the invitation she needed. She slid her arms around his neck and returned the kiss with everything she had. Their mouths were so perfect together—soft yet firm, moving in sync, his tongue dancing with hers until she conceded, allowing him full access.

There was a low moan, and she wasn't sure if it had been him or her. Both? It didn't matter. He pushed her back against the sink, and he was hard inside his jeans.

That hard length rubbed against her in a slow rocking motion that set her insides on fire. She wanted him desperately. *Needed* him. She needed their bodies to be as good together as their mouths were.

He traced kisses and nibbles down her jawline, then down her neck to the hollow of her shoulder. She could feel his teeth on her skin, and her head fell back again—this time in complete surrender. He yanked on her blouse until it was untucked from her trousers. He slid his hands underneath the fabric. Against her skin.

He had working hands—rough and calloused—but oh, so gentle. He unhooked her bra with a flick of his fingers, huffing a soft grunt against her neck as his fingers found her breasts. They fit neatly in his large hands, and he brushed his thumbs across her already rigid peaks. Her hands gripped his hair behind his head, and her whole body pulsed with aching desire.

One of his hands left her breast and slid inside her pants, then under her panties, reaching the target that was wet and hot and oh, so ready. He kissed her again, and the combination of the kiss and his hands—one on her breast and one between her legs—managed to send her into an orgasm that made her cry out as her body nearly convulsed in reaction.

He laughed, and the sound was so sexy she almost came again just from hearing it. It was a laugh of *wow*, not one of mocking anything. It was a laugh of pride. Of *I did that*. And he deserved every bit of that feeling. He lifted his head and looked at her, his eyes dancing with humor. His hand was out of her pants, but the other was still gently kneading her breast, bringing her down from the explosion that had shaken her.

"I'm never sure *what* to expect from you, Grace, but I didn't expect a hair trigger. I'll never look at this kitchen sink the same again."

Max was willing his pulse to slow before his heart leaped right out of his chest. Between having Grace fall apart at his touch, the painful swelling pressing against the inside of his zipper and the warmth of her breast in his hand... In his *kitchen*. The moment was too surreal. They needed to find a bed and shed some clothes. Right the hell now.

He kissed her swollen lips again. "The next logical step for us is—"

"A bed," she finished. He didn't usually like people finishing his sentences, but Grace had done it twice now, and it only served to make them feel more connected.

"Exactly. And fewer clothes between us." He looked deep into her eyes. "Are you sure this is what you want?"

"Very sure. Stop worrying about me, Max."

He nodded with a grin. "Yes, ma'am. Follow me."

He took her hand and led the way up the stairs to his bedroom. It was a large room, stretching across the back of the house. He'd done nothing in the coral pink room except hang his clothes in the closet and buy a new mattress for the cherry four-poster bed that had been included with the house purchase. The small master bath still had the Hendersons' rose-covered wallpaper in it.

Grace stopped in the doorway, looking around with wide eyes. "Speaking of the unexpected..."

"Yeah. Sorry. I was more concerned with Tyler's room and the downstairs. I hadn't planned on this room being seen by...anyone...for quite a while."

Her smile deepened. "Fatherhood doesn't have to mean celibacy."

"You're not the first person to tell me that. It just wasn't a priority. Until tonight." He pulled her into his arms. "So we're going to have to make do with a room decorated by an old lady. Do you think that will be a problem?"

"I don't think we'll be paying any attention to the decor."

Amen to that.

Her hands grabbed the hem of his Henley shirt and tugged upward. He helped her remove it over his head, then watched as she unbuttoned her blouse and let it, and her unfastened bra, drop to the floor. She kicked off her practical shoes and shimmied out of her trousers. He should have been undressing with her, but he found himself frozen in place.

He'd always thought Grace was attractive, with her thick blond hair and perpetually tidy appearance. Never a wrinkle in her clothes. Every hair in place. Proud and strong.

But now? As she stood there naked in front of him, with her hair a bit wild and still curling from the rain? She was as beautiful as the finest classical painting. Her figure was somewhere between slender and full-figured. Every curve was soft and oh, so inviting. She looked strong, but the strength hit differently now. There were no sharp edges to her. There was pride in her confidence to stand there waiting for him, but it wasn't the kind of pride that pushed him away. Instead, she was pulling him in.

There was only one thing that kept him from rushing toward her. It was the fear that he might not be able to stick to his promise to her. He worried that one night would never be enough with Grace Bennett.

"Is there a problem?" she asked, her voice tinged with both sarcasm and concern.

"No problem." He cleared his throat and his thoughts. "I lost track of time once I caught this view." He walked over to her. "You are absolutely beautiful."

She gave him a quick flirtatious smile, running her fingers across his shoulders and down his bare arms. "You're not so bad yourself. But I'm going to get a chill standing here naked in the middle of the room."

He ran his hands up from her waist to finally rest on either side of her neck, his thumbs lightly supporting her chin. "Sorry, I got lost in looking at you. But exploring you sounds even better." He kissed her lips softly, lingering on their warmth. The only way he could manage to pull away was to remind himself they had all night together. "I need to grab some protection from the bathroom, then I'll meet you in bed."

"Sounds like a plan."

He smiled to himself as he grabbed the box of condoms from the drawer. Grace liked plans. That's where she felt most secure. So he made it a point when he joined her in the bed to let her know what he was doing and what he planned on doing next. In the dirtiest language possible. And she loved it, if her eyes and smiles and moans were any indication.

But liking a plan didn't mean Grace wasn't still full of surprises. He hadn't anticipated she'd be this bold in bed—knowing what she wanted and saying so. He'd never guessed she'd make such delicate whimpering sounds when he sank into her, like she was experiencing something divine. The sound turned him on even more, and he didn't think that was possible. She moved with him in perfect rhythm, and rocked her hips in a way that made it very difficult for him to hang on to his self-control.

He hadn't expected Grace to be the kind of woman who used her teeth and nails to hold him where she wanted him, but he knew he'd have bite marks in the morning, as well as a few scratches down his back. He couldn't wait to see her marks on him. And damned if she didn't use some dirty language of her own. Miss Prim and Proper had a potty mouth during sex, and he approved 100 percent. She told him where to put it and what to do with it. And she was right every time.

He lasted until the moment he was up on his knees, deep inside her while supporting her hips. Her legs were wrapped around his waist, and the position was absolutely perfect. He stared down at her, her hair spread across the pillow like a honeyed flame. She met his gaze without flinching, her eyes dark and wild, her lips slightly parted. Seeing her like this—hell, *feeling* her like this—was enough to snap his resolve to make this last as long as possible. With a loud garbled cry he thrust into her and gave up the fight, closing his eyes and letting go. She met him right there, her own voice blending with his. When they finished, he eased her down to the bed and fell at her side. His entire body was limp. Boneless.

And very, *very* satisfied.

Chapter Twelve

Grace wanted to snuggle back against the heat from Max's body, but her own body simply refused to move. She'd never felt so completely spent. It was a delicious sensation. Totally sated. Happy on a level she hadn't experienced in all of her thirty-three years. And Max Bellamy was responsible for it. Who'd have guessed *that* would ever happen?

One time.

No repeats.

No relationship.

No regrets.

And no one ever knows.

They'd set very clear ground rules before coming up to his pink bedroom. *She* was the one who'd recited them down in the kitchen. They were logical guidelines. And yet…one of them was rattling around in her brain right now, and she knew it was going to be a problem.

No repeats.

She'd sincerely believed it was a good rule. A smart rule. She *still* believed that. She'd also thought it would be easy to keep. But now…? Now she was pretty sure they'd *both* find it hard to honor that particular agreement. Max moved behind her, wrapping one arm around her waist and pulling her backward against his chest. The only sound he made was a soft, contented grunt when their bodies came in contact. Then he was asleep again, clearly even more worn-out than she was. She'd always found it curious, the way men just fell asleep after sex. It had the opposite effect on her—she was energized, and her mind was spinning with random thoughts.

Although tonight, all her thoughts were on what she'd just done in the Hendersons' old bed. Max had assured her that he'd added a brand-new mattress, so it wasn't quite so weird. She gave herself a mental shake—she was going random again. She didn't want to think about anything other than how incredible they'd been together. Even now, her nerve endings were snapping and popping at the thought of what they'd had. They'd both been so eager to please each other, and so desperate for their own pleasures at the same time. It was an intoxicating combination of give and take. The look in Max's eyes as he looked down at her made something burn in her soul.

No repeats. She almost laughed out loud. There was a warm little spot inside of her that was already saying *do that again.*

Max shifted behind her. "I can feel you thinking way too hard about this," he muttered. "Why aren't you as exhausted as I am? You're making me feel old. Are you secretly twenty-one or something?"

"I'm pretty sure mid-thirties are when women are in their sexual prime, big guy, so I'm totally normal." She paused. "In that aspect, anyway."

He propped himself up on one elbow and rolled her onto her back so he could look into her eyes. "There was absolutely nothing *totally normal* about what we just did. Epic, maybe. Mind-blowing? Sure. Perfect, even? It was pretty damn close. That was amazing, Grace. *You* are amazing."

She felt her skin flushing from her chest to her face. At first, she thought he was talking about the sex. But the way he said that last sentence… The way he brushed her cheek with his knuckles, staring into her eyes as his face lowered to kiss her. It was good to know it wasn't only her who'd thought they'd just shared something really special.

His expression grew serious when he ended the kiss. "You thought so, too, right? It was good for you?"

It was her turn to touch his face, moving her fingers through the soft stubble along his cheek. "It was…shockingly good."

"Shockingly? You didn't expect it to be good?" He was only half teasing.

"I didn't know what to expect, Max. I mean, I didn't expect us to ever reach this point in the first place. But we did, and it was great. *Really* great." Epic. Mind-blowing. Perfect. Amazing. Spectacular. So many adjectives, and none felt adequate. She remembered their agreement and withdrew her hand from his face. "But I should probably go…"

"Go? Why?"

"We agreed…"

Max stared into her eyes so long she started to squirm from the intensity. She wanted him to make love to her again. It was more than *want*. It was *need*. But they'd agreed. So why did he seem so insulted? He sighed and leaned back, sending a chill across her skin.

"If that's what you really want, you know the way

out." The words were blunt. But his voice sounded... hurt? "I guess you've had your little bad boy romp, huh?"

There it was again. The hint of pain in his voice.

"What the hell are you talking about?"

He looked away. "It wouldn't be the first time some woman wanted to see what the tattooed sword maker was like in bed."

Grace sat up in surprise. And offense. "Are you suggesting that I *objectified* you? Full of yourself much?"

"I..." His expression clouded. "I don't know if I'd go that far, but Grace, there is no way I want this to be over yet, and you obviously feel differently..." He sat up, too, scrubbing his hand down his face. He took a deep breath. "I feel like we're spinning way off track here, and I'm sorry. Obviously, we both wanted to do this tonight. And I hope we *both* enjoyed it one hell of a lot." He waited for her to nod before he continued. "What I'm saying is... I want you to stay here in my bed tonight."

"It's not what we agreed to," she reminded him. "No repeats."

He pressed his lips together in a hard, thin line, then nodded. "You see, I interpreted our agreement differently— I thought the deal was one night. Which means we can *repeat* as often as I'm physically capable until morning. Which isn't going to be as often as I'd like, but I'm willing to do my best."

"And if we decide one night isn't enough?" She already had a feeling it wouldn't be.

His hand rested on the flat of her stomach, his expression still solemn, but his fingers moving softly against her skin. "I don't think more than that will work. I have Tyler to think about, and I meant it when I said I'm putting him first. My relationship with him is fragile as it is. There's no way I'm going to complicate it even further." He tapped her skin lightly with his fingers. "Besides, I haven't done a long-term relationship in a very long time, and I'm pretty sure I'd suck at it. We agreed to one night, and I think it's best if we stick to that."

She thought for a moment. Was she willing to spend the night with Max, and nothing more? She knew what she *should* do—get out of bed and go home. And yet her body didn't move. Her body wanted more of this. More of Max. And who was she kidding? Her mind, and her heart, wanted more, too. It was silly to think that *she* was the one even considering breaking their original agreement. All because she was afraid of what *might* happen. As much as she feared one night wouldn't be enough, what if… What if it was? What if spending more hours with this man gave her enough pleasure—*so* much pleasure—that it was worth getting up in the morning and pretending that nothing had changed between them?

She lifted her head and kissed him.

"One night will be enough."

It was a lie, and she suspected they both knew it. But when Max's lips touched hers, she decided she could live with that for tonight.

Max looked at his phone on the night table and groaned. It was five o'clock in the morning, which meant the agreed-to one night only with Grace was coming to an end. She must have heard him, because she shifted in his arms, snuggling closer to his chest with an indecipherable murmur against his skin.

He wasn't sure what was most surprising—that they'd

ended up in bed together at all, or that it had been the best night of sex he could remember. After their little debate about exactly what they'd agreed to, and her decision—thank God—to stay, they'd made love again. It was slower that time. They'd explored every inch of each other with lips and fingertips. They'd breathed soft, intimate words in the darkness instead of the hot and dirty language of the first go-round. It was less intense and more...comforting. Familiar. Intimate.

After what seemed like hours of foreplay, they'd come together in a quick explosion of passion that left him wondering if she'd put some sort of spell on him. He'd had plenty of sex with, admittedly, plenty of partners. Lots of fun. Lots of different approaches and different places. He wasn't one to go to bed with a woman he didn't respect and care about, so it wasn't just that he found Grace interesting as a person. But making love to her was so much...*more*. They fit together on a whole different level.

He ran his fingers across her back and stopped at the circular scar on her lower back. A bullet wound. He swallowed hard, holding on to his emotions so that he wouldn't wake her. Hearing the story had been devastating enough. She'd been *shot*. Twice. And survived.

But seeing the scars tonight—one on the left side of her chest and this one lower down her back—made him feel a surge of anger and protectiveness that he'd never experienced before. He hated that she'd gone through that, and wanted to somehow erase it from her life. He wanted to keep her safe from harm.

Keep her close.

Keep her, period.

"What time is it?" she mumbled, stretching against him with a sigh.

"It's just after five," he answered, his lips brushing her hair. "You don't work on Saturdays, do you?"

"No. But Tyler…"

"Tyler won't be home until after breakfast. He's developed a fondness for his aunt Lexi's cinnamon raisin French toast." He lifted his head to look into her eyes. "And he sure as hell isn't going to be showing up here at five in the morning, so go back to sleep."

She nodded, laying her head back down on his chest. He tightened his hold on her, kissing the top of her head. This moment, in the dark, holding Grace's warm, naked body against his, after a night of lovemaking…well, this moment was one he knew would be burned into his brain forever. He moved his hand up and down her back, and it accidentally brushed the scar again. He hesitated.

"It doesn't hurt," Grace whispered. "It's just a scar."

"I know. It's just…" He sighed. "I know it's a part of you, a part of your story. I just wish it had never happened."

He felt her snort a soft laugh against him. "Me, too. The whole thing made a mess of me."

"Not a mess," he answered. "You're anything but that, Grace. I just hate thinking of you being *shot*, of all goddamn things. Did you see him com… Oh, hell. Forget I asked that. You don't need to share any more than you want to."

He'd seen how much it had hurt her to tell him about it last evening. But he couldn't help wanting to know everything about this woman. They only had one night, and he wanted it to be more than something physical.

But getting *too* personal would only make it harder to leave this night behind.

"I really don't like to talk about it. Besides, I think maybe it's time for *you* to do some sharing, mister." She looked up at him, rested her hand on his chest and propped her chin on her hand. She was acting playful, but he could see genuine curiosity in her eyes. He didn't like talking about himself any more than she did, but she had a point—he'd told her about how he became Tyler's father, but that was it.

"What do you want to know?"

"Everything." She grinned. "Why a blacksmith? Why the tattoos?" She glanced at the dragon tattoo that covered his bicep and shoulder. "Why did you live in a motor home? Why this house in this town?" She paused. "Well, I know you came here because of your mom and sister. But tell me the rest. Or at least the highlights. Please."

He put one hand back between his head and the pillow so he could look her in the eye. "Highlights, eh? Well, I sort of fell into blacksmithing because my best friend's dad was one. They had a farm outside Des Moines, and I thought all the fire and hammering was cool. I apprenticed with him, much to my father's chagrin." That was putting it very mildly, but she'd asked for highlights. "Then I took a girl to a Renaissance fair when I was eighteen and saw a guy making knives and swords, and I thought that was cool, and…that's what put me on the path to sword making. The tattoos just sort of happened as I traveled around."

"So you went to work for a Renaissance fair?"

"No, I've never worked *for* anyone. Most of the Ren

fair performers and vendors move from fair to fair around the country. I'd rent a booth for a few weeks or months, set up the hearth and anvil so people could watch me working, then I'd pack up and move on."

Those days were over, and he only missed it a little bit, and not often.

"So did you talk in pirate talk or whatever, and wear a costume?"

"It's not pirate talk, although I guess there isn't that much difference. But yes, I laid on the Scottish brogue. I didn't wear any intricate costume, but I did wear my kilt and a linen tunic so I fit in."

Grace's eyes went wide. "You have a *kilt*?" She grinned. "I definitely want to see that."

He laughed at her enthusiasm and put on his best brogue. "Ay, ye've already enjoyed what's under it, lassie. Why'd ye need to see me kilt?"

She joined his laughter. "Oh, my God, I need to hear that accent the next time we…"

A heavy silence fell over the bed. This was a one-night deal. And no matter the temptation—and he was definitely tempted—he would not add a relationship to his life right now.

"Sorry," she finally said. "I know tonight is it."

He didn't answer right away. They didn't have long—he could already see dawn's light through the window. In a few hours, Lexi would bring Tyler home, and Grace would have to be gone. His free hand stroked her back, then he propped himself up above her with a smile. A few hours was plenty of time.

"Aye, lassie, if it's one more roll in the hay yer lookin' for, I might just be obliged to provide it t'ya." He lowered himself onto her warm, welcoming body, and she slid her arms around his neck. He gave her a kiss, then started nibbling her neck. "I'll make love t'ye 'til the sun rises."

"Yes, please," she whispered.

They both knew it was a mistake. They both knew there would never be enough *once mores* to quench their thirst.

They both chose to do it again anyway.

Chapter Thirteen

"Girl, have you been to a spa or something recently?" Maya was staring across the table at Grace. They tried to do a ladies' night out once every month or so, and this month it was Maya's choice. She'd chosen a Sunday night at 200 Wharf, Max's sister's restaurant. It wasn't exactly helping Grace move past Friday night, when she'd slept with Max. "Well, *have* you?"

"Have I what?"

"You are glowing," Maya answered. "I'm trying to figure out your secret. Did you get one of those seaweed facials at the spa in Chatham?"

Grace reminded herself that there was no way one night of great sex could possibly show on her face. Yes, her body felt different—gently aching, but also limber and still so very satisfied. But Maya couldn't know that just from looking at her, despite her knowing grin.

"That right there!" Maya exclaimed, pointing at her. "That Mona Lisa smile. That's it. That's what's different. What's got you smiling like that?" She leaned forward, her voice dropping dramatically. "Or should I say *who* has you smiling like that?"

She felt her face flush but did her best to act naturally.

"You're talking nonsense. I bought that new mattress a couple months ago, and I've been sleeping really well lately. I guess it shows." She waved her menu to change the subject. "What are you going to order? I haven't been here in a while, but I'm thinking about the crab-meat shepherd's pie special."

"Sure, it's your mattress. If you say so." Maya glanced at the menu. "Lexi's pasta is too good to pass up. I'm going for the seabass carbonara over linguine."

They placed their orders, but as soon as their server walked away, Maya went back to her questioning. And finally revealed *why* she was suddenly so interested in Grace's sleeping habits. She leveled her gaze on Grace over the rim of her wineglass. "So you're saying it's *your* bed that's giving you that smile? Because Leon told me he saw someone walking from Max's house to your house when he let the dog out yesterday morning. He said it looked a lot like you."

Grace's wineglass rattled lightly against the table when she set it down. She and Max had been so careful to make sure she left before there was any chance of his family catching her there. She'd even turned down his offer of breakfast. She'd figured the sooner she ended their *one night, no repeats*, the better off they'd be. It was before seven when they'd shared one last, gentle, farewell kiss and she'd jogged over to her side door. She'd looked back then, to find Max still on his side porch, watching her. Neither had waved or motioned to the other. They just stared until she turned away and went inside. It was over.

She'd never imagined someone else had seen them at that hour. Maya's catlike smile wasn't unkind in any way. But she was clearly expecting an explanation. For the life of her, Grace couldn't come up with one. They were still sitting in silence when their food was delivered by Lexi Bellamy Knight. Max's sister. Maya greeted her warmly.

"Wow, how's this for service?" She laughed. "The chef herself is delivering our meal! Lexi, you know Grace, right? She's your brother's—" Maya paused just enough to make Grace nervous "—neighbor."

Lexi was tall and slim, with auburn hair and smiling hazel eyes. She wore loose white cotton trousers and a matching top. Max had mentioned she was expecting, and the baby bump was visible under her blue apron. "Of course. I've seen you in here a few times, and you're one of the walkers at the beach, right? You use my mom's motel as your meeting place." She looked at the plates in her hands. "Who ordered the seabass?"

Maya wiggled her fingers, and Lexi set down the plates, then looked at Grace.

"You teach Tyler piano. He stayed with us Friday night and couldn't stop talking about how much he loves the new Disney songbook you got him."

"I'm glad to hear that. I don't usually teach young children, but Tyler is a happy exception."

"He's a good kid. He told us you also send food home with him because Max can't cook." Lexi started to laugh. "Do you really?"

"Well, sometimes I send a dish over. It's hard to cook for one, so I always have extra." She didn't want it to sound like something too weird. Maya was watching with interest. "It's just…being neighborly."

"I think it's more than that," Lexi said. Grace started

to panic—did *everyone* know about Max and her? "You're helping keep them alive, because Tyler's right— Max can't cook much more than burgers on a grill and scrambled eggs."

Grace laughed along with Maya and Lexi, but she was thinking of the meal he'd cooked up Friday night. Sharing that Max *could* cook more than a burger would be a mistake, because she'd have to explain how she knew.

"Well," Lexi said, "I have to get back to the kitchen before my sous chef tries to take over the place. Enjoy your dinner, ladies!"

They ate the first few bites in silence, but Maya hadn't given up on the conversation. She sighed as she twirled her pasta on her fork and ate it, then looked across the table.

"So…you and Max? How did that happen?"

They were in a booth along the wall, with enough privacy for Grace to answer freely. She told Maya about the power going out at the office and how Max came to her rescue. The dinner they shared. And, without any details, how they'd ended up in bed together for the night.

"And was it…wonderful?" Maya asked. She was leaning forward, fully invested in the story.

"Was *what* wonderful?" Phyllis Bellamy appeared at the table, literally out of nowhere. All she'd needed was a puff of smoke, and Grace would have believed it was magic. She and Maya both sat back abruptly, and she could feel the heat in her cheeks. How much had Max's mom heard?

"The seabass?" Phyllis answered her own question. "That *is* wonderful—one of my faves. But the crabmeat's yummy, too. More wine, ladies?"

Grace blew out a sigh of relief. Phyllis was checking on their meals, not their secrets. She and Maya both agreed to wine, and the older woman was back in a flash with two fresh glasses. She was in a fire-engine red skirt so short that Grace hoped there were shorts underneath, and sure enough, when she'd walked away she could see it was a skort. Worn over black tights and high boots. She was a 1970s vision, and the woman carried it off somehow.

"I filled them up a little extra for you." She gave them a wink. "After all, you're taking such good care of my son these days." Maya choked on her wine, coughing and laughing at the same time. Phyllis patted her back. "You okay, honey?"

Maya nodded, drinking some water. Judging from the sparkle of laughter in her eyes, she was absolutely loving this. "We *are* taking care of him, Phyllis. And loving it. Max is *such* a good neighbor to have." She looked at Grace. "Isn't he a good neighbor to have, Grace?"

Her eyes narrowed in warning to her friend, but she smiled at Phyllis. "Of course he is."

The woman beamed. "I never thought I'd see that man settle down in a house of his own, but he did it. And I think he likes it."

"Oh, I'm quite sure he does," Maya replied. Grace kicked her under the table, making her flinch, but not wiping the smile from her face. Or stopping her little game. Maya looked up innocently. "Is Max seeing anyone, Phyllis?"

"No, no. He's determined to focus on Tyler for now, but I'm hoping he'll find someone now that he's not traveling all the time."

Maya nodded, not done with her mischief. "That'll probably happen sooner than you think." Grace wondered if spilling her wine in Maya's direction might shut her up.

Phyllis's smile faded a bit. "Maybe. He's never been big on serious relationships, and that's partly my fault. His father and I didn't exactly set the best example." She paused, lost in some memory, then brightened. "But I'm not giving up on that boy of mine. His sister found happiness here, and I have a feeling Max will, too."

"Oh, I think you're right about that..." Maya started.

Grace glared at her. "I think Maya means he's finding happiness being a *father*, and Max is embracing that..."

"It's not the only thing he's embracing..." Maya muttered under her breath. Fortunately, low enough that Phyllis didn't hear.

"Grace, I hear you're helping with the school pageant this year. I can't wait to see all those kids together. How's it going?"

That was a really good question, but at least it moved the conversation away from Max. She'd been cornered last week by the assistant principal, Connie Wells, in the grocery store. Grace had sometimes played the piano for school recitals, but she'd never tackled directing the pageant. Apparently the teacher who normally did it was out on maternity leave, and Connie had begged Grace to take over. The idea of organizing that many little children made her sweat, and she'd said no at first. But... Tyler was one of those children. And Chantal.

If she went into the pageant with a plan and stuck to it, the kids would follow her lead. Hopefully. And just like that, in the produce aisle, she'd found herself in charge of the lower grades holiday pageant.

"We don't start rehearsals for a couple of weeks yet, Phyllis, but I'm sure it will be fine. I've ordered a new program to follow—*Holidays Around the World*." Connie had warned her the program might be too advanced for the age group, but Grace figured she could inspire the children to do it.

"Well," Phyllis started to laugh again. "All I can say is God bless you for taking it on. I wouldn't do it, but I'm a lot older than you."

Maya waved her hand. "Don't blame your age, Phyllis. I wouldn't touch that job with a ten-foot pole. But I wouldn't be able to do *your* job, either. How do you run around in those boots?"

A couple at another table waved to get Phyllis's attention for cocktails.

"I spent a lot of years in sensible shoes, Maya. I can handle the boots for a few hours. And I love meeting all the people here." She looked at the other table. "Be right there, folks! This job keeps me young. You ladies enjoy your night. And thanks again for all you do for Max."

Maya covered her face with her napkin to hold in her laughter, and Grace tossed a piece of bread at her. She never should have said anything. It had been part of the deal with Max. But Maya had already known most of it, since Leon saw her sneaking home Saturday morning.

She'd hoped talking it out might help her know what to do next, but when she got home later and looked out her kitchen window to Max's kitchen window, all she could think about was him pressing her against the sink and making her see fireworks when his hand slid down—

She threw her dishtowel into her sink and left the kitchen so fast that she almost tripped over Mozart. He yowled at her, then followed her into the living room and hopped into her lap when she sat down. Living next door to the man she'd agreed to never sleep with again was going to be more challenging than she thought.

Max thought he'd see Grace back in the forge, but it was Wednesday and she still hadn't stopped out there. He hadn't seen or spoken to her since Saturday morning, when he'd kissed her goodbye on his porch and watched her jog to her house.

They'd agreed to one night only, but he hadn't considered that it might mean an end to their evening chats in the forge. He enjoyed her company out here. He liked talking as he worked. Movies. TV shows. Places they'd been, and places they wanted to see. Had a terrific night of lovemaking ruined a budding friendship? Was she regretting what they'd done? He frowned, hammering a narrow length of steel that would become a cutlass for a revolutionary war reenactor in Boston.

He didn't like the thought of her having regrets. Not after what they'd shared. He set the hammer down and picked up his phone, tapping out a text.

R U OK? Missing you out here in the forge.

It wasn't long before he saw the floating bubbles of an incoming reply.

Do you think that's a good idea?

He grunted. She had a point. Still…

Maybe not. But we can keep it to just talk. The way we were before.

There was a longer pause this time, then an answer popped up that put a smile on his face.

Give me a few minutes.

Fifteen minutes later, she was walking through the door. She was in baggy jeans tonight, and an oversize sweatshirt that hung to her thighs. Did she seriously think that hiding herself was going to stop his desire for her? Not likely, considering he knew every inch of her beneath those clothes. But maybe that made her feel more secure, and he respected that. He nodded at her usual stool opposite him at the anvil.

"So…just talk, huh?" She'd brought a thermal cup of coffee, as she often did. "What are we talking about?"

"I assume you want to avoid discussing the five-hundred-pound gorilla in the room, called Friday Night?"

She shook her head sharply. "There's nothing to discuss. I mean…it was wonderful." Her eyes met his, and there were still embers of heat burning there. "But we agreed on one night. No repeats."

He set the hammer down on the anvil again and turned off the forge. Now that she was here, there was no way he'd get any work done. Everything had changed, and even the carriage house felt different with her in it.

"Agreements can be renegotiated, Grace. Can you really say you don't *want* a repeat of that?"

Her eyes went wide. "Do *you*?"

"Hell yeah, I do." He walked around the anvil and over to the stool. Her legs parted so he could step closer. His fingers combed through her hair, and he smiled at her, hoping it was a sexy smile and not a desperate leer. Because now that he was this close, he *was* feeling desperate for her.

She lifted her chin, reading his desire. "You said you didn't want to make love out here…"

His hand was on the side of her neck now, his thumb brushing against the tender skin behind her ear. Her eyes fell closed, and her lips parted. She whispered his name.

"I said I didn't want our *first* time to be out here. But the second time…"

Her hands hit his chest, pushing him back.

"No! This is a bad idea. We agreed to *once*. Not to sneaking around making love in dark corners like…" Her gaze went around the forge, and her words faltered. He stood away from her, waiting for her to figure out what was next.

"Like what, Grace? Like…lovers?"

"We are not lovers." Her conviction was fading.

"We *could* be." He held up a hand when she started to object. "Hear me out. Why can't we be lovers? Nothing serious. No big relationship. Just two adults who make love when we can, because…well…because we're really damn good together, and you know it. Why can't we keep it casual, keep it temporary and enjoy ourselves?"

She stared at him with wide, shocked eyes. The flame in his chest began to cool. He forgot who he was dealing with here. Grace Bennett was serious about everything. There was no way she'd agree to a casual, sex-only fling with him. There was no structure to that, and Grace needed structure. She wasn't the sleep-around type. She was tea and toast with the historical society. She was rules-are-rules. Their one night had been exactly that. One night. At least they'd had that, and he should be grateful for the memory of—

"Okay."

He blinked. "Okay *what*?"

"Okay to a repeat. Or more than one. But we need to talk about how—"

Max pulled her to her feet and kissed her before she could talk herself out of it. She melted into his embrace with a soft, kitten-like sigh of surrender, sliding her arms around his neck. His body was in overdrive, but he had to let his brain stay in charge here.

They couldn't go into his house and risk waking Tyler. Her house was too far away from where Tyler was sleeping. The carriage house… The carriage house had a small office in back. He hadn't used it yet, but there was an old sofa in there, draped in plastic. He turned, walking backward toward the office and pulling Grace with him, still kissing. He was addicted to her kisses. He opened the door and slapped at the light switch. She was laughing against his mouth now, and he lifted his head so they could both look around.

The old tufted velvet sofa wasn't huge, but it was big enough. He yanked off the plastic cover and was relieved to see it was actually in good shape. No stains or dust on it. It was like the Hendersons just hadn't had room for it in the house and had moved it out here to be forgotten. He patted the cushions. They were clean. It was chilly in here, though. That's when he spotted the small space heater. He plugged it in, and it hummed to life. As fast as he'd moved, he'd given them both time to think. And to doubt.

"We need to talk about this, Max."

His eyes closed in sexual frustration, but she was right. He sat on the sofa and pulled her onto his lap, lightly holding her there with his arms. "Okay. Talk."

Grace rolled her eyes. "Don't act like I'm being unreasonable. We need to be on the same page about what we're doing here. The more we find time to be together, the more chance there is that one of us might…want more. That's just human nature. People want to find partners…"

"If you're suggesting I'm going to want a partner—an actual relationship—then relax. It ain't gonna happen. And if that's what *you* want, you've got the wrong guy, Grace. I'm a good time, not a life partner."

"Because you can't commit, or just don't want to?"

He thought about it for a minute. This conversation had taken a serious turn, but he may as well let her know where he stood. "Both, I guess. Look, I've got nothing against people settling down together, but it's never been my thing. I don't know if humans are meant to do that— partner up for life. I've never seen it work."

"My parents have been together for more than fifty years," she told him. "It's worked for them."

"Well, *my* parents were together for almost forty years, and it was all a sham. My dad slept around and my mother pretended not to know. And I've seen that happen with other couples. Hell, Lexi dated a guy in

Chicago who almost got her put in jail for something *he* did. My little sister married a loser straight out of college. I'm pretty sure he got physical with her, but she's always denied it. They divorced a year later." He sighed. "If you need a long-term commitment before you'll sleep with me again, then we're done, Grace. I won't lie to you and promise something I can't deliver."

She thought for several minutes, digesting what he'd said. Finally, she began to nod. "I'm sorry that's been your experience, Max. And I'm glad you were honest about it. So what we're doing is just…physical. For fun. Not for anything long-term. Either one of us can end it at any time."

"That's right. No harm. No foul."

"And it *will* end eventually." He nodded, and she continued working through it. "And we don't tell anyone."

"If we do, people will get invested in us as a couple. Especially my mother."

"And when we eventually stop, it would hurt her." She agreed. "So secret, temporary, casual, but…" She looked at him. "Not so casual that either of us sees anyone else." He couldn't imagine wanting any other woman than Grace. He nodded in agreement again, reciting the structure of their plan back to her.

"Secret. Temporary. Casual. Monogamous. Either one of us can walk away at any time. And one more thing…" He tugged her body against his. "This is the last time we talk this much before sex."

Her laughter made the spark of desire, set on the back burner while they talked, flame to life again. He kissed her, then laid her back on the sofa and moved his hands under her sweatshirt. The bagginess was convenient now, because he had plenty of room to move under there. And...*hello*...she wasn't wearing a bra. Clever girl.

As he massaged her breasts, her hands fumbled with his belt buckle, then she shoved his jeans down over his hips. She did the same with her own jeans while he pulled a condom from his pocket. They came together, still partially dressed, and made love. Eager. Sexy. Fun. Moving as one until they both cried out and collapsed into the sofa cushions. She'd bitten him again, on the shoulder. Little minx. He looked down and caressed her face until her eyes began to focus again.

"We are really damn good together, Miss Bennett."

Chapter Fourteen

All Grace could do was smile in agreement. She was still waiting for her body to return to her control—it felt like she was still floating up in the rafters. She ran her fingers under his shirt and down his spine, closing her eyes.

She woke with a start when Max slid off of her, pulling up his jeans and fastening them. She couldn't believe they'd just made love without even undressing all the way. That was a first for her. And it had been pretty fantastic.

"What time is it?" she asked, suddenly panicked that they'd both fallen asleep out here.

"It's only nine thirty, but I need to get back to the house. Sorry to run after…"

"I guess that's the *casual* part of this arrangement." She sat up and got herself dressed again. This felt awkward—the moments *after* sex, when they weren't spending the night together. He pulled her up and gave her a quick kiss. She had an unsettling feeling that he *had* done this before. A quick roll on a sofa somewhere, then gone. But his expression was warm and tender.

"We need to figure out something a little *less* casual and more comfortable, but that was a lot of fun, Grace."

His smile deepened. "Let's do it again. Soon." He kissed her, and they headed to their separate houses. She and her neighbor were officially secret lovers. How scandalous. And exciting.

The next night, they met in the carriage house again, but the door to the small office was closed. Max pointed at the monitor screen, where Tyler was asleep in his bed.

"I originally said we couldn't use my bed, but the more I thought about it, the more I realized we *can*. Tyler sleeps like a hibernating bear. We had a thunderstorm one night last month, and he didn't even flinch— slept right through it. Plus the master bath and walk-in closet are between his room and mine, so I don't think he'll hear a thing." He put his arm around Grace's waist and pulled her in for a quick kiss. "I'll have to send you home before morning, but we'll have a lot longer than we would have out here. And be a whole lot more comfortable."

She looked behind him, noticing the forge wasn't even on.

"No work to do out here tonight?"

"Nothing that can't wait." He steered her toward the door. "Come on. I want you in my bed again."

They tiptoed up the stairs and past Tyler's room, and whisper-giggled while they undressed and crawled into bed. Their lovemaking was less frantic than the night before, and he was right—it *was* a lot more comfortable. They were learning each other's bodies—which spots were sensual and which spots were ticklish. As soon as Max realized her ribs were ticklish, he was determined to torture her. She couldn't laugh out loud or struggle because of Tyler sleeping nearby, so she ended up hitting Max in the face with a pillow. That led to a midnight pillow fight on the bed, after which they fell together and made love again. They laid together afterward, and his fingers brushed across the scar on her back.

"I know you don't want to talk about it, but if you ever change your mind…"

She didn't answer right away. It wasn't a night she liked to relive. But this was Max. He'd become her lover, but also, surprisingly, her friend.

"I never should have opened my door," she said quietly.

"What?"

Her head rested on his chest, and his arms tightened their hold around her as she spoke. "I opened my door. If I'd just stayed in my room…" She sighed, knowing that regrets now were pointless. "I heard the commotion, but it never occurred to me what was actually happening." The pops that sounded like firecrackers, people running, people screaming. "It wasn't unusual for students to start some noisy game of dodgeball or something silly in the hallway, so running and yelling wasn't *that* out of place. But to bring firecrackers inside was going too far." She looked up at him, her chin against his breastbone so she could look into his eyes and feel them anchoring her. "I guess even then I was a prissy rules-follower. Instead of minding my own business, I opened the door to tell them to quiet down."

"That was normal curiosity, Grace."

"Well, it was the wrong thing to do. He was standing right there in the hall." Nelson Drew had been dressed in battle fatigues, in green camouflage as if he was heading into the jungle. And even *that* hadn't been enough to make her see the danger. She was too startled by all the screaming to even notice the handgun until he shot someone who was crawling on the floor, then looked up and locked eyes with her. "It wasn't until he fired the gun at someone else that I realized I was in danger. I still might have had time to close the door then, but I just froze when he looked at me, trying to comprehend what was happening."

"That's a normal reaction, too."

"I opened a door I used every single day and discovered a totally different environment. Have you ever had one of those nightmares where you walk through a door or turn a corner, and suddenly you're in a land filled with zombies or something? That's what it was like. He shot me in the shoulder, and at first, it shocked me more than hurt. But I finally snapped out of it and spun away. That's when he shot me in the back. I fell, and he just… stepped over me like I was nothing. I thought I was already dead. The next thing I remember is waking up in the hospital."

"How long were you hospitalized?"

"Not long, really. I was fortunate, although it feels strange to say that. The first bullet went straight through my shoulder, and the second grazed my liver. Luckily, our livers can heal themselves pretty well. The doctors removed the damaged area, and that was that. Back to my life. But not really."

Her life—the one she'd known, the future she'd planned—had been left on the floor, stepped over by a crazed killer who'd shot her for no reason at all. She didn't even know the guy. Had never seen him before. And he'd still had the power to change everything.

"My mom said she heard you were going to be a concert pianist or something like that?"

She nodded against him, her cheek on his chest, his hand caressing her hair. "I was hoping to play in an orchestra, yes. But the thought of all that travel—new places, new doors to have to open." She sighed. "If you think I'm bad now, you should have seen me for those first couple of years. My life was nothing but one big panic attack."

"I've never thought of you as bad, Grace."

She laughed against his skin. "Not even that first day, when I recited the covenant rules to you?"

He chuckled, too. "I may have thought my new neighbor was a right royal pain in the ass, but even then, I didn't think you were a *bad* person. Just a whole lot different than me. But I'd never had a neighbor before. Not for long, anyway."

"Did you like being on the road all the time?"

Max stared up at the ceiling for a minute, trying to decide how to answer. Their conversation had been low and quiet to avoid waking his son. There was something about that quietness, or maybe it was their growing familiarity with intimacy, that was getting them both to open up.

"It was a phase of my life," he started. "And traveling fit that phase. I liked it, but honestly, the past few years were tougher. It was getting old."

Drive from state to state, find the fairgrounds, find a camping site, pray for quality hookups instead of relying on the generator, get the motor home leveled and set up. Then get the trailer set up at the event so he could do his work for an audience. He smiled into the dark. Maybe that was why he'd always liked Grace's presence in the forge. She was a very special audience of one.

"Did your friend's dad—the blacksmith—travel around like that?"

"No. The traveling was all my doing. I needed to get away from Des Moines."

"Why? Did you leave too many broken hearts?"

"Very funny, you." He squeezed her shoulders. "And no. If I'd stayed in Des Moines, I'd be running a car dealership by now. And I didn't want that."

"Your dad's dealership?"

"Ironically, it belonged to my mom's family for generations before Dad took it on. All my life, he'd made it very clear that I was expected to take over after him. But he'd never asked if I *wanted* that. And... I didn't."

"Why not?"

He chuckled, then kissed the top of Grace's head. "You sound like Tyler with all your questions. My relationship with my father has always been complicated. The more he pushed me in one direction, the more I pushed back and wanted to do the opposite. I don't know why..." He hesitated. "That's not true. I *do* know. I never wanted to be anything like him."

Grace lifted her head to meet his gaze. "You know what I'm going to ask."

"Why?" He smiled. Being here like this, warm and naked in the dark, made it easier for him to be honest with himself, as well as with Grace. "Dad always wanted me to be one of the guys, even when I was little. He'd take me to work with him on the weekends, and we'd go to dirt track car races together, and hunting and fish-

ing. I learned to golf. At first, I thought it was great—my dad wanted to spend time with me. But once I was old enough to see what he was doing…" He swallowed hard. Being honest was still hard work. "He figured if I was with him, Mom wouldn't suspect anything. She wouldn't suspect that Dad would take a seven-year-old to a bar, or to a poker game, or a strip club."

"No…" Grace breathed the word more than said it.

"I was his shield. He thought it was hilarious. I was always sworn to secrecy, of course. He'd park me in a side room when he went to the strip joint—it's not like I was stuffing dollar bills in G-strings at that age. The ladies wore their robes back there, and they were always nice to me. Sometimes *their* kids were there, too." He'd learned not to judge people by their jobs or their clothes or their lifestyles. Some of the kindest women he'd ever met were exotic dancers.

"Once I saw an opportunity to work Renaissance fairs and festivals, I jumped at the chance. I apprenticed for an older guy, then bought his setup when he retired. Dad wasn't happy, but I'd stopped trying to please him years before that. He couldn't push me into the dealership if I was never there. He finally gave up and brought one of my cousins into the business, which was a win-win for all of us."

Grace had just started to ask another question when they heard movement in the hall. Tyler was awake. Grace grabbed the blanket and pulled it up over her head, which made Max laugh. It wasn't like she wasn't still right there in his bed. His son called out in a sleepy voice from the other side of the door.

"Max? I have to go to the bathroom. The sit-down kind."

"I'll be right there, buddy."

He lifted the edge of the blanket and whispered to Grace. "He doesn't use my bathroom, so you're safe. I'll close the door behind me if you want to get dressed. He'll go right back to sleep after, and then you should probably head home. At some point, we both need to get some rest."

"I'm not sure I'm cut out for being a secret lover," she whispered back. "Too stressful!"

He chuckled. "Babe, you are a most excellent secret lover."

"Max?" Tyler called again, sending Grace burrowing back into the covers.

"On my way, pal." As he pulled on a pair of pajama bottoms and headed for the door, he smacked Grace lightly on the backside, under the blankets. She hissed something at him, but he just whistled to himself and went to help his son.

Chapter Fifteen

Grace knew going out to the forge was a mistake that Thursday night. For one thing, she went earlier than usual—it was barely seven thirty. For another, the forge was fraught with memories and temptations now. It seemed every conversation they'd had out here since they'd started this *secret lovers* adventure ten days ago, no matter how much they tried, ended up with Max pushing Grace up against a wall and kissing her senseless. Then she'd be jamming her fingers into his hair, clothes would fall off, and…well…

It had even happened in the middle of a disagreement one evening, when Grace was complaining about one of the neighbors building a backyard fence made of beige PVC panels instead of wood. It was an attractive fence, with a narrow strip of latticework at the top. And they needed it, since they'd added an inground pool in the fall, when pool companies were offering discounts. It was *not*, however, period authentic.

Unfortunately—at least in Grace's mind—the historic preservation covenants only covered the front of the properties and visible exterior surfaces of the houses on Revere Street. The *houses*, not the backyard *fences*. She didn't want to make a fuss, but she intended to bring it up at the next historic preservation meeting because she cared about her neighborhood, and it just wasn't right.

Max, of course, had argued that people needed to maintain at least *some* control over their own properties, and the debate was on. Until it wasn't. Until Grace got just a little too close and found herself swept into his arms and pressed against the wall while his hands slid under her sweater.

What had they been talking about again?

They were beginning to establish a secret lovers' routine, which Grace knew was getting dangerously close to building a relationship. She would go to the forge if she saw the lights on, or she'd wait for Max's text letting her know that Tyler was asleep so she could come to the house. Either way, they'd end up in Max's bed until the wee hours of the morning. It was a very nice relationsh— um...*routine.*

They'd even spent a Saturday night in Grace's bed, when Tyler was sleeping over at the Sassy Mermaid with Phyllis. Max and Mozart were building a cautious relationship-slash-routine of their own. She told Max that the aloof Siamese became a blithering fool for catnip, so he'd bought some tiny felt pillows of the stuff and paid it in homage to the cat. The cat, in return, allowed him not only into the house, but into Grace's room, all with great curiosity, but minimal yowling.

So, they'd broken the *no repeats* part of the original agreement. They were extremely close to having a *relationship*, no matter how temporary. They hadn't hit any *regrets* that she knew of, although she had a feeling those would show up when this adventure came to an end. Because they were very good together, and losing that would hurt. Basically the *no one can know* promise was the last one standing.

She saw the lights on in the carriage house and couldn't wait any longer to see him. She wanted to tell him about the children's pageant materials that had arrived that afternoon, and how spectacular the program was going to be—far more ambitious than anything the school had done before. She wanted to tell him how well Tyler had done playing a new song from the lesson book. She wanted to see the progress on the wrought iron bannister Max was making for one of Shelly's clients. He'd been forging iron circles of all different sizes for a week, and was going to put them together inside several long frames of iron for a contemporary look. And yes, she wanted to kiss the man. There was something about the touch of his lips that was hard to resist.

It had been a warm, dry day for November, so she didn't bother with a jacket. Her snug blue sweater over skinny jeans would be enough. Max seemed to approve when she came through the carriage house door. His eyes went dark as his gaze swept up her body, and his smile promised passion later that night. But first, she wanted to actually talk, so she parked herself on the wooden stool near the workbench.

She told him about Tyler's progress and the school pageant and what role she thought Tyler might enjoy in that. While she talked, Max was welding circles together with a handheld torch. He'd created an oversize worktable for the banister with a heavy sheet of plywood on top of three sawhorses. He had his welding shield on, and made her wear a pair of welding goggles for safety.

She felt like an old-time motorcycle moll with the round goggles on.

He was nodding as he worked, making comments here and there on her news. It was nice. Comfortable. Fun. And she was getting far too used to it already. They were becoming invested in each other's lives, and not just casually. They were moving into territory that they'd agreed to avoid, but neither seemed to be worried. Maybe they should be.

Max looked up from his work when her words trailed off. As soon as he saw her face, he turned the torch off and yanked off his heavy gloves and face shield.

"What's wrong?" he asked, walking over to her and stepping between her legs to slide off her goggles. He cupped her face. "What is it? You look freaked out all of a sudden."

The song switched on the speakers above them, and she recognized Max's favorite blues musician, Stevie Ray Vaughan, playing something sexy and slow.

"I don't know," she said. "It's *us*, I guess. It feels like everything we agreed to is just…out the window. It doesn't feel casual. Or temporary. Or detached, like a non-relationship. I know we said this can end whenever we want, but…"

"You're nervous that we're breaking all the structure we built around whatever this is that we're doing." He kissed her forehead and left his lips on her skin longer than just the kiss, as if he didn't want them to be apart. As if he knew his touch calmed her. Sure enough, she felt her panic subsiding, and he smiled against her forehead. "We both agreed that rules can be changed. We broke the *one night only* rule immediately, and that's worked out pretty well for us, I think."

She nodded. "I'm just worried about the future, Max. What if—"

He put a finger under her chin and lifted it until she was looking into his soft blue eyes. "I'm declaring a new rule right now. No worrying about the future. That's something we can't control, so worrying is just a waste of energy. We agreed this was casual—"

"But we've already broken *that* rule, too. We're involved, Max, whether we wanted to be or not."

He chewed on his upper lip for a minute, deep in thought. "You're right. We're in this deeper than casual. Deeper than secret lovers on a romp. What we have is more than just sex, and that transition happened fast. So, we're friends now, right?"

She gave him a stern look. "If you say we're friends with benefits, I swear I'll kick you in the shin."

Max's head tipped back as he laughed. "Duly noted. That phrase sounds a little like friends who occasionally scratch a sexual itch with each other. This is more than that. But we *are* friends, who have agreed to be lovers, not just sex partners. That *lover* part is pretty damn fantastic. But the *friend* part is more important to me. How about you?"

She suspected they were already more than friends. But maybe that was just her. Maybe she was the only one wondering if she was falling in love. She didn't say anything, just nodded in agreement.

"Kiss me, friend," she said with a smile. He obliged, lifting her up off the stool with his arms tight around her waist. She wrapped her legs around his hips, and he turned so she was sitting on the worktable. He leaned over her, kissing her neck, and her head dropped back, eyes closed. This table wouldn't be the most comfortable place to make love, but they could make it work.

She didn't know what made her open her eyes after he pressed her back to lie on the table. Maybe it was the pleasant jolt that shot through her as his mouth found her breast through her sweater. She moaned, not looking at anything in particular. But her brain started to notice something unusual in her line of sight. Her focus slowly came back. She was looking at it upside down, but the door to the carriage house was open.

Sam and Lexi Knight were standing there, mouths open, watching Max basically ravish Grace on top of the worktable. At eight o'clock at night. Twenty feet from his house, where his son was sleeping.

Max had no idea why Grace was smacking his back so hard. It didn't feel like excitement, even though he was enjoying the hell out of working his way down her body. Maybe she was being poked by a piece of wrought iron. The worktable may not have been the best choice for this. She hit him on the shoulder again, and he started to straighten.

"Sorry, babe. Let's go ins—"

Grace was staring in horror at the doorway.

The doorway where his wide-eyed sister and brother-in-law were standing.

His instinct was to try to hide what they'd seen, but... how? They'd caught him nearly on top of Grace, fondling her breast with his mouth while she writhed under him. What was he supposed to say—that he was giving her

CPR? On her *chest*? He took a deep breath and tugged Grace upright. She scrambled to her feet, brushing her hands down her sweater as if she was trying to come up with a viable excuse, too. She'd just been fretting about how their guidelines for whatever they were doing kept dissolving, and now the *no one can know* agreement was null and void.

His sister broke the awkward silence.

"Wow. Just...*wow*." She gestured with her hand going in a circle, wrapping up the scene. "I did *not* see this coming. And I do *not* need to see my little brother doing... *that*...ever again."

Grace's face was beet red, and she had her arms crossed as if she needed to cover herself, despite being fully dressed. He did *not* want her feeling embarrassed. He slid his arm around her waist, giving her a quick squeeze. He whispered, "It's okay," but she just stared at the floor.

"How long has this been going on?" Sam asked. "I mean, it's none of my business, but I thought you guys were nothing but an irritation to each other?"

Lexi gave her husband a wide grin. "Irritation is what makes beautiful pearls inside of oysters, honey. But I'm curious, too. How long, and *what* is this, exactly?"

Max's surprise shifted to irritation and a desire to protect Grace. "What this is, is two consenting adults doing something that's none of your business. Behind closed doors, by the way. Have you ever heard of knocking? I know why *we're* here." He nudged against Grace until she looked up at him. He winked at her, and a little bit of the tension in her body eased. He stroked her side with his thumb. "But why are *you* two here?"

"There was no other car in the driveway but yours, so

we assumed you were alone." Sam made an *oops* face. "Lexi had some tests done up in Boston this afternoon, and we were just heading home and thought we'd stop—"

"Tests?" Max asked, suddenly concerned. "Is everything…?"

"Everything is fine." Lexi patted her stomach. "It's a healthy little girl."

"A girl? Congratulations."

Grace finally managed to speak. "Congratulations."

His sister's sarcasm rose up. "I guess I should say the same to you. That was quite a position—"

Her husband touched her arm, and once again Max was impressed at how Sam could quiet Lexi when she was starting on a roll. Lexi's lips pressed tightly together, then she gave a little shrug. "Sorry. Uncalled for. None of my business."

Grace took a really deep breath, dropping her hands to her sides instead of covering her fully clothed body. Her shock and embarrassment were wearing off.

"No, it's *not*," she said, then looked up at Max. "But now that you've, um, seen us together, I don't think we can pretend nothing has happened."

"No," Lexi said, "I don't think that's a sight I'll forget anytime soon." Sam poked her, and she rushed to explain. "I'm not trying to be a smarty-pants here. I mean…yay for you two. Really. That was impressive." Sam poked her again. "What? I'm *serious*! I'm happy for you two, but… I have questions."

Max tugged Grace, and she let herself be pulled tighter into his side. He gave his sister a warning look. "Please, guys—you didn't know about us because we don't *want* people knowing. This is brand new for both of us, so—"

"So…" Lexi replied. "Maybe you should start locking doors."

Grace started to shake next to him. He looked down and she was laughing. In fact, she was laughing so hard she was wiping tears from her eyes.

"That was my fault." She looked up at Max. "We're not very good at this secret lover business." Then she started laughing again. Her body was relaxing against his, feeling more familiar. "How did we ever think we could keep this quiet in *this* town? That rule was doomed, wasn't it?"

Lexi was laughing, too. "I love that you have rules and refer to yourselves as *secret lovers*. And honestly, I love seeing you together. This—" she gestured at the two of them "—is adorable. And I will do my best to keep it on the down-low, but you are asking a lot, especially when it comes to our mother." Her expression grew serious. "But why do you think you need to be a secret? You're both single adults—there's nothing scandalous about you being a couple."

"We're not a couple." Grace said the words in unison with Max.

Lexi's mouth stayed open, and she looked at her husband, her eyes full of humor. "Sound familiar, Sam?"

He chuckled. "Yup." Sam spotted the minifridge Max had added to the forge. "Please tell me there's beer in that thing."

There was, along with bottled water that Lexi could drink. He checked the screen, and Tyler was still sound asleep. He had about an hour before he'd want to be inside. Hopefully with Grace. But for now, the four of them grabbed stools and sat around the worktable he'd laid Grace on a few minutes earlier.

He told them about the bannister project, which would hopefully lead to more high-paying jobs. He might have to reconfigure the carriage house for working on larger pieces, but it would be worth it. Lexi patted his leg.

"I'm proud of you, Maxwell Bellamy. You've worked hard for this. You're a great dad. And look at you, settling into a relationship."

"It's not a—"

"Yeah, yeah, whatever." Lexi waved off his objection. "Sam and I played that game, too. My point is, I'm happy for you."

He wasn't sure what game she was talking about, but he appreciated that his big sister was proud of him. She'd spent a lot of time nagging him to "grow up" and stop his vagabond lifestyle.

They chatted about the baby news, avoiding any more speculation about him and Grace. Lexi had been determined not to know the gender, but when they had this little scare and needed the further testing, she'd given in to Sam's desire to know.

"It *will* make choosing colors for the nursery a little easier, although I think I'm still sticking to yellow walls." Lexi was talking to Grace, and Max suddenly wondered if Grace had ever wanted children. She was giving his sister suggestions on decor, and she glanced his way. He could imagine her with a baby bump like Lexi's, talking to him about paint colors and baby names and planning a future together.

It was the first time he'd done that—thought of a future stretching out ahead for the two of them. He'd never been a believer in lifelong relationships, but right now he could see Grace and him sitting out here in the forge with his sister and brother-in-law twenty years from now. Normally that kind of thing would send his heart racing in panic. But it wasn't doing that tonight.

It felt...possible. And enticing. A lifetime with Grace.

Chapter Sixteen

"Sis, I know you keep saying it's the school pageant that has you distracted and tired." Aiden set his coffee mug down on Grace's kitchen table. "But there's more than that going on—are you okay? Is there something you're not telling me?"

It was the Saturday morning before Thanksgiving week, and Aiden had stopped by unexpectedly for morning coffee. It wasn't all that unusual—he did that sometimes on the weekends. What *was* unusual was that he'd caught Grace just coming down the stairs in her robe at nine o'clock. She hadn't crawled into her own bed until nearly four in the morning, when she got home from Max's house.

"It's not a crime to sleep in on a Saturday morning."

"Grace, I drove by the house the other night, and it was completely dark at eight thirty."

"Seriously?" She tugged her robe tighter, trying to look affronted instead of anxious. "Maybe I was out to dinner, or maybe I was having a drink with friends. I don't need to check in with you if I'm going—"

"Your car was in the driveway." He leveled a look at her. "And yes, someone could have picked you up, but…did they? Because I drove by the next two nights, and it was the same thing. Your car was here, but I rang the doorbell and no one was home. I'm not saying you shouldn't have a life, Grace. I'm the one that's been telling you to get a life for years. But you don't usually keep things from me, so I'm wondering." He sat back in his chair. "If you want me to mind my business, I will, but it won't stop me from worry—"

"I'm seeing someone." Sitting there in her robe had her at a disadvantage, and she blurted out the news. "Someone…in the neighborhood."

Aiden's face lit up at the first sentence, then looked quizzical at the last one. "In this neighborhood? Who's single…?" His eyes went wide. "Oh, wow—you and the Bellamy brother next door? The one you were fighting with?" He started to smile. "Well, damn, sis. Good for you! But why the secrecy? He *is* single, isn't he?" He paused. "Wait…he's treating you okay, right?"

Oh, yes, Max was treating her okay. So okay that, no matter how much time they spent together, she wanted more.

That evening, Grace told Max about the conversation with her brother while they finished dinner and wine at the same kitchen table. Tyler was staying overnight with Phyllis, so she'd invited Max to spend the night at her place.

"And when he asked me *why the secrecy*, I didn't have an answer. I guess I've forgotten what the point of that was."

Max picked up their dishes and turned to put them

in the dishwasher while Grace put two slices of pie on plates.

"I'm pretty sure the *no one can know* rule was your idea," Max said, looking at her over his shoulder.

"I don't think so. *You* mentioned it because you didn't want Tyler to know. But I think our friends and family can know we're…whatever…without Tyler knowing we're anything more than friends."

He met her at the table again. "Is this your apple pie? Heaven. I'm in heaven." He took a forkful and groaned. "Keep baking like this and we can tell whoever you want whatever you want."

"I'm serious, Max."

"So am I." He set his fork on the edge of his plate, then reached over to take her hand. "I agree with you. At first, I didn't know if we'd last a week, so we didn't need to get other people invested. But this…" He gestured at the dessert dishes and her kitchen. "Well, this is feeling really nice." He paused. "I'm still not a good bet, Grace. I'm not good at…hanging around. I guess I need to reword that speech now, since I don't have the motor home anymore. I have a son and a house, so I'm not physically going anywhere." He closed his eyes tightly and dropped his head. "I'm making a mess of this, aren't I?"

Grace absently brushed some crumbs off the yellow tablecloth. She'd been thinking that going public would put their relationship—no sense denying that's what it was—on more solid ground. And now Max was making it sound like he still needed to keep an escape route handy.

"I know *temporary* is the last rule still standing…"

She waited for him to look up before continuing. "And that's okay." She had a feeling it wasn't going to be okay at all, but they'd cross that bridge when they got to it.

"Grace, I want to be clear—even if *this*—" he gestured between them "—is temporary, I want our friendship to last. We live next door to each other, and I honestly enjoy your company. Your friendship."

This was feeling less okay all the time. "Are you putting me in the friend zone already?"

"No! I like the secret lovers zone way too much to give it up yet." He gave her a suggestive smile and winked. Then he lifted her hand to his lips and kissed her fingers. "But maybe it's time to drop the *secret* part. You and I are great together, so let's be great together with our friends and family. Tyler adores you, so he won't think much of seeing you around more often in the daylight hours. In fact…" He opened her hand and kissed her palm. "I was going to ask if you wanted to join us for Thanksgiving dinner."

Grace blinked. "Aren't Tyler's grandparents coming for the holiday? Won't that be weird?"

Max looked away, his eyes pinched. Then he faced her again. "Honestly? I could really use the support. Sam and Lexi are going to have dinner up in Boston with some restaurant owners they're friends with. With the baby coming, Lexi said it's their last chance for a grown-up *Friendsgiving*-style celebration for a while. That leaves me with the Cosmas, Mom, and Fred."

"And Tyler," she said with a smile.

"And Tyler." He nodded. "Like I said, he adores you. And I kinda do, too." He kissed her hand again. "I think it would help both Ty and I to have you there. I don't know what to expect from Sally and Ed. I *never* know what to expect from my mom. And Fred Knight is a complete wild card." He reached over to cup her cheek. "But you...you steady me, babe. I want you there."

It was nice to be needed. Wanted. But this felt more like a *friend* mission than a *lover* one.

"Fred, I swear by all that's holy, if you take that last dinner biscuit I will hurt you." Max's mother was glaring at her date, or whatever Fred was in her life, at the dining room table. "My grandson wanted that!"

"Well, then, the kid should have spoken up." Fred shrugged, dropping the large, flaky biscuit onto his own plate. He winked at Tyler, sitting next to him. "You snooze, you lose, little dude."

Max felt like he was watching a train wreck about to happen, and he had no idea how to stop it. He'd felt like that all day, though, and nothing bad had happened. So far, Thanksgiving had been peaceful, but it was the sort of peace that came right before a storm. At least that's how it felt to Max. He'd been on pins and needles all day.

Tyler giggled and reached for the biscuit. Fred held his fork up like he was ready to stab Tyler's fingers.

"Oh, be careful..." Sally Cosma gasped, taking Tyler's other hand. But Tyler was laughing out loud now, snatching his hand back from her, then grabbing the biscuit as Fred roared in pretend anger.

"Oh, no! He beat me!" Fred leaned back, grinning ear to ear as he clutched at his chest. The whole thing had apparently been a routine they'd done before, probably at Mom's house.

"I got you, Freddie!" Tyler crowed, waving the biscuit in the air. Everyone started to laugh, even Sally, and Max breathed out a sigh of relief. He wasn't sure how much more of this *fun* his heart could take. A soft hand brushed across his lower back. He turned to Grace and gave her a *can you believe this?* look. Her expression said she agreed. She rubbed his back with her hand, like she was trying to calm him. It was working.

His mother, on the other hand, was having a great time. She smacked Fred playfully, but not lightly, on his shoulder. "You are never gonna beat this kid to one of my buttermilk biscuits!" She leaned forward to speak to Sally. "We play that game every time he stays with us, but usually it's with cookies."

Max frowned. Did Mom just say when he stays with *us*? Who exactly was *us*? Were Mom and Fred…? He didn't have the mental bandwidth right now to go there.

Sally gave his mother a tentative smile. The two women couldn't be more different. Phyllis Bellamy was dressed fairly tame, for her. Trim brown trousers with a metallic stripe down the side and a dark orange top that looked painted on, but at least it wasn't as low-cut as most of her tops. She'd left the leopard print ankle boots at home, wearing high-heeled black pumps instead.

Sally was in a blue skirt and matching jacket over a white and green polka-dot blouse, with practical flats. Her dark hair was trimmed into a shoulder-length bob. She looked stylish, not nunlike, but compared to his mother…

As different as they were in appearance, though, the two women had one very important thing in common— his son. Things had been a bit tense all around when the Cosmas arrived two days ago. There were no confrontations, but the last time he'd seen them, they were trying to take custody of Tyler. It was a wound that hadn't completely healed.

His mom embraced Sally the moment she got out of their car, as if greeting a long-lost friend. She'd taken Sally and Tyler up to Boston yesterday, and they'd hit the highlights—the USS Constitution, the aquarium, Faneuil Hall. Meanwhile, Fred took Ed out on the water on Devlin's lobster boat. The day was a hit. Everyone had fun, and Max didn't have to play happy host until today.

Grace was still rubbing his back. He leaned toward her, turning his head to whisper softly into her ear. "Am I overreacting? Are things tense, or is it just me?"

She turned her head, looking up at him through her lashes. "It's just you. Relax. Everyone is trying, but you look like you're expecting a bar fight to break out any minute." She smiled softly. "Enjoy your meal."

He returned the smile, his forehead touching hers. She was his safe place, today and just maybe…for a long time to come. "Ty's going to stay at the motel tonight."

"Hey, you two!" His mother kicked Max under the table, hard enough to make him straighten with a yelp. "This is a family dinner, not date night. As cute as you two are, save it for later."

Max looked across the table, but Tyler was animatedly telling Ed about his day in Boston, so he wasn't paying any attention. Mom was right, though. Tyler thought Grace was Max's friend. They shouldn't get too cozy in front of him. Grace nodded an acknowledgment to his mother. Under the table, though, her hand rested on his thigh and gave a squeeze. His tension eased.

* * *

She was at his side again on Saturday, the day before the Cosmas headed home to Ohio. The holiday visit had been a success, and Grace had a big role in that. They were outside by their car before Ed and Sally drove back to the Sassy Mermaid. Sally was hugging Grace right now, as Ed stood by smiling warmly.

"It has been such a pleasure to meet you, Grace," Sally said. "When Tyler told me he was taking piano lessons, it made me so happy. Marie used to play."

"He told me that. She liked Broadway musicals."

Sally's eyes welled with tears. "Yes, she did. He told me you played her favorite song for him. I'm glad you're in his life, Grace." She glanced Max's way. "I'm glad you're *both* in his life." They all looked into the backyard, where Tyler and Chantal, from across the street, were playing with the multicolored soccer ball the Cosmas had brought him. "He's happy here, and that's all we ever wanted. We just miss him so much. With both Marie *and* Tyler gone…"

Max cleared his throat heavily, tugging at the collar of his flannel shirt. Emotions had been high all week, but not one bad thing had happened. No arguments. No sarcastic comments. And from what he'd seen, no pressure on Tyler to go home with them. That had been his irrational fear. He had full custody, but in the back of his mind, he wondered if they'd try to turn Tyler against him. Instead, Sally, and even quiet Ed, had made a point to tell Tyler how great Cape Cod seemed to be, how much they liked his house, how lucky he was to live here with his father. They really *had* changed since those fraught months right after Marie's death.

"You're welcome to visit any time," Max said. And he meant it. Tyler had been thrilled to see them, and Max, like everyone else in this little group of adults, wanted the boy to be happy more than anything else. They could build a family around that.

"Really?" Sally's eyes were wide. She glanced at her husband, who gave her a quick nod. "Because we were thinking of maybe buying a condo here on the Cape. We drove by one yesterday and looked it up online. It needs a lot of updating, but that puts it in our price range. We didn't want to do anything that would make you un-comfortable..." Her hands twisted together nervously, and Ed spoke up.

"It's just a little townhouse in Bourne. I can do all the work myself. We're getting ready to retire, so we thought we could spend a month here in the summer, come for the holidays and rent it out when we're not using it." Ed was always the practical planner.

Max had to work to keep his smile in place as he rolled the idea around. He'd been thinking more like a few short visits. A year ago, he'd never *met* these people. Six months ago, they were fighting him in family court. And now they were part of his life—Tyler's life—forever. He let out a long breath, careful not to let it sound like a heavy sigh.

Grace's fingers touched the small of his back. She'd been doing that all week, basically petting him like he was an anxious dog. Comforting him. Centering him. He smiled. He hadn't known *Grace* existed, either, not until he got here in September. And look how well *that* had worked out—for him and for Tyler. This year had been a roller coaster, but it seemed to be closing on a happier, more hopeful note.

"I think that would be nice. I know Tyler would like seeing you more often."

Grace patted his back. *Good boy.* He straightened. Another man might feel patronized, but he knew she meant it. Her approval was important to him. Everything about her was important to him. She kept fretting that she wasn't cut out for parenting, but she'd been so great at it. Tyler loved her. The kids at school seemed excited about the holiday pageant.

She laughed at something Sally said about Tyler, and the sound sent a wave of warmth through him. He'd been warning her that he wasn't a good bet for anything long-term. But now he wondered if he was as wrong about himself as she'd been about herself. Grace Bennett made a lifetime commitment seem like a surprisingly solid bet, even for him. Because he was falling in love with her.

Chapter Seventeen

"Micah, we can't have dinosaurs in the Christmas pageant."

Grace was pretty sure she'd said that particular sentence to the boy at least a dozen times this week.

"My mom says you can't call it a Christmas pageant because we're Jewish."

"You're right, Micah. I'm sorry. It's a *holiday* pageant, and we are definitely celebrating Hanukkah, too. In fact, I think your brother is supposed to be a dreidel—" she checked her list "—yes, here it is. Isaac is a blue dreidel, and *you're* going to talk about the meaning of Hanukkah. There are no dinosaurs in the script."

"What about *Kwansas*?" Naomi Wilkinson looked up at Grace with such sincere concern, but Grace had no idea what Tyler's kindergarten classmate was asking.

"*Kansas?* Like in *Wizard of Oz*?" Grace looked at the stage area, where last year's holiday pageant props were now assembled in piles. She spotted the colorful candles made of foam board. "Oh, you mean *Kwanzaa*! Yes, we'll talk about the lessons of Kwanzaa, honey. After all, this is *Holidays Around the World*. So we'll do our best to celebrate them all."

She was beginning to think volunteering for this job may have been a very bad idea. Being director, even of five- and six-year-olds—maybe *especially* of five- and six-year-olds—was a lot more pressure than just being their accompanist. But from the moment Tyler had heard she was doing it, he'd been so excited that she didn't have the heart to back out now. And she'd purchased the new pageant script online herself. She'd even bought some of the optional props. If she was going to do this, she was going to do it fearlessly. That had been the plan, anyway.

The script was written for young children, although maybe not as young as kindergarten through second grade. But it had fairly simple lines for them to recite about winter holidays celebrated around the world. All she needed now were cooperative children. Connie Wells, the assistant principal, had expressed concern over the production Grace had selected. She wasn't sure how the students would embrace standing in a line in costumes and reciting lines with facts about different cultures. Tyler's teacher, Mary Kelleher, warned they might get restless. But Grace was sure they'd do just fine once they learned their lines, and it would look so lovely with the backdrop of the planet Earth, painted onto a canvas drop cloth hanging behind them. The children would learn, but in such a fun way. The image of Earth would even have a little moon circling above it, once Max figured out a way to create that effect. He and a first-grade teacher, Kyle Henderson, were in charge of the stage props.

Max was as out of his element with this as she was, but he was giving it his best shot. She was determined to do the same. They were both changing. Growing. Their relationship—for lack of a better word—had grown past the argue-then-have-sex phase. Nearly every night had been spent together in his bed or hers. Lately, she'd been joining him and Tyler for dinner most nights. One might even say they were dating, now that more people knew about them.

"But why can't we have dinosaurs, Miss Grace? I already have a costume and everything." Micah Singer was like a dog with a bone once he got something in his head. His little brother, Isaac, was one of Tyler's favorite classmates. The two younger boys looked up to Micah in all of his second-grade wisdom. Sure enough, Isaac stepped up next to his brother.

"Yeah, Miss Grace. Why *can't* we have dinosaurs? Rawr!" He raised his hands in T. rex fashion and growled before giving her a wide grin. "Or maybe an astronaut?"

A murmur of excitement went through the three dozen children gathered around her now. *Uh-oh.* She was losing them. She clapped her hands a few times—lightly, but enough to get their attention. She liked to think of it as her *Mary Poppins* move.

"We can't have dinosaurs because this is a holiday pageant, and none of our holidays have anything to do with dinosaurs—" she looked at Isaac "—or astronauts. Save those for next Halloween, boys. But we do need some of you to be candles and dreidels and angels and elves, and don't forget—we need a bunch of you to be wrapped up as gifts. Our theme is that this is the season of giving." Surely *that* would make the children think differently.

"What's a theme?"

"Can I be a cowgirl?"

"I wanna be an astronaut!"

"Girls can't be astronauts."

"They can, too!"

"Can we be zombies?"

Grace took a deep, deep breath and held it, closing her eyes and envisioning the play coming together in three weeks. She'd get the kids on board. They'd learn their parts in rehearsals. They'd be adorable. The whole town would be captivated. Everyone would sing the songs and leave with warm hearts.

She was Mary-freaking-Poppins and this was going to work.

"Okay!" She spoke loudly enough to quiet them. "Take these papers home to your parents. This is a list of which character each of you is playing, and the costume the character requires. Please note there are *no* dinosaurs, astronauts or zombies on this list. We have a script, and we're going to follow it."

A week later, she had serious doubts that the children would *ever* follow anything, especially her lovely script. Yes, the language might be above their reading capabilities, but surely they'd be able to memorize a few lines. It's not like anyone was delivering a soliloquy. Worst-case scenario, she'd have an adult stand behind the risers and feed the lines for the kids to repeat.

The risers were on the stage, on either side of a six-foot painted world map. The second graders in her portion of the pageant were going to be standing on the risers, reciting their lines about holiday traditions of joy and kindness. The younger classes would act out the traditions in costume, from Thanksgiving's shared meals to Hanukkah, Christmas, Boxing Day and Kwanzaa.

Grace was beginning to understand why Connie had been so concerned. It was a lot of ground to cover for children this young, who had the attention spans of gnats. She couldn't keep them focused on anything for more than a few minutes. Some of the kids were trying so hard to please her, reciting their lines—*almost* correctly—at the top of their lungs, and doing their best to hit their marks on the stage. But they were a month from being ready to perform, and the pageant was ten days away.

Micah was still pleading to be a dinosaur. Latoya wanted to be a superhero. Kevin was determined that zombies *could too* have holidays, but instead of turkey they'd eat the other characters. Grace was concerned what little Kevin might be watching and learning from his teenage brother. Chantal kept pointing out that the Christmas story had a star in it, so she really *could* be an astronaut.

Grace's sense of panic was growing every day, even though everyone kept telling her it would be fine. Yesterday she'd given up on the original songs that came with the program package. Having the kids learn five unknown songs was a step too far—she could see that now. She was going to switch in some old holiday standards instead—"Jingle Bells," "Frosty the Snowman" and other easy tunes that the children knew. There was no sense in battling with new songs on top of all the distractions of the holiday season itself.

Their excitement made the kids nearly impossible to manage, but Grace was determined. That's why she

was still at the school this late after rehearsal, rework-
ing some of the bits that just weren't coming together.

The houses in town were decorated with lights, people had their trees up at home and Santa was at his
Winsome Cove workshop downtown every Saturday
in December. It was sensory overload for children—all
holidays all the time, everywhere children went. She
and Max had put up a tree in his living room the week
before, and she'd shown Tyler and him how to string
cranberries and popcorn together into garlands, the way
Grace had done as a child. As she'd watched the two of
them, racing and competing to have the longest garland,
she'd envisioned that moment happening every Christmas, for years on end.

She couldn't imagine *not* having Max be a part of her
future, which was a shock in itself. After all their ups
and downs and back-and-forths, she'd become part of
his family, and he'd become part of hers. But she still
didn't know *how* they were going to move toward that
future. She didn't know if she was ready to take on a
ready-made family. She adored Tyler, but was she *mom*
material? And what would that look like? She adored
her little house and her quiet life, too. It was a lot to give
up. Especially to give up for a complete unknown. The
unknown hadn't been Grace's happy place for a very
long time. But the unknown with Max by her side didn't
feel as scary. Then again, he hadn't *asked* to make that
future with him. She had a feeling he was still keeping
an escape hatch open for the day he decided they were
over. He'd told her more than once that it was inevitable
for any relationship.

Max was in Boston today, meeting with a potential

retailer for his blades. It was an upscale art shop on Boylston Street, where clients would be more likely to purchase big ticket items like full-size swords, even if just for decor. Max wanted to break into Boston's market, and this looked like it would be his chance. He was also looking for more home interior ironwork projects. Those jobs were more profitable, and he felt if he could get established, it would be a steadier stream of income.

Tyler was running around the auditorium with Isaac, Micah and one of Micah's classmates, Dustin Marks. They were playing some sort of good guys vs bad guys game, which hardly seemed fair considering it was little Isaac and Tyler against the older boys. But she'd been learning from Phyllis that the old saying was true. *Boys will be boys,* and they'll usually sort things out on their own. Phyllis said she'd learned while raising Max that as long as no one's in danger and the house isn't on fire, adults rarely need to interfere.

Grace ran her fingers over the piano keys. Max had looked into her eyes last night as they'd laid naked in his bed, and he told her that she'd tamed him. She began to play "Jingle Bells" and heard Tyler, somewhere in the darkened auditorium, shout-singing the words. She'd bet money it was that little boy who'd *really* tamed the wild man.

A few minutes later, as she was deeply engrossed in matching the new sheet music to the play script, three of the boys came to the edge of the stage.

"Dustin's mom picked him up. When is my dad coming home?" Tyler asked.

"Hmm?" She glanced at her watch. "Another hour or so. In time for dinner. In fact, he's bringing dinner home." Max was going to stop for some take-out Italian dinners.

"What are you doing?" Tyler was on a questioning roll. "How long before we go home?"

"I'm working on the play, Tyler. Switching out some of the songs you guys didn't like for ones I think you will. I won't be too much longer."

"Can we walk home now if Micah comes with us?"

Grace looked at the three boys over the top of her reading glasses. "Uh…no. Micah is eight—that's not old enough to babysit you and Isaac. Besides, you'd have to cross Pilgrim Street, and the crossing guard has gone home for the day."

"We're not babies, Miss Bennett!" Isaac, usually much quieter than his big brother, practically shouted the words at her.

"Honey, I know you're not. Babysit is just a word. It means someone older being responsible for someone younger. And Micah is not old enough." She frowned. "Where is your mom today? Doesn't she usually pick you up by now?" Debbie Singer was on the historical society board with Grace and had always been on time and responsible. Grace had always appreciated that.

Micah shrugged. "My aunt is supposed to pick us up today, but she's late."

"Can we go to the library?" Tyler asked.

"The school library? Miss Harrison may have gone home already, but you can go check."

"Yay!" Isaac did a fist pump, which was ridiculously cute on a five-year-old. The boys turned to hurry up the aisle to the hallway. She called after them.

"Don't go in unless Miss Harrison gives you permission!"

Lisa Harrison was nearly seventy, if not older. Never married, she lived for her job. She came off as a stern and feisty Yankee, but she'd always had a soft spot for the children she served. She'd been especially kind to Tyler. He'd told Max that his mom used to read to him every night, so now Max was doing that with him at bedtime. One of Grace's favorite things to do was stand in the hallway and listen to Max's deep voice reading *Goodnight Moon* until Tyler fell asleep.

Without the boys pounding around the auditorium and yelling, she was able to focus on the task at hand—deciding which songs would go where for the pageant. It was last minute to be making changes, but the kids knew these songs. She didn't like surrendering that particular battle, but time was running out.

She'd decided to use more generic tunes like "Jingle Bells" for the holidays that didn't include Santa Claus. She'd even rehearsed a child-friendly version of "Let It Snow" with them that afternoon, and the kids loved yelling *"Let it snow!"* over and over. This was all going to work out just fine. She played a few more songs, making notes along the way. Nearly an hour had passed when she checked the time again. She looked out to the auditorium, which was still quiet. The boys must have found Miss Harrison after all.

Grace put her notebooks into her tote bag and turned off the lights. She headed down the hall to the library, thankful that she'd had some quiet time to think through how to simplify the play and still keep all the holidays in there. She did much better work when things were quiet, which rarely happened with little boys around. Her pace slowed as she approached the school library. The door was closed, and it was dark inside. She looked through the narrow window in the door to the outside windows, and it was getting dark there, too. The library door was locked.

Her first reaction was irritation. Where would those boys have gone if the library was closed? She'd told them to come back if Miss Harrison wasn't there. Hadn't she? No. She'd told them not to go in if the librarian wasn't there. But surely they'd understand that she'd *meant* to come back to the auditorium? The halls were quiet. A janitor was vacuuming a room at one end of the hallway, and there was a light on in the office at the opposite end.

That's probably where they were—in the office. Knowing them, they'd been caught wandering around on their own and were sitting on the bench in there. She hurried that way, doing her best to ignore the very quiet whisper of panic in her heart. Three boys wouldn't just vanish from the school building. They *had* to be here somewhere.

The only person in the office was Jessica King, the administrative assistant. She looked up with a surprised smile when Grace walked in.

"Hey, Grace. Working late on the pageant? How's it coming?"

"Have you seen Tyler or the Singer boys?" The question came out more urgently than she'd intended, and Jessica straightened.

"No. Weren't they with you?"

Grace could no longer ignore her fear. Its icy grip trailed down her spine, curling around each vertebrae as it went, chilling her to her core. Those boys were her responsibility, and she had no idea where they were right now.

"Do you think they walked home alone?" Jessica asked, her forehead furrowed. "Is Tyler's dad home?"

"No. No, I don't think so. Not yet. And I told the boys not to leave."

Her head tried to take over. This was a situation. She was good at handling situations. She used to think she was good at *avoiding* situations, but clearly that wasn't true.

"Telling children not to do something doesn't always mean they won't do the thing." Jessica's voice was calm, trying to reassure Grace. But worry was clouding her eyes. "Maybe they went to the Singers'?"

Grace dropped her tote bag and pulled her phone from her pocket. Her first call was to Maya, to see if she could see Max or Tyler at the house. Her friend picked up on Grace's urgent tone and hurried across the street to check. Max's truck wasn't there, and Tyler wasn't at either house, but she promised to walk the neighborhood looking for him.

Grace called Deb Singer next, who sounded irritated when she answered.

"Yes?"

"Are the boys with you?" Grace blurted out the question like a demand. She had to know.

"My boys? Yes, no thanks to my sister-in-law. Who is this?"

Grace's knees almost buckled in relief. "It's Grace Bennett. Tyler's there, too?"

"Tyler Cosma? No. Why?"

Her knees buckled for real this time, as panic came roaring back. She sank onto the nearby bench.

"He and the boys were together..." Her voice broke. This wouldn't do. She needed to get her emotions under control somehow.

"Oh, my God," Deb breathed into the phone. "Hang on." She could hear Deb's voice raised and angry as she spoke to her sons. But it was eerily calm, the same way that Jessica's was, when she came back to the line. "Oh, God, Grace. My sister-in-law was supposed to pick Micah and Isaac up from school this afternoon because I had an appointment. I reminded her last night, and she *still* forgot. I never should have trusted her in the first place..."

"Deb..."

"Oh, right. I guess the boys got restless after waiting around, and Micah got the bright idea of walking home from school. I'm going to ground that boy for a month..."

"*Deb.* What about Tyler?"

"They told me that Tyler left the school with them, but he wanted to go to the library. I'm so sorry, Grace. The last time they saw Tyler, he was walking down the sidewalk on Pilgrim Street toward the village library."

"Okay—" Grace grabbed on to hope again "—so he must be at the library. It's only three blocks, and it's on this side of the street, so he could have gotten there safely—"

"Grace, it's Wednesday," Deb said. "The library closes early on Wednesdays. It closed at four." It was after four thirty now, and getting darker by the minute.

Tears burned Grace's eyes. This couldn't be happening.

"I'm really sorry, Grace. Micah's only eight but he should have—"

"It's not Micah's fault. It's mine." She ended the call and turned to Jessica. "I'm going to the library. But if he's not there..."

Jessica gave her a quick, tight hug. "Call me either way. If he's not there, I'll call the sheriff. In the meantime, I'll have the janitors sweep the school and playground for him, just in case. We'll find him, Grace."

Taking her car seemed silly when the library was almost in sight from the parking lot, but if Tyler wasn't there, she knew she'd need to start driving around. Her head kept saying that he was probably fine, but her heart was screaming that he might not be. She had no idea how she'd cope with that possibility. How did parents survive things like this? And she wasn't even his parent. And never should be, if today was any example of her skills.

The library lot was empty. The stairs to the white clapboard building were empty. The doors were locked. There was no one there. She got back in the car and stared straight ahead, wondering what to do next. How would she ever explain this to Max?

The sound of her phone ringing made her jump so hard she hit her hand against the steering wheel. She winced as she looked at the screen, and then the tears began to fall.

"Max..." The words refused to come.

"Hey, babe." He sounded so happy that it hurt. "I'm home, and I have a pile of pasta and pastries from the North End. Where are you?"

She swallowed hard. "Is...is Tyler there?"

"At the house? No, he's supposed to be with you." The joy began to slip from his voice. "What's going on?"

"Oh, Max... The boys were with me in the auditorium, and then they left, and I thought they were in the school library, but…" She took a shaky breath. "They weren't there, and then I thought they went to the Singers', but only Micah and Isaac are there, and now I'm at the library, but it's closed and no one is here—"

"Where is Tyler?" Max's question was as sharp and deadly as one of his blades.

"I don't know." Saying the words out loud made her start crying for real.

"Grace, are you telling me that you lost my son?"

Chapter Eighteen

Max's hands were curled so tightly into fists that he could feel his fingers losing circulation. He wanted to hit something, but there was nothing to hit except the silent walls of his very empty house. He'd hung up on Grace when she confessed she'd lost Tyler. Not as much in anger as disbelief, and a need to do a lot more than talk. He needed to *act*, but how? His son was missing.

He could hear Maya outside, calling Tyler's name, looking for him in the increasing darkness. Which was more than Grace was doing after letting a five-year-old kid just disappear on her without noticing. Maybe that was unfair, but he could hear his neighbor and he couldn't hear Grace. She'd been so obsessed with perfecting that stupid Christmas pageant, and he kept telling her she was missing that the point was for the kids to have fun. And now she'd missed the point of watching his son. She'd forgotten to actually *watch* him at all.

How do you lose a *child*? Sure, he'd heard news stories about lost kids, but that was something that happened to someone else. Not to *his* kid. He had to find Tyler. Nothing else mattered. And to do that, he was going to need help. He texted his sister.

911 Call me now

His phone rang a few seconds later.

"Make it quick," she said. "I'm one cook short in the kitchen tonight. What's up?"

"Lexi, don't let Mom know. I don't want to deal with her flipping out—"

"Flipping out about what?" He could hear the clanging of pots in the background. From the way her breath was blowing across the phone, he knew she was holding it between her cheek and shoulder to leave her hands free to cook.

"Tyler is missing. Grace lost him."

There was a beat of silence, and then Lexi's voice was coming directly into the phone. He had her full attention now.

"What are you talking about?"

"He slipped away from her at school or something. He's gone, Lex. And I don't know what to do." For the first time, emotion welled up in his throat. "I don't even know where to start."

"Honey, look," Lexi started, in full lecture mode. He was caught between not wanting to hear it and needing to have someone tell him what to do. "I don't know what you think happened, but Tyler is here at the restaurant with Mom. I'm looking at them right now." Max hit his knees so hard on the floor that Lexi heard him through the phone. "Are you okay? What the hell is going on?" Her voice softened. "Max, Tyler is fine. He and Mom came in for dinner a little while ago, and they're having a grand old time together. Why did you think he was lost?"

"Give the phone to Mom." He caught the edge in his

voice and took a breath. His son was okay. "*Please.* I'll explain later."

A few seconds later, his mother's perky voice eased the pressure in his chest. "Hi, sweetie! Tyler and I are having dinner together. His aunt Lexi is making crab cakes, just for us." He could hear rustling, and then his mother came back on the phone. "Hang on… Okay, I'm in the hall now." Her voice was less chipper. "Where were you and Grace? Tyler was all alone at the library, Max. The librarian knew he was my grandson because I've taken him there a few times. She called me because she had to close up and he was there alone. I picked him up and brought him here."

Max's chin was resting on his chest. A light breeze would have knocked him flat at this point. Relief had turned his bones to jelly.

"Grace was supposed to be watching him at school. I guess she lost track of him, along with some other little kids. Jesus…" He scrubbed his hands down his face. "I don't know what she was thinking. He's really okay, Mom?"

"He's completely fine, I promise. And that explains why he didn't want me to call Grace when I got there—he knew he'd be in big trouble. He told me she was busy. I should have known he was up to something." She chuckled. "I forgot what rascals you boys can be. He told me he was hungry, but I'll bet he was just avoiding going home and getting his little butt in trouble."

"There's nothing funny about this, Mom. I trusted her, and Grace *lost* my son."

There was a pause before she answered.

"You were around Tyler's age the first time I lost you."

He blinked. "What?"

"We were in a department store downtown, and I was checking the clearance rack for something to wear to some country club thing. I swear I turned my back for half a minute, and you were just...*gone*...when I turned around again. I screamed and salespeople came running. Ten minutes later, we found you hiding inside one of those circular clothes racks. You thought it was the funniest thing ever. I lost about ten years off my life before we heard you giggling in there."

"I don't remember that..." His brain was beginning to kick into gear again. "Look, I need to tell people he's safe. The school may have called the sheriff. I'll come there and pick him up in a minute."

"Take twenty, Max. Our dinner just came to the table and he's attacking those crab cakes, so maybe he really was hungry. I'll see you soon."

Max's first thought was that Grace should have fed him. But he'd told her he was bringing dinner from Boston. His anger with her was all tangled up with the terror that was just beginning to subside. She'd lost the most precious thing in his life. Tyler had been put in danger because of her. Because of the woman he was falling in love with. This was why relationships didn't work. People were unreliable. People always ended up disappointing each other. Even people you loved.

He rose to his feet and called out the front door to Maya that Tyler was safe. He called the school, just as Jessica had been ready to call the sheriff. He called Deb Singer, who'd done nothing but cry and apologize. Turns out she hadn't exactly known where *her* sons were, either. But he wasn't going to blame an eight-year-old kid for what happened.

He texted Grace that Tyler was okay, instead of calling her. Yes, a text was the coward's way out, but he didn't trust himself to speak to her and not lose his temper. As furious as he was, he didn't want to get in a screaming match with her, and he was afraid he might do just that. Mom had told him that story about losing him in a department store for a reason, and he needed to think about that. But right now, he needed to see and touch Tyler. Just to be sure he was real. That he was okay.

Grace called him right away, of course. But he didn't answer. He couldn't. Not until he held his boy in his arms.

Grace had always been a sound and regular sleeper. But sleep wasn't going to come tonight. Not even with the help of Sleepytime Tea. Not even when that tea was spiked with rum. Her body was still in fight-or-flight mode from losing track of Tyler earlier, and her eyes refused to close. She'd paced around the house for a while, trying to distract herself with random little tasks. Dusting shelves. Rearranging canned goods in the pantry. Writing a grocery shopping list. Annoying Mozart with her restlessness. She even took a hot bath, which she rarely did, hoping it might relax her tensed-up body.

But how could she relax when she'd done something as awful as losing track of a five-year-old? Losing *Max's* five-year-old. She didn't think she'd ever forgive herself, but worse—it didn't look like Max was going to forgive her, either. She'd called him four different times after getting his terse text saying that Tyler was safe and with Phyllis. He'd never answered her calls, and she hadn't left any messages.

What was she supposed to say? *Sorry I lost your kid? Sorry I'm so bad at parenting? Sorry I almost got us all on an episode of* 48 Hours? She dropped her head into her hands at the kitchen table. No wonder she couldn't sleep, when all she could think of was what *could* have happened to Tyler. Each scenario was worse than the last, and like a cyclone, they just kept spinning faster and faster every time she tried to close her eyes.

Tyler was safe.

He'd been with his grandmother.

Nothing bad had happened.

But that wasn't true, was it? Something bad *had* happened. Something had happened between Max and her. A trust had been broken. She was in love with Max Bellamy. And he wasn't even speaking to her.

You can fix this.

But her heart wasn't listening to reason right now. Her heart was telling her that maybe she *shouldn't* fix this. Maybe she'd been right about not being cut out to be anyone's mother. She'd known it all along—the randomness of children was more than she could handle. Adult expectations of *don't go somewhere alone* meant nothing to five-year-olds. They were so quick to think they knew better. So fearless. So naive. So willing to innocently put themselves in harm's way. And it wasn't just Tyler.

Micah and Isaac had crossed Pilgrim Street without a crossing guard. They'd crossed two other side streets on their walk home. Yes, they'd made it safely, but what if they hadn't? She hadn't been asked to watch them, but she was an adult and they'd been with her in the auditorium. Instead of worrying about them, she'd been *glad* to have the peace and quiet. She felt another stab of guilt. She'd been more productive at the expense of children's safety. She was a terrible person.

You're just tired.

That was certainly true. But facts were facts, whether she was tired or not. She was being hard on herself. But every time she started to think she was overreacting, she imagined some stranger's car door opening. A stranger's hand beckoning to the boys. A random encounter that would have changed so many lives. And she'd allowed it to almost happen. It *hadn't* happened. But almost...
Her stomach rolled. Max must hate her now.

He loves you.

Maybe. He hadn't said the words, but how could she love someone as much as she loved that man and *not* have him love her back? Her heart wouldn't do that to her. She couldn't be that wrong.

The question was, did Max *still* love her? *Should* he still love her? And if he did, should she let him? This circular thinking wasn't helping her one bit. She needed to sleep. She moved to the living room and sprawled on the sofa, turning on the gas fireplace and pulling a blanket over her. The fake crackling sounds soothed her to sleep, as did the warmth and her complete exhaustion.

She was on her second cup of coffee and third phone call the next morning when she heard a loud knock on the front door. She knew it was Max—she'd seen him walking across the driveway.

"Connie, I have to go. I'm sure Mrs. Waverly will work out just fine playing piano for the pageant. The music is right there on the piano, and she agreed to be there this afternoon for rehearsal. I'm sorry, but I think this is best for everyone." She swiped to end the call before the assistant principal could argue, then crossed another line off on her to-do list as she stood.

Max knocked again. She took a deep breath before opening the door. He looked as exhausted as she felt, with deep shadows under his eyes. He studied her face, his mouth thinning in disapproval.

"Jesus, Grace. You look worse than me. I'm sorry—"

She stepped back, throwing her hand up in front of her. "Don't! Don't you dare apologize to *me* after what I did."

He moved as if to step forward, then stopped when she didn't budge. "Grace, let me come in. We need to talk. We should have talked last night, and that's what I'm sorry about. I never should have left you alone all night."

No, you shouldn't have.

The thought surprised her. She hadn't even realized how angry she was with Max until this moment. He *had* left her alone. At the time, she'd figured it was what she'd deserved, but now her spine was stiffening.

"You could have at least answered my calls. I had to hear what happened from your sister."

"I know," he said. He rubbed the back of his neck, looking down. "I really am sorry. I… I just kind of shut down. It wasn't fair to you. Or kind." He met her gaze again. "But I'm here now. Can we talk?"

She hesitated, then stepped aside to let him in, taking in his clean, spicy scent as he walked past her. It took all her strength not to reach out and touch him. He sat on the sofa and patted the cushion next to him, but she gave a sharp shake of her head and sat in the wingback chair. She didn't trust herself to be too close. Otherwise she'd never be able to do the next item on her to-do list…

Break up with Max.

Chapter Nineteen

He hated seeing how pale Grace was. She'd obviously been crying. A lot. Max's heart constricted. He'd known how upset she'd been yesterday, and he hadn't been there for her.

"Grace…"

"No. Let me talk."

Her hands were clenched together in her lap, and she was looking down at them rather than at him. He had a feeling she'd been rehearsing whatever she was about to say, and that he wasn't going to like it one bit. Her mouth tightened, reminding him of the first time he'd met her at the picket fence between their yards, primly lecturing him on the rules he was breaking. In complete control. So unlike the woman who'd pushed him up against the forge wall and ripped the buttons from his shirt in her haste to make love to him last week. Her eyebrows lowered.

"What I did yesterday was unforgivable—"

"No—"

"Let me talk. I need to say this." Her voice sharpened. "I didn't just lose track of *one* boy, I lost track of *three* little boys. I was so obsessed with the pageant that I…"

She finally looked at him, her eyes so full of pain that he had to glance away. "I was *glad* when they left the auditorium. The first thing I thought was that I had peace and quiet to work."

"You thought they were in the school library—"

"But I didn't *know* that. I should have known for *sure*, Max. They were my responsibility, and I failed."

"Babe, you couldn't have known they'd leave the school building without telling you." He saw the wince of pain in her eyes when he called her *babe*. She must have been beating herself up all night long. "I shouldn't have shut you out last night. You didn't deserve that."

He'd been so afraid of what he might say to her last night under the stress of not knowing where Tyler was, however briefly. But he could see now that his silence had done far more damage than any words would have.

"I *did* deserve it," she said softly. "It hurt, but my God, compared to what could have happened—"

"Nothing happened." He slid across the sofa until he could reach out and take her hands in his. She fought it for a moment, then let him hold her cold fingers in his. "Look at me, Grace. Listen to me. *Nothing happened.* Everyone is just fine, except for you and me. And I'm as responsible for that as you are. The minute I woke up this morning, I knew it. I was one hundred percent focused on Tyler and me last night. In my mind, I'd put up a huge brick wall around the house and was ready to fight anything that might harm him. Look at me." This time he waited until she did. "I'm new at this dad business. I'd never felt anything like that before. The sheer terror. The way I wanted to rip this town to splinters in order to find my son. I mean, I've felt paternal feelings and love for Tyler, but nothing like—"

Grace had tears running down her cheeks. He shook his head at his verbal clumsiness.

"I'm not telling you this to make you feel any worse. It was that brand-new feeling that scared me as much as what happened. I didn't know what to do with all of that emotion, and…" He swallowed hard. "Well, I handled it badly. I should have included you *inside* that fortress I built, not outside."

"But you didn't." It wasn't an accusation. Just a statement of fact, delivered calmly. Three little words that cut sharper than any of his blades could.

"No. I didn't. But—"

"I think we need to stop whatever it is we're doing." She pulled her hands from his. She didn't look devastated anymore. She looked cool and composed and very sure of herself. Full-on Grace mode. Which meant he was in real trouble here.

"Stop what, exactly?"

"We were never going to work long-term, Max." She pulled her shoulders back, sitting up straight. "We both agreed in the beginning—no commitments, no relationships, just sex. We should have left it at that, rather than…" Her voice trailed off.

Was she going to say *rather than falling in love*? Because that's what they'd done. He knew *he* had, and he was sure she had, too. Before he could ask, she'd regrouped and started again.

"You told me once that you and Tyler were a package deal. Instant family, remember?"

"Of course."

"Well, after yesterday, it's clear that I'm not ready for that."

"Grace, you made one innocent mistake—"

"Is that how you'd be phrasing it if something worse had happened?" He hesitated just long enough for her to notice. She gave him a sad smile. "And this isn't just about what happened yesterday. It's about the future. You know me—follow the rules, everything in its place. You joke about it, but that's who I am. It's not compatible with parenthood. I'd be a terrible mother, hovering and scolding and controlling. I'd make Tyler miserable, and that would make *you* miserable."

"No—" He talked over her attempt to stop him. "I'm trying to hear you, but you need to hear me, too. You're talking about being a mom to Tyler as if it's something that will happen in the future. As if you haven't already *been* a maternal figure for him. And in these past few weeks, you haven't been at all what you just described. You've taught him how to make cookies and let him make a mess of your kitchen, you've giggled through movies with him and let him eat popcorn in your living room." He could almost see his words bouncing off of her. She was refusing to accept them. He gestured toward her. "You volunteered to run his holiday play, for cryin' out loud!"

"Not anymore."

"What?"

"Eleanor Waverly is taking over. I don't know what I was thinking, trying to manage a group of children that young. I'm not cut out for it, and I've made a mess of things. I picked the wrong program for that age group, and it's probably beyond saving at this point. But they might have a chance without me—"

"Stop it." Max straightened, his voice sharpening. "Knock off the pity party, Grace. It doesn't suit you. And neither does quitting. You're not a quitter."

"It's not about pity. I'm doing what's best for the school. For the kids. For *your* kid. And yes, it will be a relief for me. It was a bad idea from the start."

"You loved it."

"I loved the *idea* of it. I had this image in my head of this perfect pageant of perfect children and perfect music, and everyone would be..."

He sighed heavily. "I understand why you like—why you *need*—everything to be neat and orderly. Why you want people, even children, to follow rules and behave rationally. I understand why it frightens you when that doesn't happen. It makes sense after what you went through. But Grace, it's not realistic. I know that you know that." He leaned forward, taking her hands again, rubbing them to warm them. "You could have stopped living your life after being shot. You could have become a hermit and never left your house again. You could have never made friends, never made a career, never become a leader in your community. No one would have blamed you. But you *did* create a life for yourself. You never let that bastard hold you back. Until now."

She blinked a few times. "What?"

"You're using that attack as an excuse to avoid the biggest risk of all—loving me. Loving my son."

Grace huffed a soft laugh. "Too late for that."

His pulse jumped. Did she mean...?

She nodded. "I love you both. I think you already

know that. But I can't… I'm not cut out for…" She met his gaze straight on. "I just can't do it."

"You mean you *won't* do it." This emotional roller coaster was even more painful than last night's. Because Grace was *choosing* not to be with him. He sat back, thought for a moment, then stood, doing his best to harness the anger and hurt rising inside him. "Look, I'm not going to beg you to do something you refuse to do. I'm in love with you. But if you can't even try to love me in return—"

She rose to her feet and clutched his arm. "Max, I am completely, over the moon, lost in love with you. But that doesn't mean we're going to work as a…as a family. I don't want us to fail…"

"And we can't fail if we never start, right?" His irritation—or was it panic?—was rising along with his voice. Her emotions were high, too. Her eyes narrowed in anger.

"It's not just me, you know." She poked him in the chest. "You shut me out last night."

"I apologized for that! That's why I came over here, remember?"

"That doesn't change the fact that it happened. When things were at their darkest for us, you shut me out. You say I'm quitting, but maybe I just can't bear the thought of being discarded like that again."

They stared at each other for a long moment in silence so heavy that the ticking of the antique mantel clock sounded like it was echoing around them in the room. Max ran his fingers through his hair, staring down at the floor, feeling both desperate and defensive.

"Grace, I need someone who's not going to give up every time things go wrong."

There was another pause before Grace nodded slowly.

"And I need someone who doesn't shut me out when things go wrong. I know Tyler will always come first. I don't want to change that, but where do *I* fit into the equation? At your side through thick and thin, or just after dark or when it's convenient?"

"That's not fair. Tyler *is* first for me. But you and I..."

A soft smile made the corners of her mouth rise, but there was no joy in her eyes.

"I think it's just bad timing for us. You need to be focused on building a life with Tyler. You've gone through a lot of changes this year. Maybe you and I were one change too many. And that's okay." She blinked quickly. "Really. It would be different if at least one of us knew what we were doing, but...you're overwhelmed and I'm in over my head. I think we need to step back and... and hit pause."

"I don't want to do that, Grace."

"I know." She reached up and cupped his cheek with her hand. "But we each have a lot to think about, and I think we need to do that away from each other."

He wanted to fight for their relationship, but she'd made some valid points. They hadn't acted as a family last night. More specifically, *he* hadn't acted like they were family. He hated that he'd hurt Grace that way. He needed to take time to think about why he'd shut her out. Fear? Revenge? Neither reason boded well for forming a family together. He needed time, and she'd only suggested a pause. Not an end. Not yet.

"Okay. But this is only a pause. A chance to think

about what we're doing. Where we're going. This is not goodbye." He put his hand over hers, which was still against his face. "I'm not saying goodbye, Grace. I won't do that."

She pressed her lips together, her forehead furrowing. Then she nodded.

"A pause."

She didn't say more, but he knew in his heart that she'd wanted to say something else. He could see it in her eyes. She was ready to walk away. She'd agreed to the pause. But what she'd stopped herself from saying was...

We're done.

The next knock that came on Grace's door was lighter, but more frantic. She checked the time—four o'clock. Tyler was here for his lesson. He was glaring when she opened the door.

"Where *were* you today? Why weren't you at school? Micah said you *quit*, but I told him he was lying. Then Mrs. Waverly scolded me and said Micah *wasn't* lying."

"Come in, Tyler. I want to teach you the rest of that Christmas song today."

He brushed by her. "I don't want to learn a song. I want you to come back to school!" He turned, and his dark eyes brimmed with tears. "Did I get you in trouble?"

She hesitated. She'd always been honest with Tyler, and that wouldn't change now. "Well, honey, a lot of people were scared when we couldn't find you yesterday. Including your dad and me. We were upset, because we care about you so much."

Large, shimmering tears rolled down his cheeks. "I

didn't mean to scare people. I just wanted to go to the library."

Grace sat on the sofa and pulled Tyler into her lap. "But you knew you shouldn't have left the school by yourself."

"Isaac and Micah were with me." His head dropped. "At first." She didn't want to pile on, so she stayed silent. He finally looked up at her. "I'm sorry, Grace."

She hugged him tight, and he began to sob on her shoulder. If telling Max to leave broke her heart, this little boy was shattering the remaining pieces into dust. She held him, rocking back and forth as he cried, making soothing noises without saying anything. She didn't trust herself to speak without breaking into tears herself, which would just upset him more.

So she held him, and told herself this was why she wasn't cut out for parenthood *or* step-parenthood. Children broke rules—testing boundaries was part of being a child. But that testing, and the consequences, like this sobbing child and the argument with Max… Well, that was too much for her to bear.

"Hey! Grace, wait up!" The voice was familiar, and she wanted so much to ignore it. But Lexi Knight was five months pregnant and was still fast enough to catch up as Grace walked the beach. She turned and waited as Lexi jogged the last few steps.

Grace had hoped for some alone time, but she realized now that she should have anticipated company when she walked past the Sassy Mermaid Motor Lodge and saw Phyllis waving cheerily at her. She'd bet money Phyllis had immediately called her daughter.

It had been five days since she'd told Max they were on pause. He'd honored that, not calling or texting. One afternoon, he'd been outside as she pulled in after work, and he'd given her a casual wave, as if they were barely acquaintances. It was everything she'd asked for. It made her feel miserable.

"I didn't think I was going to catch you," Lexi said with a smile as she caught her breath. "This little basketball—" she patted her bulging stomach "—puts me off balance when I try to run these days."

"Should you be running at all?" Grace heard the judgment in her own voice. "I'm sorry, I didn't mean—"

"To suggest I shouldn't have tried to catch you?" Lexi smiled as they started walking together. It was a chilly December day, but it was sunny and the winds were almost nonexistent for once. It was the proverbial calm before the snowstorm being predicted for the weekend. "You did look like you wanted to be alone," Lexi continued, "but it was either me or my mom, and she'd have been way more pushy than I'll be."

Grace stared out at the ocean, with soft rolling waves lapping the beach. "Your mother is one of a kind," she conceded.

Lexi laughed. "That's one way to put it. Look, you know what I want to talk about, but first—how are you?"

"I'm fine."

"Ooh...*fine*. Hitting the pause button is that bad, huh?"

The Bellamy women were nothing if not direct. There was no point in trying to convince Max's sister that she was happy she and Max were through. Lexi had seen them together, and she'd never believe it.

"To be honest," Grace started, "it's been hard for me. But it was the right thing to do."

"Dumping my brother? Tell me why you think that was right—" she put her hand on Grace's arm "—and to be clear, I'm not here to defend him to you. I'm genuinely curious what happened. The two of you seemed solid."

"I guess looks can be deceiving." She'd thought they were solid, too. "We both had our doubts about this relationship to start with, and we were right. It just isn't going to work. I'm not cut out for being responsible for children, and he's not cut out for commitment. It was always going to end at some point, and after I made such a mess, it was time."

"How did *you* make a mess?"

"Seriously? Did you not hear that I lost the man's son?"

"That wasn't your..." Lexi's hesitation pierced Grace. "Okay, you lost track of him, but everything I've read and heard about parenting..." She patted her belly again. "And I've been doing a *lot* of research. Anyway, I've learned it's not that uncommon. Kids misbehave. Parents don't pay attention for a nanosecond."

"But that's what I'm not cut out for. Dealing with misbehavior and the unexpected. That's why I decided a long time ago to not even think about becoming a mom. Something like that triggers every fear inside of me. I was a wreck."

"Max doesn't blame you—"

"Max *should* blame me, and he *did* blame me that night. He was furious."

Lexi stopped and faced Grace. "He was *scared*. Just

like you were. And the whole time, Tyler was with my mom and perfectly safe. Nothing bad happened."

"But it *could* have."

"But it *didn't*."

Grace refused to concede, walking off. "Children are too much responsibility for me to handle. Give me a spreadsheet or sheet music, and I'm fine. All those lines give me structure. Kids?" She threw her hands up. "Zero structure."

"But you were running the school holiday pageant, with lots of no-structure children."

"You're proving my point. I failed at that, too, and quit. I'd lost control of those kids."

"Your only failure was in quitting. The kids all miss you and want you back."

She looked at Lexi. "How do you know that?"

"Because Max took your place."

She stopped cold, her mouth dropping open in surprise. "*Max?* I left Mrs. Waverly in charge of it."

"Girl, Eleanor Waverly is pushing eighty! She can pound the piano keys, but she can't control that many children alone. So Tyler volunteered Max, and he stepped in to organize things while she plays the music."

Grace closed her eyes, turning her face to catch the sun's warmth as she tried to envision Max with that many kids. A smile twitched at the corners of her mouth. It was an unfamiliar sensation after the past week.

"And how is that going?"

Lexi shook her head and laughed softly. "About as good as you're imagining. He looks exhausted, but he says they're all having fun. He said something about dinosaurs…"

Grace smiled for real at that. They turned to head back toward the Sassy Mermaid.

"That supports what I said before—Max has embraced fatherhood, and it's beautiful to see. He's a natural with children. But adult relationships…"

"Oh, yeah," Lexi nodded. "Max is pretty bad with those. Didn't my mom or I ever tell you that? He's an idiot."

"Well, I wouldn't say—"

Lexi cut her off before she started defending him. "No, he's an idiot. For real. Back in his twenties, he used to insist that humans weren't meant to have monogamous relationships. He said it wasn't natural. That's why he's always ready to cut and run."

"Because of your father?"

Lexi's face looked pinched, then she nodded. "He's never seen a successful relationship to model himself after. Even though I was older, Max saw more of the problems in our parents' marriage than I did. Probably because he was a boy, and hung out with our father more. Our dad fooled around a lot more than I realized until I was in my twenties, but Max always knew."

Grace nodded, remembering when Max told her the stories. "Your dad used to swear him to secrecy if another woman was around, telling him not to tell your mom. He told Max that was what men did, like it was some kind of bro code to cover for each other."

Lexi muttered a curse. "Did I mention Max inherited his idiocy from our father? I didn't know Dad outright told him to lie to Mom, though. Ugh!" She swore again. "I'm trying to keep my relationship going with our dad, but he sure doesn't make it easy. He came to my wedding with his latest Sweet Young Thing on his arm. She's not the one he claimed to be in love with when he divorced Mom, but he insists *this* one is the real deal. I'll give him credit—unlike the last one, she's older than his three children by a few years." She looked at Grace. "But you can see why Max isn't very confident about commitment."

"I *can* see why. Just like there's a reason for my attachment to order and consistency. The problem is that those two things aren't compatible. I need a deep commitment, and he can't give it. And he has a child, which means he needs someone who's flexible instead of rigid. We aren't right for one another."

"That's a load of bull."

"Excuse me?"

They were at the base of the stairs up to the motel property. Because of the warm day, there were more dark, shiny seals sunning themselves on the rocks than usual. A few of them raised their heads to look at Grace and Lexi, then their heads dropped again, uninterested.

"Grace," Lexi started. "You and Max both have good reasons *not* to be compatible. And they're genuine, valid reasons. Max hasn't seen a committed relationship work long-term, and you had a horrible experience when rules weren't followed, so you need structure."

They headed up the wooden stairs. Grace didn't speak until they reached the top. She followed Lexi to the observation deck built above the rocks and they sat in the Adirondack chairs there.

"I'm confused," Grace finally said. "You called BS on me, then repeated all the reasons why I'm right about us not being compatible."

Lexi held up one hand and shook her head. "I didn't say you *were* incompatible. I said you both have reasons *not* to be compatible. You each also have one big reason to *be* compatible."

Grace's forehead furrowed. "What's that?"

Lexi gave her a pointed look. "Come on. You're in love with each other. Anyone who knows you can see it."

Her heart jumped in her chest, fanning a spark of hope before her head spoiled it. "Love can only do so much."

The breeze blew Lexi's auburn hair around her face, and she pushed it back behind her ear with one hand, staring out at the ocean. The silence between them stretched to the point of being uncomfortable before she looked at Grace, her expression still serious.

"Love can do whatever you give it permission to do. It can change you, if you let it. It happened with Sam and me. It can happen with you and Max, too."

Chapter Twenty

On one hand, Max was glad for the distraction the school pageant provided. It was keeping him too busy to spend all his time missing Grace and wondering if she was right about them never working. Maybe she *had* just been another temporary port in the storm of his life. Maybe they'd always been destined to be temporary, as they'd agreed at the start. Or maybe he'd keep missing her with every fiber of his soul for the rest of his life.

And on the *other* hand, this pageant was very likely going to break him. He'd figured out how to deal with *one* little boy, and he was feeling good about how things were going at home with Tyler and him. But right now he was looking at a couple *dozen* little boys and girls, and it was terrifying. So many opinions, spoken so very loudly. Sometimes through tears. It was…a lot.

But he'd agreed to step up to replace Grace, and he was a man of his word. At the time, of course, he'd made some assumptions he could now see were not true. He'd assumed the pageant was rehearsed and ready to go with a few more practice sessions. That was *not* the case. The script Grace had purchased was too advanced for these kids, and apparently she'd told some of them that she was going to rework it. But then she'd quit, without leaving any notes on what to rework.

Mrs. Waverly had been at the school for so long that Sam said she'd been his second-grade teacher. She could play piano well enough, if not with Grace's artistry. She was small and wiry, always in dresses, with gold wire-rimmed glasses and short silver hair framing her face.

The woman had no interest in getting creative with the program. She'd tap the sheet music sharply with her pencil whenever he tried changing anything, even if it was just shortening the songs by a verse or two. He had five days left to make this thing work. He was beginning to understand why Grace threw in the towel.

"Micah, I'm sure you'd make a great astronaut, but what does that have to do with *Holidays Around the World*?" That was the title of the program.

"Space is all around the world," the boy replied. Pretty smart for a second grader.

Tyler nodded enthusiastically. "Yeah! And dragons were on the world."

Micah's little brother, and Tyler's pal, Isaac joined in. "And *zombies* are in the world!"

There was a chorus of voices.

"I could be a fireman—they're on the world, too!"

"I wanna be an angel. Does that count?"

"Can I be a butterfly?"

"Can I be a bear?"

"I could be a bumblebee!"

"Okay, I get it." He held up his hands. "But those aren't holiday characters. You're supposed to be angels and snowmen and dreidels and candles."

Chantal King was sitting on the floor, and she looked

up at Max, her beaded braids brushing her shoulder. "Why can't I be a butterfly Kwanzaa candle? And Tyler could be a dragon snowman!"

Max dropped his head in defeat, his eyes closed tightly. He had to make this work somehow. There had to be a way to keep almost all the kids happy. He thought about Chantal's suggestion. Would it be against any laws to have them talk about holidays while in costumes that didn't match the holiday? *Could* there be a zombie dreidel?

"Max?" Tyler's small hand touched his arm. "Grace said she was working on easier songs that day she was here late. Stuff we already knew."

"Grace must have taken those notes home with her, because I haven't seen them, son."

Tyler was beginning to bounce back from the change in things between Max and Grace. He'd skipped a few piano lessons but said he wanted to go back next week. It would be awkward, but Max and Grace were grownups who could put their problems aside for Tyler. They could pretend everything was fine twice a week for his sake. Tyler pointed to the piano where Eleanor Waverly sat, waiting for someone to tell her what to play.

"Her notes are in the big book," Tyler said. Eleanor flipped through the pages and started to shake her head because nothing was there. Then a sheet of paper fluttered out from the back of the book. She held it at arm's length, squinting through her glasses.

"This might be the new music list," she said, waving the paper. Max went over to check it out, biting his tongue not to ask why she hadn't looked for it before, when he'd *asked* if she'd seen any notes from Grace.

The list had references to pages of dialogue in the program, but instead of all the original, more advanced songs, Grace had added a list of familiar tunes in her neat handwriting. "Jingle Bells." "Frosty the Snowman." "Menorah Candles." The last one had a note in parentheses—*tune is "Twinkle Twinkle Little Star."* He could work with that.

The kids had a point. They could be dressed as anything and still sing the songs. They'd just have to figure out an explanation. He turned back to Tyler and his band of misfit toys... Wait just a minute. That was it! Whatever their characters were, they could be *toys.* Like the movie, but for Christmas and Hanukkah and all the other holidays.

This might just work!

"Okay, gang." Max waved to get their attention. "If I can figure out a way for you to be whatever you want to be, will you work extra hard to learn these songs?"

The kids all cheered, except little Amelia Mendez.

"But I *want* to be a Christmas angel!" Tears welled in her dark eyes.

"Honey, you can still be an angel. About the only thing we'll have to think twice about is the zombies."

Negotiating with five-year-olds was simple, he realized. You just gave them whatever they wanted in the first place, then figured out how to work around it. Easy-peasy.

Mrs. Waverly cleared her throat behind him. "This is a *Christmas* pageant, not Halloween."

"This is a *holiday* pageant, with multiple holidays being celebrated. And I have a plan." The elderly woman didn't look convinced, but she sat back and started flipping through a different songbook.

"I have music for the songs Grace chose," she said. "We'll have to copy the lyrics for them."

They came up with a plan for the next rehearsal, and he told the kids that he'd create a new, simplified script by then. When the bell rang, they rushed out of the auditorium in a noisy, chaotic gaggle of energy. Mrs. Waverly followed them far more slowly.

He was going to need help. He was a blacksmith, not a writer. His first thought was to call Grace, but there were two reasons he couldn't. First, he'd promised to give her the space she wanted during their pause. It went against every grain of his being, but if that's what she wanted, he had to give it to her. Secondly, going off script would be against everything she valued. He could imagine her saying *the script is there for a reason.* He smiled as he picked up the music books the kids had left all over the stage.

He loved her love of structure and order. He hated the reasons behind it. Hated that she'd come so close to being murdered by a random stranger. But her desire for order was part of her story. She'd used it as her armor so she could face the world and live her life. And it worked. Maybe too well, but he still understood it.

What he hadn't figured out was how to break through that armor and convince her that she could trust him to stand by her. Yes, he'd blamed her for Tyler's disappearance. Said things in the panic and heat of the moment that he regretted. And then, he'd just…*accepted* her decision to end things. It was her choice to make, so he had no choice but to honor it. Pushing her to change her mind would be wrong. *Wouldn't it?*

He'd had dinner with Sam and Lexi two nights ago, and they shared what broke them up at one point—Sam's downright phobia about change because of a trauma in his past. And what brought them back together—a giant gesture on Sam's part to win Lexi back. He'd made a bold change in his life to convince her he was ready to commit.

Max dropped the programs in a box and went backstage in the auditorium to see what props and costumes might be available there for the new pageant plan. He understood what Sam and Lexi were saying, even if he'd always thought big, bold gestures like that only worked in the movies. He wasn't a grand gesture sort of guy, though. Granted, he didn't have a lot of experience with healthy relationships, but in his mind, neither person should have to *prove* their love or commitment. Good relationships should just...work.

Maybe he'd been right years ago when he'd claimed that humans weren't created to be monogamous. Maybe even good relationships just...ended. That sounded logical when he ran it through his head, but his heart had something to say about it. His heart couldn't imagine a future without Grace Bennett in it. And not as just some vaguely polite neighbor who waved and walked away.

Grace, Tyler and Max felt like a *family*. He checked the costumes on a hanging rack and made some mental notes on which ones could be used as toy characters. Tyler would want to be a dragon, which wasn't a problem, since he still had his Halloween costume at home.

Max thought about Halloween night, when Grace had

opened her door and pretended to be so frightened at Tyler's costume. She and Max had laughed together, and her smile had lit up the night for him. They'd shared their first kiss by then, and he'd burned with anticipation for more than that. Sure, they'd agreed *not* to go any further. But that agreement had fallen by the wayside within days.

He paused, his hand on feathery white angel wings. Did that mean there was hope for this damn pause to come to an end? Or had she already decided that a family was truly too much for her? She'd always been worried about it. *Chaos monsters.* That was how she'd viewed children. And yet, she'd stepped up and agreed to lead the holiday program at school, pushing herself way outside her comfort zone.

He moved the angel costume to hang near the snowman costume. What had *he* done to go outside his comfort zone with Grace? Had he treated their relationship as something permanent? Or had he always, in the back of his mind, figured it would end eventually? Which meant he hadn't acted any different with her than with any other woman. They slept together, they had meals together, they did fun things together. But had he *committed* anything to Grace at all? Had he shown her how much he loved her, or had he just glided along, letting nature take its course?

There was a wooden chair in the costume room, and he reached for it as his legs went weak. Damn it, had he simply…let Grace go? Did he think it was what he deserved? Should he do something—grand or small—to make it clear how much he wanted her back in his life? For the long haul. He pulled his phone out.

"Mom?" he said when she answered. "I need help. Advice. A knock on the head. Something. Anything." He took in a ragged breath, panicked at the idea of losing Grace for good. "Can we talk?"

"Come right over, honey. Tell me what you're thinking, and I'll decide what you need most. Hopefully *not* a smackdown, but if so, I promise I'll do it."

His hand was shaking as he slid the phone back in his pocket. He already knew what he needed most. He needed Grace.

Grace did *not* want to go to the school pageant. For one thing, she was embarrassed that she'd quit so abruptly. For another, she knew Max had taken her place, and it would be too painful to see him there. They still hadn't spoken much, just a few hellos. Max had continued to be respectful of their pause. And Grace continued to be annoyed by that. Illogical, but she couldn't help it.

She'd had good reason to end things—she wasn't cut out for any sort of parenting role, and that was a job requirement for anyone dating Max Bellamy. And now, it seemed Max hadn't been that into her, anyway. He'd just…stopped when she asked him to. As if it was no bother. As if he hadn't really fallen in love with her after all. As if she'd misread everything.

So no, she had zero desire to be at the school pageant.

And yet, here she was—walking through the school entrance, along with half the residents of Winsome Cove. It was Maya who'd forced the issue. Not physically, of course, even though she had her arm firmly locked with Grace's right now. She'd insisted that Grace would be full of regrets if she missed it. Not only was Tyler going to be in it, but so was Chantal, who Grace had known since birth. And Grace had come to know all the other children, and they would all want to see her there—especially Tyler.

Then Tyler himself had begged her to come when he saw her outside a few days ago. Grace had assured him that the change in her relationship with Max had nothing to do with anything Tyler had done, and that his father and she were still friends and neighbors. The boy used that to say that if they were friends, then she should come to the pageant to support Max.

"It's a secret," Tyler had whispered.

"The pageant? Honey, the whole town knows it's happening this Friday."

"No, what we're *doing* is a secret!" He'd leaned in close to her side. "There are going to be monsters, but don't tell anyone, because it's a secret!"

Five-year-olds had a very loose relationship with the definitions of some words, and she had to smile at the way Tyler seemed to think whispering the news made it a secret. She wondered if he was just making up the whole idea of monsters, but his excitement seemed genuine.

"Tyler, how are there going to be monsters in a holiday pageant? You mean snow monsters, like in the Rudolph cartoon?" Even that was something that hadn't been in the program when she left.

"Well, yeah, he'll be there, but *other* monsters will be there, too! Martians from space, and—" his eyes were wide as he whispered again "—I'm gonna be a dragon. But it's a secret."

Grace had managed to resist Maya's pleas until that conversation. Curiosity got the best of her, and she'd agreed to come. But she insisted she was going to stand in the back of the auditorium, where she could slip out if she felt the urge. Where she wouldn't be seen by many people. She was still feeling bad about the whole quitting thing. That wasn't like her. She'd panicked after losing the boys that day, and once she'd quit, there was no good way to rescind it without looking even more ridiculous.

And now there were monsters in the holiday program...

"Grace!" Phyllis Bellamy shouted her name across the packed school lobby. "Come on over—we saved you a seat!" Phyllis was waving wildly, which was unnecessary considering she was dressed in a battery-operated Christmas sweater that had literal blinking tree lights on it. Something sparkly, like tinsel, was clipped into her hair, which was looking a little more holiday red than pink at the moment. The woman truly did not care what anyone thought of her. Grace begrudgingly admired that about Phyllis. Fred Knight was at her side, watching Phyllis with a mixture of awe and trepidation. He looked like a man handling explosive material, who wasn't at all sure what was about to happen with it.

But he was there, in public, as Phyllis's apparent date. Grace had never known Fred well, but he was a fixture in Winsome Cove, and she knew this was *way* out of character for him. His wife had been gone for years now, so it wasn't that unusual for a man to begin dating again. But Fred had been known for his surliness *during* his marriage, even though he worshipped the ground his late wife had walked on. Since her death, she'd heard he'd become even crustier. And yet, at Thanksgiving dinner, he'd been playing jokes with Tyler. There was a softness in his eyes these days that said something had changed him. That Phyllis may have changed him. The Bellamys had a way of doing that to people.

Maya patted her shoulder and gave her a not-so-subtle shove in their direction. "They saved a seat for you, hon. Don't be rude to family."

"They're not my—" But Maya and Leon were gone into the crowd. Leaving Grace with no choice but to wave back at Phyllis and head her way. Lexi walked up at the same time that Grace did.

"Well, look who decided to show up!" She started to give Grace a sharp look, then immediately laughed and hugged her. "Oh, crap, I can't even *pretend* to be mad at you. Blame it on the baby hormones—my truth meter is at one hundred percent these days. But be warned, sometimes that includes truth that hurts. Sam said he didn't think I could *get* any more forthright, but here I am, going for it!" She held Grace at arm's length. "I'm mad that you two haven't fixed this yet, but it's good to see you."

"Leave her alone, Lexi. She and Max will figure things out eventually." Grace started to protest, but Phyllis talked right over her. "Wait until you see what Max cooked up with these kids. I helped with a few costumes, so I got to see the dress rehearsal—it's adorable."

"I heard something about a dragon?" Grace said, as Phyllis enveloped her in a hug. "But I'm told it was a secret."

Phyllis squeezed her tight and laughed. "I warned Max that the more he told those kindergartners *not* to tell anyone, the more those kids would *have* to tell someone." She stepped back and waved a hand in Fred's direction. "And Fred decided to join us."

She shook the hand he extended. "Nice to see you here, Fred."

He scoffed. "*Surprised* to see me here, you mean. Well, me, too. I thought my school play days ended when my son graduated, and Devlin's pushing forty. But some people won't take no for an answer." He looked straight at Phyllis, who just shrugged.

"My *grandson* is in this pageant. And since your nephew is married to my daughter, that makes Tyler your…cousin-in-law…or nephew once removed or… something. He's *family*. And people show up for family. Period."

"Is Sam here?" Grace asked, trying to move away from all the family talk.

"Oh, sure. He and Devlin are helping Max backstage. Carm is back there, too." Phyllis waved a finger at Fred. "I still say there's something between Carm and your boy. But they're all Team Max tonight." She paused. "Someone had to be."

"Mom!" Lexi gasped. "You just scolded me for saying I wanted them to fix things, and now you're the one making her feel bad." She patted Grace's arm. "Although I'm sure if you went backstage, they'd accept your help."

Grace shook her head sharply. "I'd just be in the way. Besides, we all know how inept I am with children."

"That's a bunch of nonsense, and you know it." Phyllis was serious. "None of us know what we're doing when we become parents…" She winked. "Or stepparents. But we learn. And we get help from other parents. And we see what the children respond to best." She nudged Lexi with her shoulder. "This one was my head-strong but responsible oldest child. She was stubborn, and Lord knew she had a temper from day one, but she responded to being needed. She liked being a leader, so I worked with that and used it to motivate good behavior."

"Gee, thanks, Mom." Lexi rolled her eyes.

"With my middle child, Max..." She frowned. "Max was headstrong, but much more independent. He didn't want to lead, but he sure didn't want to be bossed around, either. He preferred doing his own thing, and I did my best to allow that, as long as he was safe. And my young-est, Jenny... Well, she's—"

"—the princess," Lexi finished.

"I really tried not to spoil her," Phyllis protested with a laugh.

"We *all* spoiled her, Mom. I treated her like one of my dolls. Max was ready to fight any kid who even thought about giving her trouble." Lexi shrugged at Grace. "But somehow she didn't grow up to act spoiled."

"She's a teacher, right?" Grace asked.

"Yes," Phyllis said with a proud smile. "She knew she wanted to be a teacher before she started high school. And she wouldn't let anything, or anyone, stop her." She turned back to Grace. "My point is, every child is dif-ferent, and you figure out what's important to them and what motivates them, and that becomes part of your ap-proach."

"Phyllis, that sounds very wise, but also terrifying. At least to me." The lights dimmed a few times in the hallway outside the auditorium. "I'm the one who quit the school pageant because I couldn't handle the chal-lenge, remember?"

"You handled the kids just fine. You had a bad moment." They headed into the auditorium. "My son reacted badly to your bad moment. And you've both given up on each other far too easily." They took their seats, closer to the stage than Grace would have liked. As the lights dimmed a final time, she wondered if that was why Max hadn't tried to talk to her. Had he given up on them? Had she?

The curtain was just beginning to rise when she whispered to Phyllis, "If we both gave up, then the relationship wasn't strong enough to start with."

"Phfft!" Phyllis huffed, ignoring someone shushing them from a few rows back. "The relationship is just fine. It's *so* fine that it scares you both half to death. One of you will have to *do* something about that."

Chapter Twenty-One

Max watched as Sam tugged the rope that opened the red curtains shielding the stage. He wasn't breathing. Didn't want to watch. Couldn't look away. This would either be an epic disaster or a hilarious success. The kids, in all their various costumes, were lying on the stage like toys scattered beneath a Christmas tree. The tree was represented by a hastily painted curtain that Devlin and Carm had created with spray paint, glitter and fake pine garland. The audience began to giggle at the sight of a dragon—Tyler—lying on his side along with the other characters. Chantal was an astronaut. There were three dinosaurs. Two firefighters. A puppy. And, in addition to the non-holiday characters, there were also some sheep, angels and Tyler's friend Isaac, dressed as a dreidel. All lying down. Waiting for him.

It wasn't too late to make a run for it. But Sam must have read that thought, because he put his hand in the middle of Max's back and shoved him hard enough to send him stumbling onto the stage. His arrival brought more laughter from the audience.

Max was in costume, too—a long-tailed red jacket and tall hat, decorated by his mother and sister to make him look like the nutcracker from the famous ballet. Minus the tights, of course. His darkest jeans would have to do. Bright red circles were painted on his cheeks. He was in this thing now. No place to go but forward. He clutched a stack of index cards in one hand. They contained the entire script for the evening.

He took a stiff bow, waving his arm at the stage like a ringmaster. "Welcome, ladies and gentlemen!" He shouted the words and heard snickers from the kids at his feet. That made him smile, and smiling helped him relax. He wasn't expecting perfection, but they'd rehearsed enough this week that he thought—he *hoped*—they could pull this off. He raised his arm again. "The title of our program is *Holidays Around the World* and we know that holidays for children mean one thing.... *magic*. This time of year holds many holidays. We'll be visiting these holidays through the eyes of children. Or, I guess I should say through the *toys* of children. We associate kindness and children's gifts with many of our favorite holidays, including Christmas, where we find our toys gathered under the tree."

This was where the toys were supposed to start coming to life. But no one moved. He cleared his throat. "I *said*, it's *Christmas*, where we find our toys gathered under the *tree*!"

He nudged Tyler's foot, and the little dragon jumped up. As soon as he moved, the other children followed, standing to cheers and laughter from the audience.

Tyler began shouting his lines, even though microphones hung above the stage. "I AM A CHRISTMAS DRAGON!"

"Christmas *present*," Max whispered.

"I mean Christmas PRESENT!" There was scattered applause, and Tyler relaxed a bit and stopped yelling. "At Christmas, we give presents to people we love. Especially little kids!" More laughter at the subtle hint. Max whispered a few more lines to his son, who recited them. "The tradition started when kings brought gifts to a baby. Then Santa Claus came along with gifts for children."

Max pointed to Chantal, who stepped forward in her astronaut costume.

"I'm an ASTRONAUT!" She followed Tyler's example for volume. "I fly around the world! And I found *other* holidays!" Max whispered more lines for her to echo. "In India, they have *Dwally* before we have Thanksgiving!" She waved a battery-operated candle in the air.

Max reached forward to turn the candle on, then spoke to the audience. "Diwali is a Hindu holiday."

There was a huddle of children dressed as candles who now came out onto the stage, dancing the best they could in the cylindrical costumes. Devlin had the job of standing in front of the stage, making sure no one stumbled off, and he spread his arms wide to shoo the candles back a few steps.

Chantal shouted her last line. "*Dwally* has LIGHTS!"

Max laughed along with the audience. "Diwali is a festival of lights, and uses candles, just like Christmas does. And speaking of candles…" He pointed to Isaac, the dreidel, who stepped up and turned around like a spinning top as Max talked about Hanukkah. Max had to plunk his hand on the boy's head so he didn't fall over in his enthusiasm for spinning.

And so it went. The children shout-talked briefly

about Diwali, Thanksgiving—complete with pilgrims—Hanukkah, Christmas, Boxing Day and Kwanzaa. How they all used lights or candles in some way, even if just on the dinner table. How they all, at least from a child's point of view, had an element of giving attached to them. They sang one verse from a song for each holiday. There were a lot of giggles, only a brief moment of tears—when a snowman tripped over an angel. Max had to whisper so many lines to them from his index cards that his throat was sore.

The program was wrapping up, and he was grinning right along with all the other adults when he spotted Grace. She was sitting next to his mother, but he hadn't noticed her the first time he looked for Mom. Two of the little firefighters had been having a shoving match on stage, so he'd just waved quickly to his mother and broke up the two young girls before things got more physical. But once the singing started, things were less complicated for his emcee duties. He had time to look around.

This time, his eyes had gone straight to the blonde sitting between his mother and sister. She was watching the children, her eyes wide and hands clasped in delight as the candles, now wrapped in rich colors for Kwanzaa, twirled around him on stage as the other children sang. He couldn't look away from her. Not even when Devlin shouted a warning to the candles to stay away from the edge.

"Max! Catch the purple one! *Max!*"

Max flinched, then jumped to grab the girl in the purple candle before she twirled right off the stage. Once she was securely with the other candles, he looked for Grace again. She was staring right at him now, and her gaze stabbed him like a blazing hot sword fresh out of the fire. Not with pain, but with a sharp realization that he'd been a complete fool to think he could walk away from her. She was smiling, but there was a hesitation in her eyes. She wasn't sure of him.

This would be the last damn time *that* happened. Because he was suddenly more sure than he'd ever been in his life.

Grace was mesmerized by this wild, unpredictable and totally charming children's pageant. The costumes, so colorful and completely unconnected to each other. The stage, that changed with different backdrops for each holiday. The children, all *so* excited to be the characters they'd told her they wanted to be. And…it *worked*.

Max—handsome, smiling Max—had given in to the children, but figured out a way to make it all make sense in a nonsensical way that was adorable. And brilliant. He'd had help—Devlin was dashing around the front of the stage, acting as a human safety net. Phyllis had leaned over early in the program to explain how she and Lexi had created Max's nutcracker costume with some thrift shop finds and lots of glitter. She said they'd also helped with the children's costumes, and that Sam was managing things backstage.

It was completely chaotic. Loud. Colorful. It was also educational and respectful of each holiday. More importantly, most of the children looked *thrilled* to be there. Little Tommy Milton looked terrified, as usual, but he was in the back row where he could escape if he really felt he needed to. His lips were moving a little, so he was at least trying to sing. Grace smiled. Max had even been able to get poor, shy Tommy to be part of this.

They'd gone way off the original script. They were only using a handful of the suggested costumes—a list which had never included dinosaurs. She should be losing her mind right now at the audacity. Instead, her hands were clasped under her chin as she took in every chaotic detail. She loved every bit of it.

Especially the sexy nutcracker emcee in the too-small red jacket and the ridiculous plastic top hat covered with tinsel and glitter. She thought he was ignoring her at first, when he gave a quick wave to Phyllis, then looked away. But the surprise on his face when their eyes met just now told her that he'd somehow missed seeing her before. His mouth opened and closed a few times, like a guppy. He barely snapped out of it in time to catch little Ava Langley in her Kwanzaa candle costume right before she danced right off the stage and into Devlin's arms.

With that crisis averted, he'd looked back to Grace. And he'd smiled. Not a polite, neighborly smile. Not quite a peel-your-clothes-off smile, either—although there was heat in his eyes. But also...affection? She straightened. Love? Her heart jumped and leaped inside her chest. Could it be love? Not love on pause. Not love being careful. Not love living in fear.

The children finished singing the Menorah song. They looked up at Max, but he was still staring at her. Devlin said something, and Max blinked, looking back at the children. He cleared his throat, glanced back to Grace, then his smile deepened. He was going to go off script again, she just knew it. She leaned forward in eager anticipation.

"That was great, kids!" He joined in the audience's applause, then raised his hand for quiet. "Ladies and gentlemen, dragons and angels… I'd like to say something before this collection of misfit toys sings their last song." There were chuckles all around, but Grace wasn't laughing. She was waiting, barely able to breathe. He looked straight at her.

"Some of you may know that I've been seeing someone from Winsome Cove—my neighbor, Grace Bennett." There were a few gasps and giggles as heads turned toward her. "But then something happened, we handled it badly, and…well…she put us on pause. Ended what we had." There were sounds of sympathy. "And I let it happen. I mean, of course she had every right to do it, and I respected that, but… I gave up. I told myself that relationships are for fools, so of *course* it was over. It was inevitable. Better now than later, you know?" He paused. So that *was* why he'd walked away like it meant nothing to him. He hadn't fought for them because he'd been convinced they were doomed.

"But I was wrong. And so was she, but hey—I can only control my end of things." There was more laughter, but less of it, and it was less certain. Max shook his head. "My sister told me I'd need to do some grand gesture to win Grace back. My brother-in-law here—" he pointed at Sam, who was standing at the edge of the stage "—well, *he* redecorated his whole *house* to show my sister how much he loved her. But what am I supposed to do? Make an extra pretty sword for her? Look at her, folks. She deserves the world, but—"

"Get to the point, Bellamy!" Fred Knight yelled out the words, then gasped and coughed when Phyllis elbowed him hard in the ribs. He waved her off, though, and called out again. "You're rambling, boy. Do you love her or not?"

There was more laughter now, and Grace waited for Max's answer.

"This is my grand gesture, Grace." He spread his arms wide in the middle of the stage. "This is me, standing in front of the whole town, dressed like a nutcracker and telling you that I love you. I miss you, and I want us back. I want us together. Forever." He waved his hands. "Hell, forever isn't enough. I'm standing here and pronouncing that I want you by my side for *longer* than forever. We can do this, Grace. I believe in us. And I promise never to give up on us again, if you'll do the same. I love you." He gestured around the auditorium with his hand. "Grandly."

There was a burst of applause, and even the children were clapping. All Grace could do was nod, her vision blurred with tears. Max gestured to Mrs. Waverly to begin the final song, "We Wish You a Merry Christmas." Sam stepped out and led the singing, shoving Max toward the steps leading off the stage. He bolted down those stairs, and Grace met him in the aisle. He lifted her up and swung her around. Then he led her out of the auditorium and into the now quiet hallway. Where he took off his top hat and kissed her.

All of the pain and hurt of the past few weeks poured through that kiss and vanished in the face of the love they felt. Max's strong arms around her felt like home. When they parted, his hands cupped her face.

"We never do that again, okay? We never give up on *us*."

She nodded, sniffling over her happy tears. "Never."

He kissed her wet cheeks. "Do you remember when I told you about playing harmony with Tyler? How I described it to him as two people making one song better?" She nodded again, more slowly this time. "Well, that description works for us, too. Our lives are better together. We are each other's harmony." He paused with a frown. "Does that make sense? That you and I can blend together and create one unit?"

Grace giggled. "Somehow it *does* make sense, although I'd prefer we don't talk about ourselves as a *unit*." She stared into his warm blue eyes. "But I'll take your dubious analogy one step further. When more instruments start playing in harmony, the song gets even better."

Max looked confused, and she punched his arm. "I'm talking about *Tyler*. The three of us…"

Recognition dawned on his face. "The three of us will be in harmony."

"Maybe not every minute, but yes. We'll be better together." She laughed again—the joy just kept bubbling up. "Neither one of us are making sense, are we?"

"We're just wrapping too many words around something that's very simple. I love you, and you love me. That's all that matters. The rest is details, and as much as I know you love details, you might have to learn some flexibility, sweetheart."

"You mean the kind of flexibility that has kids wearing Halloween costumes to a Christmastime pageant?"

Max puffed out his chest and slid his arm around her

shoulder proudly. "That was a stroke of genius, don't you think?"

"That was you giving up against those children, wasn't it?"

His laughter echoed in the hall. "It was. I figured if you can't beat 'em, join 'em and make it work somehow."

"It was brilliant." She went up on her toes to kiss him. "Crazy, funny, chaotic and brilliant. Let's make a deal—you step up and handle the chaos of our lives, and I'll keep things running as smoothly day-to-day as I can."

"I think that's a great plan..."

He was swooping in for another kiss when the auditorium doors opened and families came pouring out. People were excited to congratulate them. Phyllis was still crying, and Lexi hugged Grace so hard she could barely breathe.

"Grace!" Tyler, still in costume, ran through the doors and spotted them. He rushed over and wrapped his arms around her legs, looking up with a bright smile. "Did you see it, Grace? We were *toys*! That was the secret! Did you like it? Did you like Daddy's surprise for you?"

Grace and Max stared at each other. Phyllis covered her mouth with her hand, her eyes wide. Lexi did a little fist pump behind Tyler.

Daddy. He'd called Max "Daddy" for the very first time. Max let go of Grace and lifted his son, the dragon, high into the air before wrapping him in a bear hug. Tyler accepted it at first, then wiggled free enough to look at Grace.

"Well, did you like it, Grace?"

She put one arm around Tyler and one around Max, giving them both kisses. Tyler made a face and rubbed his cheek, but Max leaned in and planted his own kiss there, making the boy squeal in laughter.

"Tyler, I not only *liked* it—I *loved* every minute, every song, every costume and every speech. Especially that last one from your daddy." Max's eyes were glowing with emotion and unshed tears. "I love *you*, Tyler, and I love your daddy, too. Very much."

"You're not mad at each other anymore?"

"No, son," Max answered. "We never should have been mad in the first place. We made a mistake, and we're going to try very hard not to make it again." He shifted Tyler on his hip and looked directly into his son's eyes. "Would you be okay if Grace spends more time with us? Like...*all* of her time?"

"Can she bring her big piano? And Mozart?"

Grace moved closer into Max's embrace. "I'll bring the piano, and I'll definitely bring Mozart."

"Hooray!"

"So we're doing this?" she said softly to Max. The hallway was beginning to empty again as families headed home.

"Oh, we're definitely doing this, my love. After all, I just told the whole town about it."

Epilogue

January 31

Max was hammering, but not in the forge this time. He was in Tyler's bedroom, putting a picture hanger on the wall near Ty's bed. Grace, Phyllis, and Sally Cosma were watching.

"You know, it doesn't take four people to hang a picture," Max pointed out, feeling their eyes on him.

"Never mind us," Grace answered. "Just keep hammering."

It only took another tap to secure the hook. He turned to take the framed photograph from Sally. She handed it to him with a smile, then took a shaking breath. Max hung Marie's picture on the hook and stepped back.

"She was beautiful, Sally." Phyllis put her arm around the other woman's shoulders.

The large photo was a candid shot of Marie sitting on a tree swing on the Cosmas' farm. She was wearing a yellow ruffled dress, with her dark hair soft on her shoulders. She was holding Tyler on her lap, when he was two years old. They both smiled up at the camera, with the sun on their faces and the cornfields green behind them. Max hadn't been there, of course, but he could tell it had been a happy day. Marie had loved their son, and now Tyler would see his mother's love every morning when he woke, and every night when he went to bed.

Max felt a hand brush against his back and turned to pull Grace close. The Cosmas had driven back to Cape Cod to close on their townhouse. That was a good thing for Tyler, even if Max was still sorting out his feelings.

Ed and Sally had welcomed Grace into Tyler's life. In fact, it had been Grace's idea to put pictures of Marie in Tyler's room. Max hadn't officially proposed to her yet. But soon. There was a diamond solitaire sitting in a small square box in his dresser drawer, and Valentine's Day was coming.

Phyllis and Sally had continued their unlikely friendship. Sally was calico, cotton and cornfields. His mother was leopard print and neon hair. But they were Tyler's grandmothers, and that made Tyler one very lucky little boy.

"Thank you, Max." Sally nodded toward the picture. "It means so much to us that Marie won't be forgotten. It's hard having Tyler so far away, but now we'll be able to visit a lot more often."

Max looked around. Where *was* Tyler?

Grace read his mind. "He's outside with Chantal, waiting for more snowflakes. Ed is keeping an eye on them."

They'd had a slightly white Christmas, with just a dusting of snow. They hadn't had much since then. But there was a winter storm headed their way this week, with the promise of five or six inches of white stuff. Enough to sled on, and enough to make a snowman or two.

Sally walked over to the photo of Marie. She kissed

her fingertips, then put them on the image, over Marie's smile. They all stood in silence, not wanting to interrupt the moment. Sally turned to face Max and Grace.

"Marie knew what she was doing when she put your name on Tyler's birth certificate. We had no idea she'd done that. But she *knew*. She knew that if something happened, you would be a good father to her boy." She reached out and held on to Grace's arm. "And she would have wanted you here. She would have wanted a family for Tyler who loved him."

Grace blinked a few times, then nodded. "Thank you for saying that. I do love him very much." She glanced up at Max. "And I love his father, too."

Whatever was left of Max's hard feelings toward Marie's parents disappeared. A peace finally settled over his heart. It had been one hell of a year, but the new one was off to a pretty good start.

Grace poured two glasses of wine. Tyler was spending one last night with the Cosmas before they headed home to Ohio. Her house was quiet, and Max was waiting for her to join him by the fireplace.

The plan was for her to gradually move into Max's larger house, but they didn't have a timeline on it yet. She didn't know what they'd do with her house—sell it or rent it. As much as she usually liked a good plan, she simply wasn't worried about it.

She smiled when she carried the wineglasses into the living room. Max was sitting on the love seat by the fireplace with his eyes closed, and Mozart was curled up on his lap. She sat next to them, and Max sat up, holding Mozart in place before taking one of the glasses.

"I think your cat likes me."

She nodded. "That's a good thing, because I like you, too." Max raised his arm, and she slid over into his embrace, being careful not to disturb the cat. "That was nice, what Sally said today about how Marie would want this for Tyler."

"We keep adding to our harmony."

She gave a soft laugh. "Someday we'll have our own little orchestra harmonizing together."

Max went still. "Are you...?"

Grace laughed out loud this time, earning a disgusted glare from her cat. "No, I'm not pregnant. You know I'd want to plan something *that* major. But...someday. When we're ready."

"I'd like that. A lot."

She rested against his shoulder, and Max kissed the top of her head. She wanted a lifetime of these moments—snuggled with Max, feeling safe and loved. And she knew she'd have it. She'd found the little box in his dresser a week ago, while putting away his socks.

She couldn't wait to say yes.

Yes to a ready-made family.

Yes to growing that family.

Yes to the future.

Yes to love.

* * * * *